A CALL TO ARMS

—◆—

P.G. NAGLE

Also by P. G. Nagle

The Far Western Civil War Series

Glorieta Pass
The Guns of Valverde
Galveston
Red River

A CALL TO ARMS

P.G. NAGLE

Evennight Books
Cedar Crest, New Mexico

A Call to Arms
Copyright © 2014 by P. G. Nagle

ISBN: 978-1-61138-386-7

Published by Evennight Books, Cedar Crest, New Mexico
an affiliate of Book View Café

Publication team: Vonda N. McIntyre, Phyllis Irene Radford, Judith Tarr, Chris Krohn

Illustrations: P. G. Nagle
Cover design: Beetiful Book Covers

Book View Café Publishing Cooperative
P.O. Box 1624, Cedar Crest, NM 87008-1624
bookviewcafe.com

For Lynne

Acknowledgments

I owe thanks to many people for their help in bringing this book to publication. Ken and Marilyn Dusenberry provided valuable feedback about army life during the Civil War. Vonda N. McIntyre and Phyllis Irene Radford provided thoughtful editorial input, and Chris Krohn and Judith Tarr caught a great many proof errors.

As ever, I am grateful to my colleagues at Book View Café for their support. I must also acknowledge Emma Edmonds herself, who has been a source of inspiration to me for many years.

"*I would rather have been shot dead*, than to have been known as a woman and sent away from the army under guard as a *criminal*."

—*S. Emma E. Seelye*

Washington, D.C., 1883

Mr. Glass looked up as a tall, inelegant woman entered his office. She wore a sober black dress of modest and unfashionable cut, and a trim hat with the veil drawn over her face.

Soldier's widow, he decided. God knew Washington was overrun with them still, almost twenty years after the war.

The eyes of the three men waiting to see his employer followed her as she approached Mr. Glass's desk with a slightly halting step. Mr. Glass set his pen in the standish and stifled a sigh.

"May I help you, madam?"

"I am here to see Congressman Cutcheon," she said in a voice both quiet and rather firmer than he'd expected.

Mr. Glass reached for his ledger book. "The Congressman is fully occupied today. You may make an appointment for next week."

The woman coughed—whether it was a gesture of discretion he could not tell, for she raised a handkerchief to her lips beneath the veil—then spoke again, quietly.

"If you would be so kind as to tell him I am here, I believe he will see me at once. It is in regard to a matter of which I have written to him, as have several others—"

"Madam, the Congressman receives many letters. All are dealt with in due course."

She paused for a moment, drawing a breath. "I understand, but I have traveled a great distance at considerable expense to come here. I have not the means to remain indefinitely."

"You have my sympathy, madam," Mr. Glass said politely, if rather insincerely. "However, I am afraid I cannot favor you before others who have already been waiting."

1

He nodded toward the three men, whose expressions had gone from curious to resentful. The lady paid them no heed.

"If you will just give him my name, I will be content to wait as long as he requires."

Seeing that he would not be rid of her until he acceded to her wishes, or at least gave the appearance of doing so, Mr. Glass drew a slip of paper toward him and picked up his pen. "Very well, madam. Your name is?"

"Seelye. S. Emma E. Seelye."

He recorded it in his elegant hand. "And your husband's name, Mrs. Seelye?"

"My husband's name is of no consequence to the Congressman. I am here on my own behalf."

"If you are here about a pension—yes?" Mr. Glass paused to judge the effect of his discernment upon her, but her veil prevented him seeing whether she was surprised. "Then your husband's name is needed."

"I am here about a pension," she said in her quiet voice, "but not for my husband. He did not serve during the war."

Mr. Glass looked up at her, frowning. The fact that she was here, instead of at the Pension Office, implied that she was seeking intervention from the Congressman to overcome some obstacle to the normal, tedious process of collecting a soldier's pension. If she sought to claim the pension of a brother, father, or some other relative, the knot could be tangled indeed. Mr. Glass knew his employer disliked such problems.

Before he could compose a phrase of courteous dis-couragement, the door behind him opened and several voices, bidding cheerful farewell, intruded. Four men, all connected with various members of Congress, took their leave of each other as they departed Congressman Cutcheon's office. The door closed, and the gentlemen strolled toward the outer hall, two of them deep in debate, the others nodding to Mr. Glass. The woman standing before his desk watched them, and as the last of them passed her, she spoke.

"Jamie."

The man addressed—Mr. Reid, who was an aide to Senator Dalton—halted, then slowly turned, a frown on the face that a moment before had been smiling and carefree. He stared at the woman, his nostrils flaring as if, like a hound on the hunt, he could identify her by scent.

"Do I know you?" he said, the slight trace of a Scottish burr to his voice.

She raised her hands and put back her veil, revealing a countenance more handsome than lovely, and weathered by not a few years. Yet still she was striking, Mr. Glass observed without reservation. Her hair was dark and neatly pulled back from her face, though a strand had escaped to curl at her temple. Her eyes, dark and commanding, gazed steadily at Mr. Reid.

"It's Frank," she said simply.

A convulsive swallow moved Mr. Reid's throat.

The sound of a polite cough distracted Mr. Glass from this interesting scene. One of the waiting visitors had risen from his chair and taken a step toward the desk, raising his eyebrows in inquiry. The other two sat watching Mrs. Seelye and Mr. Reid with unabashed curiosity.

The door behind him opened again and Mr. Glass was distracted by his counterpart, Mr. Whitfield, who spoke in a discreet murmur.

"The Congressman will see the gentlemen from Detroit, now."

Mr. Glass hastened to usher the three men into the Congressman's office, hiding his annoyance and curiosity and fear that his chance at learning more was lost, but he need not have worried. When the door was safely closed again and the office now empty of all observers save himself, it did not appear that Mr. Reid or Mrs. Seelye had moved.

"What are you doing here?" Mr. Reid said in a tight voice.

"I have come to claim my pension and back pay," said Mrs. Seelye. "I need the money."

A corner of Mr. Reid's mouth turned up wryly. "And you expect to get it?"

Her head remained high and her eyes flashed momentarily, but her voice as she answered was cool. "I hope to, with the aid of many of my old friends."

"Old friends," he repeated, and gave a laugh that to Mr. Glass sounded bitter. "I did not know you counted Congressman Cutcheon among them."

"I do not, but I hope to prevail upon his sense of justice. I am only asking what is my due."

A silence stretched as they stood, gazes locked, the tension between them palpable in the air. Mr. Glass scarcely dared to breathe, wondering what would happen next. At last the woman turned away from Mr. Reid and faced the desk again.

"The name you want to give the Congressman is Franklin Thompson, Company F, Second Michigan Volunteers," she said, smiling slightly. "He will recognize it."

Mr. Glass hastily sat down and scrawled the name, rather less elegantly, beneath the first. He glanced up at Mrs. Seelye, preparing to ask her relationship to Mr. Thompson.

"You'll never get it," Mr. Reid said.

Mrs. Seelye's head came up, though she did not turn. Her lips pressed together in annoyance, and a steely look came into her eyes. Beyond her, Mr. Glass saw Mr. Reid's sardonic smile.

"Frank Thompson was a deserter."

Emma seethed within, but schooled her face to keep it from showing. She knew well how to do that—she had spent years keeping her true thoughts and feelings hidden. It was most unfortunate to have encountered Jamie here, for she was uncertain what he would do. He might block her; he was one of the few who could do it. He had the power to ruin her if he chose.

Bitterly she regretted having called his attention to herself. She should have let him pass, but on seeing him she had spoken his name without thinking, and the damage was now done.

She turned to face him, knowing his remark had been a challenge. He seemed almost unchanged to her—a few strands of silver in his beard, but his hair still sleek and ruddy gold, his frame tall and energetic, eyes biting blue, the creases at their outer corners the very same he had borne in the army, if a little deeper.

He seemed misplaced here in the hallowed halls of government. She saw him still in uniform, striding purposefully through the camp, calling out orders in his clipped voice.

She could not allow herself to become lost in such memories. They were gone forever, those times, and she was here for a purpose. She looked at Jamie, who waited like a boxer for the answer to his first blow.

"Desertion is a harsh word," she said.

She saw his slight, sharp intake of breath, and knew that she had struck home. She forbore to smile.

"There were mitigating circumstances," she added.

Jamie's mouth twisted wryly. "Were there?"

"Yes. I was ill. I could not risk going into a hospital."

"How strange, you being so fond of hospitals."

Jamie eased his weight back onto one leg, his hip cocking out to the side. It was a stance he used when enjoying an argument. Emma glanced at the Congressman's bewildered secretary, then back at Jamie.

"It is unkind to mock the work I did out of Christian charity," she said.

"You being such a virtuous Christian."

"In my heart, I have always sought to be faithful to Christ, to work for His glory. My conduct after the war proves this. I have letters from many that say so."

Jamie made no answer. The secretary cleared his throat.

"Mrs. Seelye, if you would, please explain your connection with Private Thompson."

Before she could answer, Jamie cut in again, the ironic smile widening on his face. "Oh, it is the most intimate connection possible."

The look of shock on the poor secretary's face must have pleased him. Emma fixed Jamie with a glare. He would have it out, then, here and now. Well, she should not be surprised. This argument had been waiting, unfinished, for twenty years.

She turned to the secretary, holding herself collected, refusing to rise to Jamie's cast. "I am Franklin Thompson," she said. "That is the name I used when I served in the army."

The secretary blinked several times, confusion writ upon his face. Behind her, Jamie laughed. The secretary's glance shifted to him, imploring.

"Oh, 'tis true," Jamie said. "That is the one statement she has made that I can verify as truth. She served in the Second Michigan as Frank Thompson." His gaze shifted to her, eyes narrowing. "And on April 16th of 1863, Frank Thompson deserted."

"You cannot have been surprised," Emma replied coolly.

"Surprised? No. Disappointed, certainly."

"You expected me to remain?"

Jamie's face hardened. "After all your protestations of patriotism and desire to support the Union? Yes, I expected you would suit your actions to your word."

"I served for two years. I would have served out the war had I not fallen ill."

"You seemed well enough to me, that day."

As she drew breath to answer, a fit of coughing took her. She cursed silently as she struggled to control it, covering her mouth with her handkerchief, tasting the bitter tang that had plagued her ever since she had contracted malaria. No doubt Jamie took it for dissimulation on her part.

The truth was that she was still unwell. The fits of illness had cost much of her strength, and in recent years the old injury to her leg had begun to trouble her. She had come to claim the money owed her by the government, money she had forgone until now, because she was uncertain whether her health would hold until the day when she might sorely need it.

"Mrs. Seelye—" began the secretary in a plaintive voice, but he was not allowed to continue. Jamie came to the desk in two quick strides.

"Mrs. Seelye, is it? And when did you assume that name?"

"I assumed it upon my marriage," Emma said sharply.

"Oho! I pity the unfortunate gentleman. That is, unless he is conveniently deceased?"

She had no wish to bring Linus into this discussion. She was very glad, considering how the visit was going, that he had taken their sons to see the sights of Washington that day. Linus was a gentle soul, too yielding for this kind of confrontation.

"He is quite well, thank you," she said, watching Jamie sidelong. "Better than I."

Jamie looked disconcerted, as if he had truly believed her marriage was a lie. The mirthless smile returned. "But still unable to support you without the aid of a pension."

Emma turned to face Jamie squarely. "What business is it of yours? What does it matter to you that I make this claim? You washed your hands of me the day you left the army!"

Jamie's brows drew down into a frown, not of anger, but of distress. She knew the expression well, and it almost undid her. She had expected him to have forgotten it all, put the memories away from him, after so many years, but apparently he had not.

Into the silence of his reaction the secretary dropped a discreet cough. "As I was about to say, Mrs. Seelye, I wish to be sure that I understand your request quite perfectly. You say that you served as a private soldier in the Second Michigan Volunteers?"

Emma turned to him, ignoring Jamie once more. "From 1861 to 1863, yes."

"And you are here to request help of Congressman Cutcheon in claiming your pension?"

"I need his assistance to have the charge of desertion struck from my record."

"I see." The secretary picked up the page upon which he had written her two names, peered at it, then set it down again and looked up at Emma. "I must say, madam, I find it hard to credit that a woman such as yourself could have enlisted in the army without detection."

"Oh, it was easy." Emma couldn't help smiling. "It was early in the war, and the medical inspectors were none too choosy. But I doubt I would have had difficulty in any case. You see, I had already been living as a man for two years."

The War: Flint, Michigan, 1861

"M r. Thompson, you arrange your entertainments most delightfully," said the elder Miss Little over a dessert of apple crumble. "I have never enjoyed a concert more!"

Emma bowed in her seat. "Thank you, Miss Little. I endeavor to please. Did you like the Mozart concerto best, or the Beethoven?"

"The Beethoven was a little ambitious for the abilities of the orchestra," Mrs. Little remarked, raising her glass to sip at her Madeira.

The dining room at the Casino Hotel, the best establishment in Flint, was filled with warmth and the quiet murmur of contented patrons. Dark wood paneling and rich velvet hangings gave the room a cozy feeling, and lamplight glinting on the several crystal goblets and wine glasses at each place attested to the lavishness of the fare. Emma had brought her guests there for supper after the concert, and was pleased to have won their approval.

"I liked the patriotic songs best," said Miss Little, her dark eyes glittering with enthusiasm. "You will think my tastes too simple, but I found them thrilling."

Emma smiled politely. Patriotic fever was high, just now, with the uncertainty caused by the recent secession of several Southern states. Miss Little's preference did not surprise her.

"The supper was also quite elegant, and tastefully chosen," said Mrs. Little, whose frail, blonde looks she had passed to her younger daughter, but not to the elder. "You must prosper well in your business, Mr. Thompson."

Emma fixed her with an interested gaze. Mrs. Little, if she guessed aright, was looking to settle one of her daughters.

"I am happy to say that I do, ma'am," said Emma, smiling with private amusement. "There is a great appetite for books in this part of the country. I have sold more in the last year than I did in the previous, when I was first the top salesman for my employer."

The ladies made polite noises appreciative of this accomplishment. Emma turned her attention to the youngest, who was but fifteen and prettily shy.

Miss Daphne Little had spent much of the evening in a state of tongue-tied awe. Emma had included her in the invitation out of kindness, thinking she was just of an age to wish to take part in adult entertainments, without knowing quite what she should do in such a situation. Her presence also made the invitation to her elder sister seem less particular.

"Do you like to read, Miss Daphne?"

Miss Daphne cringed a little at being addressed directly, then nodded. "Mother lets me look at her magazines."

A rustle of taffeta from her mother's direction made Miss Daphne give a start and glance up. Her eyes widened with alarm as she looked back at Emma.

"And I read in the beautiful Bible you brought for us," she made haste to add. "I read in it every day!"

Emma smiled to reassure her. "I'm glad you enjoy it, Miss Daphne."

"The Bible is indeed wonderful," Miss Little the elder put in, "and I am also enjoying *Jane Eyre*." Her voice held a hint of smug satisfaction, that her parents trusted her to read the novel without fear of its turning her head.

Emma observed her, a vivacious girl of seventeen, fairly bursting out of her skin at the prospect of claiming her place in adult society. Eager to marry without understanding the toll it would quickly exact from her.

Emma thought of her own sisters, who were older than she and had wed while she was still young, younger than Miss Daphne. How quickly they had faded, become weary and despairing like their mother, under the burdens of matrimony.

A sudden anger at Mrs. Little filled Emma's breast. She hid it by toying with her coffee cup, stirring her coffee and sipping it. It had gone cold, and tasted slightly bitter.

Miss Little continued talking of *Jane Eyre*, freely expressing her opinions of the characters and the writing. Emma listened with half an ear, her annoyance fading to sadness as she realized Miss Little was beyond rescue. She would wed, as she was so eager to do, and from then on live in her husband's shadow.

Miss Daphne was not yet ensorceled by the attractions of men, though there was a spark of unformed curiosity in her. Emma watched her covertly as she scraped a last bit of dessert from her dish. Miss Daphne had the appetites of a healthy young girl.

"I encourage you to read as much as you are able," Emma said when Miss Little paused. She addressed the remark to Miss Daphne, who looked back at her with guileless interest. "It was a book that inspired me to make my way in the world."

"What book?"

Emma smiled. "Perhaps I will bring it to you one day."

Miss Daphne's eyes lit with excitement. Emma glanced at her mother and saw suspicion, though Mrs. Little was quick to hide it with a smile. The mother would willingly give up her younger daughter to the charming Bible salesman, Emma thought, though the girl was but fifteen. Emma had to hide another flash of anger at the thought.

"What do you think of the situation at Fort Sumter, Mr. Thompson?" Mrs. Little asked.

Emma looked at her, mildly surprised that she would bring up the subject in her daughters' company. Fort Sumter was on everyone's mind, though, even hundreds of miles away here in Flint.

All the rhetoric of secession and disunion had come to balance on the knife's-edge of Sumter. Lincoln had refused to hand over the fort to the fledgling Confederacy. The poor garrison there had been without supply for weeks, blockaded by the Confederates, and was surely near to starving.

"I think it must be very dire," Emma replied. "I hope the relief convoy is allowed through."

"And if they are not?" Miss Little asked, eyes wide. "Will it be war?"

Emma regarded her, suspecting her breathless excitement to be fanned by a romantic view of warfare. "I very much fear that it will."

"What will you do in that case, Mr. Thompson?" asked Mrs. Little. "Will you return to Canada?"

"I have not decided, ma'am."

The question troubled her. She had gone over it in her mind many times. If war broke out, as a young man in good health and wishing to do right, Frank Thompson might well be expected to enlist. She doubted she would retreat to Canada; she cared too much about this fine country, which had been the source of her independence, to turn her back when it was threatened with dissolution.

But could she bear arms against her fellow man? She knew how to handle a rifle—growing up on a farm had taught her that, along with other skills that were convenient to her disguise—but she had never contemplated aiming a firearm at another human being.

"One thing is certain," Emma said with more lightness than she felt, "you will hear a great deal more patriotic music if there is to be war, Miss Little."

Having thus turned the subject, Emma whiled away the remainder of the supper with innocuous conversation, assisted by the willing Mrs. Little. When they rose from the table Emma escorted the ladies home in her carriage, accepted an invitation to visit on the following Saturday despite Miss Little's threatening to play the piano for her, and bade them all a cheerful good evening.

Mr. Little, who had no taste for concerts, welcomed his family home again at the door, favoring Emma with cursory thanks and a mistrustful glance. Emma shook his hand firmly, smiled, and went her ways.

She drove home, bestowed her carriage and saw to the horses, then sought the room she rented from the Reverend Mr. Joslin and his wife. The Joslins had already retired for the evening and the house was quiet; dark save for the lamp left burning low beside the stairs. Emma carried it up to her room.

Shutting the door, she let out a small sigh. Home at last, sheltered from suspicious glances. Her room was a refuge, small as it was and filled with stacks of books and order forms. She was safe here.

She took off her good suit and untied her neckcloth, thinking over the evening as she prepared to retire. The Littles were pleasant enough, though she found she did not really enjoy the elder Miss Little's company. It was important, however, to appear to show some interest in young ladies. To avoid them might occasion remark, and she was careful never to attract that sort of attention.

Two years, it had been, since that first terrifying day when she had cut her hair off short, dressed in men's clothing, and stepped out into the streets of Moncton with her brand new case of sample books. She had been so apprehensive of discovery that she had hurried away from the city and waited in the woods for concealing dusk before she dared to approach a farmhouse. Fearful of denouncement and arrest, she had instead received a courteous welcome, and had sold her first Bible to those trusting folk.

She had never looked back.

Once, she had paid a visit to her family. She was careful to arrive during the day when her father was sure to be away from the farmhouse. She went in her man's attire, and had been sitting with her mother, her sister Frances, and her poor sickly brother Thomas, for half an hour before her mother recognized her.

She doubted she would ever wear skirts again. She had cast them off, and no longer owned anything that might be considered a lady's property.

She had kept only one possession from her early life: the book that she had mentioned to Miss Daphne. Smiling, she opened her trunk and sought for it beneath the clothing, drawing out the small volume and holding it carefully in both hands.

The binding was cracked and beginning to come apart. A faint, musty smell of deteriorating paper arose from the pages. The book was cheaply made, nowhere near the quality of the elegant volumes upon which she made her living. But it was the most important book she had ever possessed, saving only the Bible.

The title was fading from the worn cover. She opened the book to its title page, admiring the picture of a woman in trousers holding a Jolly Roger. *Fanny Campbell, the Female Pirate Captain.*

How well she remembered the day she had received it, a gift from a peddler who had sheltered overnight from a frightful storm in the Edmonsons' home. He had given it to Emma, the youngest child, before going on his way. She had never seen a novel before. If her father had known of it he would surely have taken it away from her, but she hid it in the pocket of her skirt and went out to work in the fields with her sisters.

Opening that book had opened Emma's eyes to a new awareness of possibilities she had never considered. She and her sisters had taken turns reading, then become so engrossed in the story that few potatoes were planted that day.

When Emma read of Fanny Campbell's decision to cut off her curling locks and dress as a man, she felt as if an angel had touched her with a live coal from off the altar. The problem of her life was solved.

It was not until some years later, when her father demanded that she marry a neighbor—a widower much older than herself—that she had actually escaped the farm, and not even then had she donned men's attire. She had first gone to Salisbury and worked in a milliner's shop, then moved to Moncton and opened her own hat shop with a friend. It was the constant fear that her father would find her and drag her back to marry his horrid old neighbor that had led her finally to take the step she had so often dreamed of.

And to discover the freedom a young man enjoyed.

She could dine when and where she pleased, go wherever she wished without escort, and answer to no one but herself. With the sample books she had requested from W. S. Williams & Company in Hartford, Connecticut, she traveled all about New Brunswick, meeting folk of all kinds and taking their orders for Bibles, illustrated histories, and other books.

She earned more money than a poor farm girl could ever have dreamed of. Each success increased her confidence, so that now, two years later, she was perfectly at home in the role of Franklin Thompson.

She turned the yellowing leaves of the novel in her hands, remembering the fire it had lit in her heart. An early passage caught her eye:

> *Fanny Campbell was a noble looking girl. She was none of your modern belles, delicate and ready to faint at the first sight of a reptile; no, Fanny could row a boat, shoot a panther, ride the wildest horse*

in the province, or do almost any brave and useful
act.

How those words had thrilled her, confirming that there
was worth in a girl who was able to do such things. She
herself could handle a rifle or an axe with equal skill, and
rode as well as her father. *Fanny Campbell* had convinced her
that she could base a life upon those abilities—a life that was
bound to be full of interest and adventure—rather than resign
herself to being a wife and mother. Could this book inspire
Miss Daphne Little to a similar conviction?

Perhaps, but she dared not give it to the girl. Even if Miss
Daphne kept the book a secret, it might cause her to suspect
Frank Thompson, and that Emma could not risk. She was
taking some risk even keeping the book, but she had not so
far been able to let it go.

There was one other way she might rescue Miss Daphne:
marry her and take her away from Flint, thereafter to set her
free upon the world, perhaps even become her mentor and
guide. While the thought of carrying off a marriage amused
Emma, she knew she could no more do that than give
Daphne the book.

Suppose Miss Daphne felt cheated upon learning her
husband was not a man? The girl might actually wish for
children, as her sister so plainly did. Might wish for the
drudgery of motherhood and all its attendant woes. Frank
Thompson would be a kinder husband than Isaac Edmonson
had been, but could never sire children.

No, Frank Thompson could not marry. Not only would it be
dangerous and uncertain, and perhaps unfair to the young
lady, it would make a mockery of a Christian sacrament, and
that Emma would not do. The other fire that burned in her,
now that her freedom was assured, was the fire of Christ's
teachings.

She longed to devote herself someday to missionary work.
Frank Thompson would do well, she thought, bringing the
teachings of Christ to those living in the darkness of
ignorance. She was putting some of her earnings by against
just such a venture, though for now she was content in Mr.
Joslin's congregation. They were something like a family to
her, a great comfort after her self-imposed isolation.

She closed *Fanny Campbell* and carefully hid it again in the bottom of her trunk before saying her prayers. She included all the Littles in her requests for God's guidance and protection, her concern especially for the two Misses Little.

Miss Daphne would have to find her own inspiration, but at least Emma had been able to encourage her to read. She was curious enough, Emma thought, to seek out works beyond what her mother might consider strictly appropriate. Smiling on the thought, Emma climbed into bed and drifted to sleep.

The next morning she was walking to the telegraph office to place her book orders when she heard the news of Fort Sumter's fall. A boy in the street was hawking newspapers, shouting hoarsely that Lincoln had called for 75,000 volunteers.

With a sinking heart, Emma hastened to purchase a paper from him. Others crowded around the boy, buying papers as fast as he could sell them, blocking traffic in the street. Emma walked away slowly, eyes fixed on the description of the shelling and surrender of the fort.

It was war, then. Miss Little's romantic hopes were fulfilled, and Emma's quandary descended upon her with full force.

She knew she would not leave America. There must be a role for her, a part she could play in the coming calamity, a means by which she could serve her beloved adopted country. What it would be, she was uncertain.

She finished reading the article and looked up, becoming aware of her surroundings once more. She knew with a sudden certainty that she could not continue blithely in her comfortable existence, peddling books while the country tore itself apart.

Sadly, in sober contemplation, she turned away and walked back to the Joslins' house. When she reached it she found the Joslins sitting in the front parlor with Mr. Morse and two other gentlemen from the church.

"Mr. Thompson," said Mrs. Joslin as Emma looked in the parlor door. "You have returned very quickly!"

"Yes, ma'am," Emma said sadly.

"He has heard the news," said Mr. Morse, gesturing toward the paper in Emma's hand.

Emma met his gaze. Energetic and active, William Morse was a leading member of the Reverend Mr. Joslin's congregation. He was also captain of the Flint Union Grays, a militia company to which he had tried more than once to recruit Emma. Emma had politely declined, having no wish to draw attention to herself by marching in parades or sporting a uniform at picnics and dances. Now, though, the militia would be called to a different task.

"The Grays are going," Morse said, holding Emma's gaze. "I have written to the governor, and will take the company to Detroit to enlist in the infantry regiment. Do you join us?"

Emma could not hide a frown of concern. She had expected this—it was inevitable now that the war had begun that she would be pressured to enlist—but she had not yet decided how to respond.

"I do not know," she said. "I need time to consider."

Mr. Morse's brows rose slightly. "Well, do not take too long. We are holding a recruiting meeting in a few days."

Emma nodded, and because she felt that to leave the parlor would call her courage into question, she sat down and listened to Mr. Morse planning the details of the Grays' journey to glory. She learned that the other two gentlemen, Mr. Prentiss and Mr. Jordan, with whom she was acquainted from church, were also officers in the Grays.

Governor Blair was raising a regiment of volunteers in accordance with President Lincoln's proclamation. Ten companies would be formed, and Mr. Morse intended the Grays to be one of them. Their number was not near the required one hundred men, so recruitment was necessary, but Mr. Morse was confident he would quickly make up his numbers.

"There is a fervor in the streets already," Mr. Prentiss said with suppressed excitement. "One can see it."

"One can hear it," Mr. Jordan added drily. "All the talk is of going to Washington, to be a part of crushing the rebellion. We must hurry or we'll miss the fun."

"We'll have no trouble filling up our company." Mr. Morse glanced again at Emma, but she made no comment.

Mrs. Joslin had sent the maid for an extra cup and saucer when Emma had joined them, and now she poured coffee and offered it to Emma with a smile. "You are wise to consider carefully, Mr. Thompson. I imagine you may be concerned what your family will think."

Emma regarded her, and gave a slow nod, though in fact she was certain her family expected never to see her again. For her part she wished never to see her father again. Her mother and sisters she missed, and Thomas.

Poor Thomas, the only boy, whose sporadic fits made him useless for farm work. Their father thought him stupid, though Emma was sure he was not. Gentle Thomas. She smiled a little, thinking of him. She had chosen Frank's surname in his honor.

Recalling her company, Emma sipped her coffee and tried to pay attention to the conversation. The men were discussing firearms now, speculating whether the government would arm the regiment with the newest rifles or some less magnificent gun. Her thoughts drifted again to Thomas, who handled firearms so poorly that their father would not permit him to hunt, declaring him a waste of powder.

Emma was a keen shot. She'd learned eagerly, as she'd learned everything her father wished of her.

The youngest, and probably the last of his children, she had bitterly disappointed him by being born female. He had reacted by demanding things of her he never asked of her sisters, and being robust in health and larger than her siblings, Emma had made no protest. She actually enjoyed such chores as chopping wood and hunting or fishing for the stew pot. Yet nothing she had ever done, though she tried in all earnestness to please him, had mitigated Isaac's resentment.

What would he think, she wondered, if he learned his youngest child had gone for a soldier?

She shook her head and took another sip of coffee. Isaac would never know of Frank Thompson's exploits. He would certainly not appreciate them if he learned of them, and Emma had taken care that he should not.

"I would join you," Mr. Joslin said to Mr. Morse, "but I fear I am too old, and too burdened with responsibility." He glanced at his wife, who had shown momentary alarm.

"No, no," said Mr. Morse. "Thank you, Reverend, but I am sure there are plenty of young men who do not have such obligations."

"We can still help," said Mrs. Joslin, looking relieved. "I will organize the ladies in our congregation to prepare some little comforts for the Grays to take with them."

Her husband nodded, glancing at Emma. "We should send a Bible with each of them."

"I haven't a hundred Bibles on hand," Emma responded promptly, "but I will gladly donate as many as I can."

"Thank you, Mr. Thompson." Mr. Joslin made a slight bow

in her direction. "And perhaps the ladies can inscribe them with an appropriate sentiment."

"'Put your trust in God, and keep your powder dry,'" suggested Mr. Morse.

"Oliver Cromwell," Emma said.

Mr. Morse looked at her. "You are well read, Mr. Thompson."

"I regard it as necessary to my success."

Mr. Morse gazed at her for a long moment, then suddenly smiled. "I hope you do decide to join us, Mr. Thompson. I think you would be an asset to the company. I'll not press you, however."

"Thank you."

Emma had to resist the urge to bite her lip. She appreciated the tribute, but she dared not let it sway her. The fact was, enlisting in the army would be far more dangerous than anything she had done in the guise of Frank Thompson.

To be thrown together with a hundred men, no doubt living and sleeping in close quarters, was a risk that made her quail. The possibility of discovery, of the disgrace and perhaps even abuse that might follow, frightened her far more than secessionist bullets.

She listened to the others discuss the coming war as she silently wrestled with her own internal conflict. When the guests departed after another half-hour, she retired to her own room and looked at her samples and papers.

Her employer would be displeased if she abandoned her work. She supposed he would have to accept it with a good grace, but it would mean a loss of income to him, as well as to her. A soldier's pay was far less than she earned as a salesman.

That night, as she undressed, she made a discovery that served to give her even greater pause: her monthly bleeding had begun.

She was prepared. She kept a bolt of soft cotton cloth—ostensibly to clean and protect the books she sold—from which she cut a strip to roll up and use to block the bleeding. She had done this for many months, but each time it was a reminder that her disguise was not perfect.

If she were a soldier, this would be a chief danger for her. She could not carry a bolt of cloth to war, nor trust that she would find a substitute whenever she might need it. She tried to imagine washing out her cloths for use again, but could not see how to do it without risking discovery.

Her body mocked her; it reminded her that the life she lived was a lie. Her flesh had been formed for a different fate.

Clenching her teeth, she put on her nightshirt and slid between the sheets. She had rejected that fate and all its inequities. Her life was her own, and she would never submit to the dominance of a man.

In the following days, the fervor of excitement about the war increased tenfold. Almost nothing else was talked of, and as Emma rode out to deliver books, she was asked for news at every place she stopped.

The Flint Union Grays filled up their number at a meeting on the courthouse steps. All Flint turned out in attendance. Emma was present, but did not put in her name. She listened to the rousing speeches, applauded with the rest of the town, and donated a hundred Testaments, hastily ordered from Hartford at her own expense, to provide the Grays with moral armament to accompany their more martial equipments.

It was done; the company was full. They were not accepted into the First Michigan Volunteers, for there were more than ten militia companies in the state vying for the honor, but the governor quickly began organizing a second regiment in reserve. The Grays were ordered to rendezvous in Detroit to be mustered into the Second Michigan Volunteer Infantry by the end of April.

Emma watched the preparations for their departure with mingled feelings of relief and regret. Many of her friends from church had joined the Grays. Damon Stewart, a clothing merchant with whom she'd enjoyed discussions of commerce, had signed up. Flint would be lonely and dull when the Grays went off to war.

On the 29th of April, a parade was held in the Grays' honor, followed by speeches and music and much fanfare in the town square. All Flint was there to celebrate the company, who would travel by train to Detroit in the morning.

The Grays were resplendent in their new uniforms, ten-

derly made by loving mothers and sisters. Their faces shone
with pride and excitement. Speeches were given, patriotic
tunes played by a brass band, and the Testaments were
presented to the soldiers by the Reverend Mr. Joslin.

Young ladies bedecked in red, white, and blue made much
of the new-minted soldiers. The Misses Little were both
present, among a delegation of ladies who went round and
pinned a rosette reading "For Union and for Constitution" to
the breast of each soldier.

Emma nodded and smiled a greeting when she chanced to
catch Miss Little's eye. Miss Little hesitated, then lifted her
chin and turned away, bestowing her attention and her
smiles upon one of the Grays. Emma hid her laughter in a
sudden fit of coughing.

Miss Daphne was not so particular as her sister. She came
straight up to Emma with her basket of rosettes, regarding
her with childlike speculation.

"You didn't get into the Grays," she said.

"No, I didn't."

"Was it because you weren't tall enough?"

Emma's brows twitched. She was not unduly short for a
man, being tall for a woman.

"Ah—not quick enough. The company filled up at once."

"Oh. Don't feel bad, Mr. Thompson. You aren't the only
one."

She gestured at the surrounding crowd, the good folk of
Flint, who certainly outnumbered the Grays. Emma smiled at
Miss Daphne's youthful assumption that every man in town
must wish to be a part of the militia company.

"When are you going to bring me that book?"

A stab of dismay struck Emma. She should never have
mentioned *Fanny Campbell*. She looked at Miss Daphne,
trying to frown.

"Did I promise to bring it? I thought I said 'perhaps'."

"Well, will you bring it? Please?" Miss Daphne begged
prettily.

"It is a novel, Miss Daphne," Emma said, noting the approach of Mrs. Little. "Your parents might not wish you to
read it. In fact, you might not care for it at all. It's about a
pirate captain."

"Oh, but I love adventure stories!"

"Good afternoon, Mr. Thompson," said Mrs. Little, joining them.

Emma bowed. "Good afternoon, ma'am. Your daughters are both looking lovely today."

"Thank you, sir." She reached out to twitch Miss Daphne's red and white sash, which had fallen askew. "Daphne, dear, your sister needs more rosettes."

Daphne's face fell in disappointment, and she moved rather languidly away, casting one backward glance at Emma. It was the book she was thinking of, Emma knew.

"You decided not to enlist," Mrs. Little said.

"I hesitated too long, ma'am. The company filled almost at once."

"You could always join another company, I suppose."

Emma regarded her, trying to decide if she meant to mock Mr. Thompson for lack of courage. Mrs. Little's face showed nothing but a polite interest in the decoration of the soldiers being conducted by her daughters and the other young ladies.

"Ah, but to serve among strangers, instead of the good folk of Flint. It would be a disappointment," Emma said.

"Do you go to Canada, then?"

Mrs. Little was regarding her, now. Emma met her gaze steadily.

"I think not, ma'am, though I have not yet decided what to do."

"That is a decision in itself."

Mrs. Little moved away, then, to greet two other ladies who were passing near. Emma felt a strange impulse to defend herself, and thought rather less of Mrs. Little for not allowing her the opportunity. She shook it off, however. Such arguments could have no benefit.

As the evening drew near the celebration moved indoors, where it continued with a supper for the Grays, more music, and more speeches. Emma joined wholeheartedly in the cheering, and the next morning, along with many other citizens of Flint, she escorted the Grays to the depot to see them off.

Emotion welled in her as she shook hands with many of her friends and bade them farewell. To the oft-repeated strains of *The Star-Spangled Banner*, they boarded the train, waved from the open windows, and were gone.

A hush fell over Flint. All the color and excitement had ended, and though people went about their daily lives with cheerful determination, there was a tension in the air.

Emma began more and more to regret her decision to stay behind. She had not the heart to take up her business again. She delivered the remaining books she had received, but collected no more orders.

More and more, she felt she could not stand idly by. She had become convinced that she, too, must have a duty to perform, must find some way to serve the Union cause. She spent long nights in solitary contemplation, pacing her room as she weighed the alternatives.

If only she had gone further in her pursuit of becoming a missionary, she could have volunteered to serve as a chaplain, and perhaps been safer from discovery in that position. That was a futile hope, however. No doubt plenty of chaplains had already offered their services. A soldier's pay, though it was less than Emma's income, would be attractive to many.

She might assist in one of the hospitals. She should retain her alias if she sought this work, for she felt she could tend to the needs of sick and wounded men with less embarrassment to them and to herself as a man than as a woman. She had no idea how to go about volunteering for such work, however. Perhaps she would travel to Washington and see what fortune offered.

Or she could follow Mrs. Little's suggestion and enlist with some other company of volunteers, but her heart sank at the thought. If she were to be thrown into close company with a group of men, she would be safer with those who already knew and accepted Frank Thompson than with strangers. The Flint Union Grays had been her best chance of that, and the opportunity had passed.

She was sitting in the parlor with the Joslins one evening after supper, reading aloud to them from the latest New York newspaper, when a knock fell upon the front door. As the Reverend Mr. Joslin received frequent visits from members of his congregation, Emma at first paid no heed, but the sound of a familiar voice in the hall made her pause and raise her head.

The maid came into the parlor. "Mr. Prentiss is here to see you, sir."

"Mr. Prentiss? Show him in," said Mr. Joslin.

Emma folded the paper and set it aside. Bernard Prentiss, who had marched away in splendid martial array with the Grays, now entered the room dressed in a plain suit and carrying a book.

Not just a book—a Testament. One of Emma's Testaments. She looked at his face as Mr. Joslin stood to greet him.

"Reverend, forgive me for intruding," said Mr. Prentiss. "I came to return this to you." Looking somewhat haggard, he offered the book.

Mr. Joslin accepted it slowly. "What has happened, Mr. Prentiss? Have you left the Grays?"

"I have. The War Department is no longer accepting regiments for three-month enlistments. They demand three-year terms, now, and I cannot commit to that. I have a wife and small child—"

"Yes, of course," said Mr. Joslin. "Quite understandable. It was valiant of you to volunteer at all."

Mr. Prentiss gave a wan smile, and his glance crossed Emma's. She felt a tingle suffuse her, spreading down her forearms to the tips of her well-manicured fingers.

"Are others returning, Mr. Prentiss?" she asked.

He nodded. "A handful. Captain Morse was with us on the train—he's come to fill up the vacancies. Perhaps one of them can use that," he said, gesturing to the Testament.

"We will see that it goes to a soldier," said Mr. Joslin. "Thank you for returning it."

"I am only sorry...it is not that I am afraid," said Mr. Prentiss in a strained voice.

"Of course not."

Mr. Joslin laid a hand on his shoulder and escorted him out, talking in soothing tones. Emma looked at Mrs. Joslin, quietly knitting in her chair.

The mantel clock began to strike the hour. Seven o'clock. The chimes fell heavily into the quiet evening; it seemed to Emma they were tolling a change. As the last of them faded, she stood.

She heard Mr. Joslin's returning step behind her. Mrs. Joslin glanced up. Emma turned to face them both.

"If you will excuse me," she said, her voice sounding hoarse in her ears, "I have just thought of a call I would like to pay."

Mr. Joslin, returning to his chair, raised an eyebrow. He laid the Testament on the table beside him, next to the paper from which Emma had been reading. Emma's gaze rested on the gilt letters on its binding.

"I will bid you good night, in case you have retired by the time I return."

"Good night, then, Mr. Thompson."

Mr. Joslin's gaze was steady, and showed curiosity, though Emma knew he would never pry. She shrank from telling him where she meant to go—she was as yet uncertain what would pass. With a slight bow, she hastened from the room.

The evening was cool, but not chilly enough to warrant putting on an overcoat. Spring had arrived in Flint. Emma noted flowers blooming in the front garden Mrs. Joslin fussed over with such pride, and in the neighboring gardens as she walked down the street. She looked at Flint with an altered perception, noting each pleasant house and garden, each place that was the site of some fond memory.

She turned her steps to the Casino hotel, not knowing where better to go. She regretted not having questioned Mr. Prentiss further, but the man was distraught as it was. She suspected this was the place to come, and when she inquired at the front desk, she learned she had guessed correctly.

"I believe you will find him in the dining room," the clerk told her.

"Thank you," Emma said, and made her way there.

Few patrons were in the spacious dining room at this hour. Emma's gaze swept the room, passing over empty tables laid with fresh linens for the morning, and came to rest on a gentleman dressed in a suit of dark blue, dining alone. She approached the table, her heart beating rather quickly.

"Captain Morse," she said, bowing slightly as the gentleman looked up at her.

He looked older, somehow, though he had scarce been

gone a month. His hair and mustache had been trimmed somewhat shorter, the hair just brushing the upstanding collar of his jacket. The shoulders of the jacket were adorned with straps of a lighter blue.

Emma realized with a small shock that this was a uniform. She had seen Morse in his Grays uniform many times, but he seemed to wear this one differently, as if it was merely clothing instead of what amounted to a costume.

"Pardon me for intruding on your supper," Emma added.

Morse's brows rose slightly, then he smiled. "Not at all, Mr. Thompson. Will you join me?"

Emma hesitated, her nervousness making her restless, then she thanked him and sat in the opposite chair. Captain Morse gestured toward the wine bottle between them, inviting her to share it. She shook her head. Morse picked up the bottle and replenished his glass.

"What may I do for you, Mr. Thompson?"

Emma found it hard to say what was in her heart, so she resorted to commonplace chat. "I heard you had returned ... Mr. Prentiss called on Mr. Joslin this evening."

"Ah. Did he tell you to find me here?"

Emma shook her head. "I remembered that you had given up your lodgings last month, so I thought you must have come to a hotel."

Morse nodded, watching her expectantly. Emma drew a deep breath.

"I understand you are here to fill some vacancies in the Grays."

"Yes."

"I would like to put my name in for one of them, if I may."

Morse regarded her steadily. "It's for three years, now," he said.

"I know."

Their gazes held, and Emma felt she was being measured. It was a feeling she often endured, yet still it made her heart skip.

"What changed your mind, Mr. Franklin?"

"It hasn't changed. I would say, rather, that it took me a while to make it up. I knew I must serve the Union, but I was unsure in what capacity I might serve best."

Morse sliced a bite of his roast and regarded her as he

chewed it. Emma found she was clenching her hands in her lap, and made herself lay them flat on her knees instead.

"Well," Morse said, "as a friend of ours has said, it is wise of you to consider carefully, especially now. This three-year enlistment took everyone by surprise. Some companies lost nearly half their number. I'm lucky I only lost a few."

"Do you think it will take three years to beat the Rebels?"

Morse laughed. "I doubt it. More likely we'll be home for Christmas."

Emma smiled, reassured by his confidence. Morse reached a hand across the table, returning the smile.

"Welcome to the Grays, then, Mr. Thompson."

Emma shook hands, her heart rising in her breast. For the first time in many days, she felt she had done right.

Washington, D.C., 1883

Emma watched the secretary, whose expression had gone from confusion to astonishment to something near indignation as she explained the circumstances leading to her enlistment. The indignation did not surprise her; she had encountered such reactions, and worse, before. It was one of the reasons she had kept her service a secret from her present acquaintances, though once, just after she had left the army, she had been quite famous for it.

This man, Mr. Glass, who could be no more than twenty-five, would have been a mere child when her book was published in 1865. It was no wonder that he had not heard of her. By the time he could read, the excitement over the war had no doubt faded, and too many memoirs been written for anyone to read them all.

She glanced at Jamie, wondering if he had read hers. Probably not, as he had gone to Scotland in 1863. She had not heard of his return—had not expected it, in fact. Yet here he was, plainly at home in the halls of government.

"I wondered how it was you succeeded so well in your deception," he said, blue eyes hooded as he gazed at her. Cold words, but there was less venom in his voice as he said them.

"I have wished sometimes that I was even more success-ful," Emma replied.

Jamie's eyes narrowed. Had that stung him? Good.

"It was no trouble, for the most part," she added, glancing at Mr. Glass. "It was hardest at the first, of course. By the time I reached Detroit with Captain Morse, I was quite nervous that I would be discovered, but no less determined to try."

"I should think you were nervous!" declared Mr. Glass. "How you dared, I cannot imagine! It is one thing to dress as

29

a man—I do not say it was right, though I understand your explanation—but quite another to present oneself as fit for a soldier!"

Emma laughed. "I was more than fit, Mr. Glass. I grew up on a farm, remember. I could handle firearms better than half the Grays."

"And yet you rarely did so, during your service," said Jamie.

Emma faced him, squaring her jaw. "Because I was serving in other capacities."

"Other capacities," he echoed, and the bitter smile twisted his lip.

"Dare you mock me? When I risked my life over and again on the field?" Emma's anger flared and she stared at Jamie, breathing hard.

Jamie blinked, the smile falling away, leaving an expression of sadness in its wake. "I never questioned your courage," he said in a voice gone strangely quiet. "I would say, looking back, that you had rather too much of it for your own good."

Her anger faded as quickly as it had come, replaced by an unexpected swell of affection. How strange that all the old feelings—the anger, the fondness, all of it—had not died as she had thought, but had only been slumbering.

"Perhaps so," she said, and could not help the smile that tugged at her own lips. "I always loved an adventure."

The War: Fort Wayne, Michigan, 1861

No parade or brass band saw Captain Morse and his handful of replacements off from Flint. No uniforms adorned the recruits; no young ladies celebrated their departure. As they boarded the cars in silence, Emma thought with slight wistfulness of Miss Daphne, of all people.

Emma had spent the better part of the past two days in making arrangements for her departure. She sold her horses and carriage, shipped her sample books back to Mr. Hurlburt with a letter explaining her decision to enlist, and packed spare clothing and the few things she wished to keep in her trunk, which the Joslins had agreed to store for her. *Fanny Campbell* remained buried within it, secured by the trunk's stout lock. Emma had considered sending the book to Miss Daphne anonymously, "from a friend," but decided it was still too great a risk.

She had purchased two dozen pocket handkerchiefs and stowed them in her valise. They would earn her some teasing, perhaps, and the reputation of a dandy, but they were worth that cost. She would find a way to clean them if she could; if not, she must purchase more. A great expense for a soldier, but luckily she had money of her own.

Now, as she watched Flint slide away on the rails, fading behind clouds of black smoke from the locomotive, she had occasion to think of those acquaintances to whom she had not had time to say goodbye. The Joslins had promised to make her excuses to any who inquired after her. Emma did not expect many to do so—the Littles would probably not do so—but she wished she had been able to say farewell to Miss Daphne. She contented herself with hoping that the girl's spirit would survive society's attempts to crush it.

She had her own survival to think of, now. She was going into unknown territory. It set her heart afire with the thrill of danger and kept her nerves on edge.

She joined in the conversation of the other recruits, consisting mainly of self-congratulation and speculation. The latest newspapers from the east, all filled with descriptions of preparation for war, were passed around and discussed. When the train deposited them in Detroit, Captain Morse led them toward the river about a mile, to the sprawling brick buildings of Fort Wayne.

The fort had never been occupied by the army, but now the 2nd Michigan Volunteers had taken it over. Emma looked in vain for the gray uniforms of Flint's own. All the soldiers she could see, drilling in groups on the parade ground or practicing with their muskets, were dressed alike in the same dark blue worn by Captain Morse.

"This way," Morse said brusquely, leading them between buildings. "The Quartermaster will issue your kit."

The Quartermaster did so, providing each of the recruits with a uniform, cap, boots, canteen, haversack, and musket. Thus burdened in addition to the small valise she had brought with her, Emma followed Captain Morse and the others to the barracks assigned to the Grays, now designated Company F of the 2nd.

"Just stack your things for now," said Captain Morse. "You'll be at liberty to find bunkmates after drill."

Emma stood gazing down the length of the building at the wide bunks, five high, that smelled of freshly-sawn wood. There were ten sets of bunks, five on either side of the aisle.

Emma swallowed. How could she sleep beside a man and maintain her deception?

She followed her fellow-recruits' example and set her things against the wall, taking a moment to examine the musket. It was a smoothbore, not the most recent design. Captain Morse, standing nearby, caught her eye.

"No rifles?" Emma asked.

"These were what Colonel Richardson could get," Morse replied. "We may get rifles in Washington."

"The Quartermaster gave us no ammunition."

Morse grimaced. "You're to drill without it. The government doesn't want any of the recruits to injure themselves."

Emma gave a huff of scoffing laughter. Morse's face twitched in an unsuccessful attempt to hide a smile. Though the captain seemed to be trying his best to keep a distance in accordance with his rank, it was impossible to forget old friendships.

"Dress out, now," Morse said to them all, resuming his air of authority. "When you are ready you will join the rest of the company at drill."

Emma carefully propped her musket against the wall, hiding a rush of anxiety. This would be the first test of her ability to keep her incognito. She glanced at the others, hoping to find them all distracted with their own new uniforms.

Private Rawley, a boy of eighteen whom Emma had first met that morning, called after the departing captain, "Excuse me, sir, where may we change?"

A moment's silence as Captain Morse turned, raising an eyebrow. It was broken with laughter from the other recruits.

"Wants a dressing-room, he does," said Private Green, giving Rawley a good-natured cuff on the shoulder.

Rawley flushed, then stepped to the nearest window and drew the curtains closed before beginning to unbutton his coat. The others continued to chide him.

Emma removed her own coat. She would have liked a dressing-room too, but she kept it to herself. As swiftly as she could, she pulled on her new uniform over her shirt and long underwear. The blouse, which closed with four brass buttons down the front, and the trousers rode well enough, being cut loosely so as to fit a variety of men. The boots, she found when she sat on a nearby bunk to put them on, were too large.

She pulled off the boot she had tried on and sat frowning at it. Unhappily, this attracted the attention of Private Rawley.

"Look at those dainty feet of his," Rawley said. "Pretty as a girl's!"

A stab of fear made Emma freeze.

"March a few miles in those and your feet will spread to fill 'em," said Green, grinning.

Emma joined in the following laughter, then opened her valise and took out a spare pair of socks. By stuffing these into the boots she was able to make them fit somewhat better.

"That's a handsome Bible," said Green, stepping toward her bed to admire the book in Emma's open valise.

"Thank you." She picked it up, offering to show it to him out of long habit. It was a gilt and leather-bound Carriage Bible, larger than the Testaments she had donated. Heavier, too, of course, but she could not bear to part with it, or with the Psalms.

"That's right, you're the Bible salesman," said Private Shelley, joining them as he buttoned up his blouse. "I remember. You came to our house last fall, and delivered us a new family Bible in time for Christmas."

Emma smiled at him, grateful for the support. "I hope your family enjoys the book."

"Oh, they do. It's beautiful, much bigger than this one," Shelley added, showing Emma's Bible to the others.

"Why'd you leave selling books to go for a soldier?" asked Green.

"Why did you leave masonry?" Emma returned. "I imagine you made more than a soldier's pay."

"I expect we are all here for the same reason," said Private Howell, a tall, slender fellow whose dark beard and piercing eyes made him look to Emma like a mountain man. He had been quiet for the most part, until now.

No one chose to disagree with him. They all regarded one another, and Emma felt the tightening of a new-formed bond of unity among them. She was glad of it.

Footsteps—boots clomping on the wood floor of the barracks—intruded on the moment of fraternity. Emma glanced up and saw Mr. Turver approaching.

"Hello, boys," he called. "Welcome to Company F. I am Corporal Turver, come to bring you out to drill with the rest of the company. Fall in."

Emma hastily put her Bible and clothing into her valise, and stowed it against the wall. Catching up her musket, she joined the others following Corporal Turver out to the parade ground.

The rest of the day was spent in drilling, learning the manual of arms, and more drilling. Emma saw many familiar faces among the company and was gratified to be made welcome. At midday they were dismissed to dinner in the fort's vast mess hall, and as she was standing in line to be served, she felt a hand on her shoulder.

"Frank! I thought that was you I saw come in with the fresh meat! Welcome!"

Damon Stewart, her mercantile friend, beamed at Emma and pumped her hand. His brown hair took on a reddish cast against the blue of his uniform blouse, and he had grown a mustache.

Emma smiled back. "Thank you."

"I half thought you had decided to go back to Canada."

"Not that, no. I knew I must serve the Union. I am glad to have been given the chance to do so with the Grays."

Damon grinned. "Now we shall have some good debates! Have you got a bunkmate?"

"Not yet."

"Then share with me. Mine skedaddled."

Emma thanked him, nervous but also relieved. Damon was a good friend. She need only take a little care, and she would be safe with him.

He joined Emma at the table and told her what the Grays had been up to for the past month, largely learning to move as a unit and respond quickly to commands. Emma listened with interest to this and to the camp gossip, the soldiers' chief form of entertainment.

"We hear that we are to go to Washington tomorrow, or next week, or at the end of June," Damon told her. "Believe whichever you will, but most of us prefer to believe in tomorrow."

As it happened, the morrow produced no summons to the capital, but it did produce a summons to the medical examiner for Emma and her fellow replacements. They went all together, the seven of them standing up nervously in a line waiting to be declared fit for service.

Emma had kept her overlarge boots, though her feet had begun to get blisters from drilling in them, in the hope they would help her pass the examination. She had not counted on anyone taking notice of her hands, though, and was startled when one of the examiners, walking along the line of soldiers, took hold of her wrist and raised it, turning her hand over to reveal the soft palm.

"What sort of living has this hand earned?"

Emma met his gaze and smiled, hoping he could not feel

the quickening of her pulse. "Well, up to the present, that hand has chiefly been engaged in getting an education."

"Hm."

The examiner turned her hand over again, peered at her neatly-trimmed fingernails, then let her go and moved on to the next recruit. Emma let out her breath slowly, the nape of her neck tingling.

She was passed, along with the others, much to her relief. The next morning she went to the Quartermaster to trade her boots for a smaller pair, which brought on a renewal of teasing about her small feet.

"Ah, our woman's gotten a better pair of slippers," said Private Rawley, who seemed anxious to prove his own hardiness.

Emma held still for an instant, then to her private amusement, Damon Stewart defended her. "The size of a man's feet does not affect his ability to fight," he said.

"Or to run," said another.

"The only running I expect to be doing is toward the Rebels," Emma replied, lacing her new boots tight.

"There's a fierce lad!"

The teasing continued, but in a good-natured way, and Emma responded with equal cheer. She no longer feared suspicion from her fellow soldiers. They had accepted her, and as long as she was careful, she would be safe.

One way in which she must be careful was in finding relief from the calls of nature. The sink provided by the army for the soldiers' use was far too public, being only a long trench with a pole suspended above it for a seat. Her dismay upon learning of this, that first day, was compounded by the urgency of her physical need.

Fortunately, she spied a fellow soldier slipping behind a convenient bush to relieve himself. The bush, being closer to the barracks than the sink, was apparently a preferred spot, for when Emma strolled past it an unmistakable aroma assailed her.

She bypassed this location, and also the sink, and decided to develop a habit of taking long walks in the woods in her free time.

The days passed quickly. The company spent many hours at drill, and amused themselves with conversation in the evenings. Emma considered offering to lead prayers in the barracks, but decided it would be best not to draw attention to herself. She did read in her Bible every night, and often discussed it with others who shared her devotion.

When she had been with the company for two weeks, the order to move to Washington arrived. Much excitement ensued, and a flurry of furloughs were issued to allow the soldiers to pay farewell visits to their loved ones. Emma did not request a furlough. She had made her farewells, and was content.

She was lying on her bunk, reading a newspaper, when Private Howell approached. Emma glanced up as Howell sat on the neighboring bunk.

"No sweetheart back in Flint, young Thompson?" he said.

"No," Emma replied. "Nor you?"

"Nor I."

Emma lowered her paper, wondering what Howell wanted. He sat gazing out of the window at the grounds, which were shaded in gathering dusk.

"They all say it will be a grand rout," Howell said in a musing tone. "Do you think so?"

"I don't know," Emma said.

"I do wonder...if the outcome is so certain, why did the Rebels bother at all to secede?"

The subject was one oft debated among the soldiers, but Emma had never heard it stated in quite this way. She thought for a moment.

"They must believe they are acting in the right," she said at last.

"Then God's justice will fall on them like a mighty hammer," said Howell, his voice suddenly harsh.

Emma regarded him, then slowly nodded. "So it will."

Howell nodded also, his expression one of satisfaction, then he stood up and went away. Emma watched him go back to his own bunk, several beds down the row.

God's justice. She believed in it, and pitied the Rebels.

On June 6th the regiment boarded steamers bound for Cleveland, accompanied by the cheering of a number of the good people of Detroit, who had come to see them off. In Cleveland they were met with more cheering as they marched from the wharf to the depot.

Crowds of well-wishers stood on the platforms at every depot they passed. When the train stopped long enough, the soldiers were offered baked treats, lemonade, and even kisses from some of the bolder young ladies. Emma began to feel compensated for not having been fussed over when she had departed Flint.

All day and night the train continued eastward. Late the next day it reached Harrisburg, Pennsylvania, where the regiment marched into Camp Curtis. Here they were issued tents, and she and Damon lost no time setting up theirs, then hastened to prepare for afternoon parade.

After supper, Emma put her cap atop her haversack, took off her boots and set them by the foot of her bed, then crawled beneath her blanket. She lay on her stomach, watching out the open front door of the tent as the regiment settled in for the night. The aroma of campfires and the rich, green smells of the fields filled her with a sense of well-being. Somewhere in the camp a banjo plinked out a tune.

"We're to be issued ammunition tomorrow," Damon said. "I heard it from the quartermaster."

Emma thought quietly about that. Tomorrow they would reach Baltimore, where in April the first Union troops to pass through the city had been attacked by a mob of Southern sympathizers. The same ugly fate might await the Second.

"Did you read in the paper that the tracks in the middle of the city have been torn up?" she said.

"Yes. We'll have to march across town to the Washington train." Damon turned on his side, propping himself up on his elbow. "Do you think that is the reason for giving us live ammunition?"

"Perhaps." Emma turned her head to look at him. "Or maybe it is just time that we stopped 'playing soljer' and took up our real duties."

"Playing? Is it a game to you, then?"

Emma glanced down and pressed her lips together, holding back a smile. "Not a game, no."

"I think to some of them it is," Damon said quietly.

Emma made no answer. She thought perhaps some of the

men pretended it was all a game, so as not to be afraid. She herself was afraid, but for reasons that differed from most.

The next morning they struck their tents, received their issue of ammunition, and got back on the cars, the new cartridges riding heavy in the boxes on their belts. The mood in the cars was less jubilant, save for a few men who maintained a stream of rather antic hilarity. Green was one of these. Emma listened in silence.

Sixteen miles from Baltimore the train halted and the men were ordered off it to form a column in the road and load their weapons. Emma could now perform the manual of arms in her sleep, or so she thought, yet still her hand trembled a little as she poured the powder from her cartridge into her musket and rammed the ball home. She had loaded guns countless times for hunting, but this time if she fired, it would be at a man.

It was wrong to kill, according to God's law, but in war this rule was suspended. Emma had not resolved the paradox within her heart. She wanted most ardently to support the Union, yet she shrank from slaying its enemies. She would have to resolve herself, she knew.

As they took up the march, the ranks fell quiet. No cheery songs rose up as they had during the march across Cleveland. Maryland was divided, and though the army held Baltimore, many of the citizens were for the South.

Just outside the city, the column made a brief halt. Captain Morse came down the line, looking over his company.

"If anyone in the town undertakes hostilities against you, you are to fire upon them," he told them.

Emma saw his grim expression and her heart sank. To fire upon civilians was a terrible prospect. She silently prayed that it would not be necessary.

They moved forward again, marching into Baltimore all in step, aware of the faces gazing at them from the windows. Farther into the town the streets were lined with people watching the march. Emma saw their angry expressions and knew alarm.

"More damned bluebellies," someone in the crowd

muttered.

Emma pretended not to have heard. Her hand felt slick on the butt of her musket. The day suddenly seemed hot.

Movement caught her eye; someone in the crowd raised an arm. The next moment a rock flew toward the column, toward E Company, marching just ahead of the Grays. A sharp, angry cry followed. Emma saw the soldier who was struck, a corporal, raise his musket.

And fire.

Baltimore, Maryland, 1861

"Keep your ranks! Keep your ranks! Forward march!" The order bellowed along the column by voice after voice. Emma swallowed.

Lieutenant Farrand, nearest her, sounded hoarse already. His face was sheened with sweat, and he scowled fiercely at the Grays, who regained their pace after a moment's faltering and marched on.

Some angry shouting was going on among the citizens of Baltimore, but Emma could not make out the words over the continuing orders to keep ranks. She faced forward and ignored the crowd, though her skin prickled all over.

No more rocks were thrown, no more shots fired. After what seemed an eternity of tense marching through the hot sun, the regiment arrived unmolested at the south side of Baltimore, where a train waited to carry them to Washington.

Emma breathed a sigh of relief as she climbed into one of the cars. She had feared a repeat of April's riot, all the way up until the Second had reached the depot. With silent thanks to God for preventing such a horrible event, she took a seat on the far side of the car and gazed out of the window, glad to be leaving Baltimore behind.

Damon joined her, saying, "That was a near thing."

Emma nodded. Her throat was dry and tight with the tension of the march. She sipped from her canteen.

The company was subdued until the train began to move. As they left Baltimore behind, the soldiers' voices rose in discussion, eagerly sharing details about the rock-throwing incident. The atmosphere of tension dissipated, replaced by something of the merriment that had prevailed on most of the journey, though not quite as carefree.

"I am glad we did not have to fire on civilians," Emma said.

Damon gazed at her. "Afraid, Frank?" he asked softly.

She squared her shoulders and met his gaze. "I am not afraid to face the enemy. I think it is wrong to fight our own people."

Damon gave a snort. "They looked like enemies to me. Sounded like 'em, too."

"Maryland has not seceded."

"Technically, true." He shook his head. "You are right, it would have been unfortunate. All for the best that we had no need to fire."

By the time they reached Washington, the soldiers of the Second were exhausted by travel and excitement. They descended from the cars into a city filled with military activity.

Emma had seen lively cities before, but never one as lively as this. Soldiers marched through the streets and lounged on the grounds of the Capitol, officers on showy horses attracted the admiration of the local ladies, and everywhere there was talk of war.

The Second spent a night in quarters, and were reviewed the next day by President Lincoln and General Scott. Emma longed for a look at the President, but only saw him from a distance.

Having been approved for service, the regiment marched through the city to a camp in the countryside overlooking the Potomac. Here they formed a brigade along with three other regiments—one from Massachusetts, one from New York, and another Michigan regiment—all under the command of the Second's own Colonel Richardson.

The soldiers busied themselves in setting up their camp, and soon settled into a routine of daily drill, visits to the city, and yearning for letters from home. Emma and Damon continued as tentmates, and spent many evenings talking round campfires with others of the company. Emma felt at ease with Damon, who seemed to have decided to take "young Frank" under his wing.

She found she enjoyed camp life, though she avoided some of the soldiers' more popular spare-time pursuits, such as drinking and gambling. Instead she sought out prayer meetings and lectures whenever they occurred.

She also took advantage of the passes to visit Washington which were generously distributed by superiors anxious to combat the soldiers' boredom. She eagerly acquainted herself with the halls of government, the Smithsonian Castle, all the monuments and museums and other places of interest.

In mid-June, a wave of typhoid swept through the Second, sending many of them to the hospital tents. Emma began to spend her evenings there, giving water to sick soldiers, washing their faces, writing letters for them, or merely listening to their frustration at being ill. She found she had a knack for calming troubled spirits, for bringing ease to restless men struck down by an enemy at which they could not strike back.

She felt she was being of use. If it was not exactly missionary work, it was still God's work, still a work of compassion.

Now and again a sick soldier would speak to her of God—sometimes shyly, as if only his weakness had brought him to think on such matters—and she would talk with him of Christ and the righteousness of serving one's country. She began to bring her Bible to the hospital and read to those who wished to hear. It seemed to comfort.

She was doing so one evening when the surgeon, Dr. Palmer, came up to where she sat and stood looking at her. He had made his rounds of the tent earlier, and the man to whom she was reading was in no distress. Emma felt the back of her neck prickle, but she finished the chapter she was reading before looking up at the surgeon.

"A word with you, Thompson," he said, gesturing toward the tent door.

Emma closed her book, said a brief farewell to the sick soldier, and followed the surgeon out of the tent. Had she somehow betrayed herself? She could not think how, but the fear of it ran chill down her spine.

Dr. Palmer led her to the dispensary tent, a smaller wall tent where the medicines were kept and where the surgeons remained when they were not visiting their patients. Inside, the smell of tonics and herbs was pleasantly pungent. The hospital steward was measuring out a dose of some medicine, and Dr. Lyster, the Second's other surgeon, sat at ease, reading. Emma held her Bible tightly and waited.

"You have been spending a good deal of your time in the hospital, Thompson," said Dr. Palmer.

Dr. Lyster looked up and closed his book, taking an interest. He glanced at Emma, then smiled slightly as he looked at Dr. Palmer.

"Yes, sir," Emma said to Palmer.

"We appreciate your efforts to make the men more comfortable."

Emma cleared her throat. "Thank you, sir. I am happy to do it."

Palmer and Lyster exchanged a glance. Emma looked from one to the other. Had her voice given her away? She never sang in camp, and she thought her speaking voice passed as that of a young man, but perhaps it had been a mistake to read to the sick. She felt a trembling threaten to start in her arms, and held them tight to her sides to fight it.

"How would you like to be assigned to regular hospital duty?" Dr. Lyster said.

Emma blinked. "Sir?"

"You would still drill with your company, but your duty would be here otherwise. We are allowed four men to nurse the sick. Would you be willing to make it your regular work?"

Relief washed through Emma's limbs. "I would be glad to, sir."

"It will mean odd hours for you—night duty, at times. You will have to sleep during the day on those occasions."

Time alone in the tent she shared with Damon. A bit of privacy.

"I would not mind that," Emma said.

"Excellent!" said Doctor Palmer. "I will speak to the colonel about your assignment."

"Thank you, sir." Emma smiled, delighted in her good fortune.

Hospital duty was not a sought-after detail. Most soldiers would rather dig ditches than tend the sick, but Emma did not mind it. Certainly the fetid smells of the hospital were uncomfortable, even when the greatest care was taken to maintain them as clean as could be. Cleaning the men who had soiled themselves from being too weak to rise was also unpleasant, but little more unpleasant than the tending of infant babes.

Emma had learned at a young age how to do that, having been called upon to assist her sister shortly after the birth of her first child. She had not found the baby as charming as her sister did. Tending the soldiers who suffered from typhoid or dysentery was much the same as caring for a sick baby, except that the men she aided seldom screamed.

She enjoyed the work, and continued to receive praise for it. She knew also that when her regiment saw battle, she would be able to help the wounded.

Perhaps the best advantage of hospital duty for her was the opportunity to slip her soiled handkerchiefs into the laundry. The first time she did this she covertly watched the contrabands who did the washing, but they seemed to think nothing out of place.

In the dispensary tent, she cast a covetous eye on the shelf full of bandages. These would be a last resort for her, if she were ever in dire need.

July Fourth was a day of celebration and picnics. All regular duty was suspended in honor of the nation's independence, though some talked of the irony of that celebration when the country was struggling over whether the southern states should be allowed to secede. It made for interesting discussions in the mess.

The summer wore on, and Washington was ever more a center of military activity. More regiments arrived, making the area all around the capital into a giant camp. Dress parade was frequently attended by onlookers from the city, who often brought picnics.

Some of the men were restless for a fight. The same conversations went round and round—when will marching orders arrive? Emma was content to await events.

One morning she returned to her tent after a shift of duty in the hospital and found a letter from Flint lying on her bedroll. This surprised her to no end, for she had made no attempt to maintain a correspondence with anyone there. At first she thought it must be from the Joslins, but the hand was neither Mr. Joslin's firm strokes nor his wife's elegant script. The writing was light, well-formed, and simple.

Damon, wakened by the first call, fumbled sleepily with the brass buttons of his blouse. "That arrived yesterday."

Emma glanced at him, then back at the letter. It bore no name with the return address, only the street number, which seemed familiar. Emma frowned, trying to recall who it might be.

"Aren't you going to open it?" Damon said, pulling on his boots. "I want the news from Flint."

Emma turned the letter over and opened it, smoothing the folds out of the page. "Dear Mr. Private Thompson," it began.

It was from Miss Daphne Little.

Emma read it through quickly, knowing she and Damon must assemble for roll call. Miss Daphne had joined the other young ladies of Flint in an effort to remember all the young men of the Grays—she said as much, artlessly, and went on to hope that Private Thompson was well and in good spirits. Emma was touched, and could not help but smile.

The letter contained little in the way of news. Flint was as it always was, and the talk was all of war, which Miss Daphne did not scruple to say she found dull. Since it was brief, Emma read the letter aloud to Damon as he finished dressing.

He grinned slyly. "I think Mr. Private Thompson has an admirer."

"I think Miss Daphne Little is a trifle young," Emma replied. "She is but fifteen."

"That is not too young. Not for you, Frank."

Emma said nothing, merely folded the letter and slipped it into her pocket, then reached for her musket.

She had been Miss Daphne's age when her father had sought to marry her off. Remembering it brought back the anger she had felt.

Emma went out with Damon, stood through the roll call, then returned to the tent to rest until drill. She would answer Miss Daphne's letter in the afternoon, she decided as she lay drifting toward sleep. Such kindness should not go unthanked.

Some few days later Emma was on duty in the hospital tent when a wild whoop went up through the camp. She went to the tent door and looked out. The hospital was on a slight rise, and she could see down along the orderly streets of tents in the Second's camp. Men were standing there in clusters, talking excitedly. Now and then one would dash along a street.

Emma turned to Dr. Palmer, who had come out to stand beside her. "What is it?"

"Marching orders," the doctor said. "I have just received them. We advance on Manassas tomorrow."

"Oh."

Emma looked back at the excitement in the camp below. The prevailing mood was joyful. Emma felt no desire to celebrate. She could only think of the suffering to come.

Glancing back into the hospital tent, she looked at the empty beds—more than half of them—and imagined them filled with wounded. The storm of war that had been so long gathering was about to break.

Washington, D.C., 1883

"How convenient for you," Jamie said, not quite sneering. "You were already in a position to stay behind and watch over the sick."

"I did not stay behind," Emma said calmly, determined not to allow Jamie to goad her. "I marched with the Second the next day. So did the surgeons. There were fewer sick in the hospital then, and they left one man to tend them."

Jamie's brows drew together in a frown. "You were at Bull Run, then?"

"Yes. We were sent to Centreville, then went on to try to find a crossing of the Run. We had reached Blackburn's Ford when the Rebel artillery opened fire on us."

Jamie nodded, the animosity gone from his face. "So you were in the advance."

All at once, constraint fell away as they shared the memories etched on their souls. No longer were they at odds; they were two veterans talking of the war.

"We were pinned by artillery fire for half a day," Emma said. "That was Thursday. On Sunday we were in reserve at Centreville."

"We were at Henry House Hill." Jamie's eyes darkened, looking into the past. Emma felt a rush of sympathy.

"That was when you were captured," she said softly.

"Yes."

His face hardened and he looked away. He never had liked to talk of the months he had spent in a Confederate prison. It had been fresh in his mind, when they had first been acquainted, but he seemed no more reconciled to it after twenty years.

"We were all so innocent, before then," Emma remarked.

She became aware of Mr. Glass watching her. He knew

nothing of the hardship of war. He was young, confident, and wholly ignorant of the savage brutality of which man—of which he himself—was capable.

A sudden weariness of spirit came over Emma, and she moved to a chair and sat down. Jamie glanced toward her; she thought she saw a momentary concern in his eyes, but then his face closed again, as if he had drawn a curtain across his heart.

"So you remained in reserve during the worst of the fighting," he said, the bitter edge returning to his voice. "How fortunate for you."

"I was not idle. I volunteered to help in the field hospital." Emma shuddered; she could not help it. "That first time was the worst," she murmured. "I had no idea how it would be."

The War: Centreville, Virginia, 1861

Sunday, the 21st of July, dawned with a rumble of thunder that never faded. Unnatural thunder, herald of a tempest that bore a rain of lead, a flood of blood. Artillery fire continued in the distance, never ceasing, and soon the wounded began to arrive.

The field hospital where Emma had volunteered to work was in a small stone church in Centreville, hastily commandeered by the surgeons upon the brigade's arrival a few days before. The pulpit and altar had been moved aside to make room for the surgeons' tables. Pews were stacked against the wall, and stocks of bandages, lint, and other supplies made ready.

The first wounded were victims of artillery fire, bleeding from shrapnel wounds, flesh torn and raw. They moaned as they were brought in and tended, the unluckiest of them soon beginning to scream under the surgeon's knife.

Emma's heart hammered as she ran for bandages, brandy, and water. Her nerves were as tense as if she were herself under fire, but it was the pain in the eyes of the wounded that pierced her, the screams that raked her soul.

A ghastly heap of severed limbs began to pile up outside the church—she saw it when she went to refill the half-dozen canteens she had scrounged to bring water to the wounded. It made her gorge rise, but she had no time to indulge in weakness. Too many waited patiently, in pain, for the simplest attentions. She went to the nearby stream to draw water, taking care to go well upstream from the hospital, then hurrying back to the church.

A man was brought in raving, both his legs smashed irreparably above the knee. He was laid on the floor at the end of a row of wounded, but his agonized thrashing threatened to harm his neighbor. Emma, who had been washing the face of that neighbor, grabbed at the newcomer's flailing arm and was astonished at the strength in it. He nearly pulled her off her knees.

"Here, move aside!" said one of the soldiers who had carried the poor fellow in.

Emma yielded her place to the larger man. It took both him and his fellow stretcher-bearer to hold the unfortunate soldier down. Dr. Palmer came over and looked at him briefly, shook his head, then went on to someone who could be helped.

Emma watched in horror as the poor man shrieked and wept, his head thrashing back and forth, practically beating against the stone floor as he cried out to God to release him. Inflammation soon granted his wish, to the dreadful relief of all. He was carried out again, laid with the other dead in a heap more grim than that of the lost arms and legs.

No time to bury them. Emma turned her face from the horrors outside the church, offering what comfort she could to those yet clinging to life. Working without rest, scarcely conscious of the day wearing on, she moved from man to man, offering water, bathing fevered brows, joining broken voices in prayer.

One man she came to was plainly close to death, his face white and grimly set against his pain, though he bore it in silence. He shook his head slightly when she offered water, eyes beseeching as he looked up at her.

"Do you think I'll die before morning?" he asked.

Emma gazed at him, blinking back a sudden threat of tears as her throat tightened. She would not deceive him; he had the right to an honest answer.

"I think so," she said, nodding. "Has death any terrors for you?"

"Oh, no." He smiled, the smile of one looking forward to rest after long toil. "I shall soon be asleep in Jesus."

Night descended and the roar of artillery finally ceased, but the crisis continued in the hospital. Lanterns were lit and the surgeons went on with their grisly work. The church was now filled, as were the other buildings the surgeons had claimed, and still the wounded kept coming.

An assistant surgeon collapsed against the wall, overwhelmed and exhausted. Emma watched him sink to the floor, and was about to go to him, when a harsh voice stopped her.

"You there. Thompson. Come here!"

It was Dr. Palmer who had called her, his hands drenched in blood to the elbows, rolled sleeves stained dark with it. With a sodden rag he wiped the blood from his empty table. It spattered like rain upon the stone floor.

Uneasy, Emma approached him. "Yes, sir?"

"You'll have to help."

"I don't know how—"

"Put him here," the surgeon said to two men carrying a third.

They placed their burden on the table and left. Emma stared in horror at the soldier's mangled foot, still covered by part of a boot, whose top dangled around his ankle.

"Put that bucket underneath," Dr. Palmer told her. "That's right. Now hold him down. Rogers will hold his legs. No, across the chest, and mind he doesn't get his arms free. You may have to sit on him, if he's too strong for you."

Glad to be able to turn her face away, Emma flung her body across the soldier's. She had thought he was insensible, but soon learned otherwise. His moan rose to an agonized cry and then to a shriek that made her squeeze her eyes closed, wishing she could cover her ears. The man's body beneath her rocked slightly as the surgeon plied his saw.

"No more! No! Please! Please—aaaaaah!" cried the man, ending in a wordless howl. He thrashed, and she leaned all her weight upon him.

When the rocking finally stopped, the man was sobbing, rasping with each breath. Emma slowly eased her weight off of him.

"I'm sorry," she whispered, though she doubted he could hear.

"That'll do," said Dr. Palmer. "Go out to the wagons and find Warren, send him in to me," the surgeon said. "You're too small to hold them."

Emma swallowed, ashamed of the relief she felt. She obeyed this order, then retrieved her canteens and returned to making her rounds, glancing in the direction of the battlefield as she moved from building to building. At sunset, on the heights above the town, she had seen troops stack their arms and throw themselves on the ground to rest. Now the darkness hid them, and still the agonized screams rose from the church as the heap of discarded limbs grew higher.

Mr. Brown, the Second's chaplain, caught Emma's arm as she was returning to the church with freshly-filled canteens. Like Emma, he had spent the day offering comfort to the wounded. His sleeves were stained with blood, his face pale in the light spilling from the open doorway.

"The army has retreated toward Washington," he said, frowning in dismay. "We are abandoned."

"That cannot be true!" Emma said.

"It is true. We must follow them, or be captured."

"No!"

The threat of capture held its own terrors for Emma, but they were overshadowed by dismay at the thought that the army would abandon its wounded to the enemy. She looked at the church and the other hospital buildings, thinking of the helpless men lying within.

"I cannot believe they would desert us," she said. "They have moved their camp, perhaps. I will go and see."

"Frank!" the chaplain called after her, but she was already striding up the road to the heights.

A few minutes brought her to the ground where she had seen the men stacking arms. It was indeed abandoned. Thinking she might find them by searching the field, she strode across it, and soon spied a glimmer of flame.

A campfire. Only one, but perhaps others were nearby. Emma hastened toward it, seeing as she came near that the fire was tended by a solitary figure.

A woman crouched beside the flame, feeding it with sticks, coaxing heat from the coals beneath a battered pot filled with water. Nearby stood a huge heap of blankets, haversacks, and canteens that she had evidently collected. Emma recognized her as she came near; it was one of the washerwomen who followed the army, married to a soldier in the Second though Emma could not remember who.

The woman's hair was a wild tangle, and she wore a soldier's overcoat. She glanced up as Emma entered the circle of firelight.

"Good evening, ma'am," Emma said. "I am looking for the army's camp. Can you tell me where it lies?"

"I don't know anything about the army," the woman said irritably. "I am cooking my husband's supper, and am expecting him home every minute."

Home? Emma glanced around. As far as she knew, the field was empty save for the woman's campfire. No tent stood nearby, not even a horse or a mule.

The woman suddenly sat up and smiled. "See what a lot of things I have got for him?"

She gestured toward her pile of battlefield spoils. Emma closed her eyes. This woman was wounded, she realized, as surely as any of the men in the hospitals. Wounded in her soul. She had lost her mind, from grief, perhaps.

"Ma'am," Emma said gently, now convinced of the danger of their situation. "The army has gone. The enemy will surely come here soon. We must leave if we are not to be captured."

"No, my husband will be home soon. I must wait here for him."

She stirred her pot of water with a stick, paused to peer into it, then stirred again. Emma begged and pleaded with her, but nothing would move her. At last Emma gave up and started back toward Centreville.

She had gone only a short distance when she heard the clatter of hooves behind her. Turning, she saw a squad of cavalry stopping at the poor mad woman's campfire. They were not Union troops, she was certain. Cold fear washed through her limbs.

Hide, or be captured. The washerwoman would not think to conceal Emma's presence from the Rebels, not in her fuddled state.

Emma glanced at a fence nearby. The field beyond was too open, but there were several large piles of brush close against the fence. In the darkness, she might hide beneath one and escape the cavalrymen's notice.

The horses' hooves sounded again. Glancing back, Emma saw the cavalrymen approaching, following the washerwoman whom they compelled at gunpoint to precede them. A drizzle of rain was beginning. Emma crawled beneath the nearest brush pile and lay still, watching as the horsemen came closer.

"You're sure he came this way?" a man's voice demanded.

"Oh, yes," said the woman, her voice high with fear.

"Because if you're lying, we'll shoot you, old woman."

"It's the truth! It's the truth! He walked right down this hill!"

The horsemen halted not ten paces from where Emma lay. She shivered, more with fear than with cold, though the rain dripped from her cap and ran into the collar of her shirt. She held her breath, watching and listening.

There were five horsemen in all, and their leader now commenced a heated argument with the washerwoman, who wanted to go back to her fire and wait for her husband. He threatened again to shoot her, and she began to cry. Emma was sorry for her, but dared not try to intervene. To do so would be to give herself up a captive.

The leader sent three of his men searching along the fence, and Emma cringed, her heart thudding in her chest so loud she feared it would give her away. Darkness, the rain, and the brush pile protected her, though. At length, the cavalrymen left, taking the poor washerwoman with them.

Emma lay silent, counting a full five minutes before she dared emerge. Crawling out of the brush, she stood shivering for a moment, looking and listening.

The fire had guttered, or else the cavalrymen had extinguished it. She heard no more hoofbeats, but she could not deceive herself that the Rebels were gone. They would come, more of them, and take Centreville. She hastened back to the church.

Only one lamp remained, its light far too feeble to fill the church, nor even reach the door. Emma stood in the doorway listening to the groans of the wounded.

"Water," someone said feebly nearby, and another took up the plea.

Emma hastened to find a canteen. It was empty. She collected a dozen more and carried them outside in the rain to fill them. Returning, she gave canteens to those who could lift them, and helped those who could not to drink.

"Did Chaplain Brown leave?" she asked a man who was well enough to sit up and drink.

"Yes," he said, gasping between long gulps at the canteen. "and so must you. The chaplain said we would soon be in the hands of the enemy. You will be taken prisoner if you stay."

For a moment Emma considered it. If she might be allowed

to continue to care for these poor suffering men—but no, she could not take the risk of discovery.

"If you do stay the Rebels will not let you do anything for us," the wounded soldier told her, as if he had read her thoughts.

Others murmured agreement, urging Emma to go. Her heart breaking, she filled all the canteens again and gave them to those who could use their arms. Turning to go, she was called back by the feeble voice of a young officer from Massachusetts, who lay near the wall. Emma came to him and saw that he held a gold locket in his hand.

"Will you please to open it?" he said, holding it out to her with a trembling hand.

He was dying, Emma realized. She opened the locket, which contained a portrait of a lovely young woman holding a baby in her arms, and held it up so the officer could see. A name and address were printed on the opposite side of the locket.

The officer seized Emma's hand and dragged it closer, gazing feverishly at the locket, then pressing it to his lips. Emma waited, thinking he would give her some message for his family, but he only kissed the portrait again and again.

Outside a rumble that was not thunder arose, coming nearer. Horses.

"Go," whispered another soldier nearby. "You must go!"

Emma put the locket away in her pocket and slipped out of a window at the rear of the church. Rain brushed her cheeks. She pulled her coat closer about her.

Glancing toward the streets, she saw that they were already filled with Confederate cavalry.

The rain was falling more heavily now, and the ranks of dark shapes moved through the abandoned town like so many demons. Emma climbed over a fence and cut across a field, keeping as far from Centreville as she could.

Crossing several more fences and fields, she skirted the town for a mile and more until she came out upon the Fairfax road. Here there was no sign of the Confederates as yet. They would be occupied some time in Centreville, no doubt, securing their wounded prisoners.

Emma closed her eyes, saying a brief prayer for the safety of those brave men. Not a one of them had bemoaned his cruel fate, nor begrudged her the freedom to escape it.

She dared not linger, for she was still in danger of being captured. She set off along the road, running as far as she could, then walking to rest until she had strength enough to run again. The rain soaked her uniform, and at times she paused to turn her face skyward and catch some of it in her mouth, as she had left her own canteen with the wounded.

She had no food; the rations she had been issued were long gone. Her haversack was empty of all but her Bible and a number of letters and remembrances she had accepted from the wounded, promising to send them on to loved ones.

The sky lightened as dawn came, though the sun struggled feebly against the continuing rain. Emma trudged wearily on, passing signs of the army's scrambling retreat all along the road. Wagons lay broken and overturned, their contents spilled in the road or alongside it, some with the horses that had pulled them lying dead in the traces. Ambulances that had carried civilians from Washington in picnic spirits to view the battle, now foundered in mud with broken wheels or axles, ruined and blocking the roadway.

Emma wondered idly what had become of those sightseers, then decided she didn't care. It had been foolish of them to come to the battlefield as if it were merely another review. The spectacle to which they had been treated was no doubt unlike what they had expected.

From what she could see, the retreat had been no less than a rout. She could have wept for the waste of the broken wagons and ruined supplies, and did weep a little for the poor men she had left behind in the church.

She found her regiment at noon, encamped on a farm at Arlington. Exhausted, her boots nearly worn off her feet, she wandered through the dismal, rain-soaked camp until she found her company huddled around sputtering fires beneath some spreading oak trees.

"Frank!" Damon cried, jumping up, a blanket clutched around himself.

Several others exclaimed, bidding "Frank" welcome. Emma thanked them and edged closer to the fire, holding out her chilled hands.

"You're wet through," Damon said. "Here, take this." He took off his blanket and, despite Emma's protests, wrapped it around her shoulders. "We thought you'd been captured," he added, frowning in concern.

"I nearly was, I think," Emma said.

"Ho! Got a story to tell, have you?"

Someone shoved a tin cup of coffee into her hands, and room was made for her beside the fire. Emma sat down with a weary sigh, grateful to be among her comrades again. She wrapped her hands around the hot mug and swallowed a mouthful of the scalding coffee, then told her friends about the hospital in the stone church, her encounter with the washerwoman and how she had hid from the Confederates, and her wet and weary journey on foot. It was not so grand a tale, but the Grays heard it appreciatively.

"Lucky you weren't taken," said Shelley.

"I know it," Emma said.

"Ah, he was just lollygagging," said Green, grinning as he reached over to clap Emma on the back. Her coffee sloshed onto her knee.

The Grays then told Emma their own stories, mostly of the dubious behavior of the rest of the army during its disgraceful retreat. Deserters there had been aplenty, and cowards who scrambled out of harm's way, their oaths to flag and country forgotten. None from the Second Michigan, of course.

Emma was proud to learn that the Second had been the rearguard, and though the Grays' description of the retreat consisted mainly of grumbling, it seemed to her that they had conducted themselves well in that duty. While the bulk of the army hastened away in disarray, the Second had kept order and halted time and again to face off the enemy, protecting the retreat.

Emma's thoughts drifted as the stories gave way to boasting and foolishness. The soldiers amused themselves with ridiculous tall tales, but Emma felt the shadow of dread beneath the laughter.

This war was now in earnest. What everyone had assumed would be a swift victory had instead been an ignominious rout. Far from over, the effort was scarcely begun. Emma saw a long, dreadful fight ahead.

Three years. She had promised three years of her life to this. She had not really expected she would be called upon to serve so long. Home for Christmas, Captain Morse had said. Now she knew that was merely a dream.

The Second returned to its old camping ground, and Emma and Damon reestablished their shared tent quarters. The first evening there Emma took out a candle and stuck it into the socket of her bayonet, shoved the blade into the ground beside the cracker box that held her few belongings and doubled as her table, and began writing letters.

The first was to the young mother in the portrait inside the gold locket. Emma took the locket from her pocket, opened it, and copied off the address, then turned the page over and set up the locket where she could look at it. Writing slowly, for her hands kept threatening to tremble, Emma told the poor widow of her beloved's demise, there in the rain-lashed church while the Rebels marched into Centreville. Her throat tightened as she wrote, remembering him, and all the others.

She folded the letter around the locket, then set it aside and drew another page toward her. She had many more remembrances in her haversack—letters, locks of hair, scraps of ribbon, buttons. Tiny treasures, sent with love from out of the dark despair in that stone church. She heaped them on a corner of the cracker box, and began to work her way through them.

"What is all of that?" Damon asked, coming in and taking

off his coat.

Emma told him. Damon's brows drew together. When she had told the Grays of her adventures in Centreville, she had not emphasized the despair of wounded men in the church, but the pitiful little pile of remembrances gave mute testimony.

"These might be the last messages their families will receive," Emma said, touching a lock of sandy hair. Some of them certainly were, she knew.

Damon gazed at them and a swallow moved his throat. "Can I help?" he said quietly.

Emma glanced at the pile, knowing her own memories of the words that went with the keepsakes were fleeting. "You could get some more writing paper from the sutler," she said. "I don't think I have enough."

"I will," he said, shrugging into his coat again.

He went out without another word. Emma listened to his receding footsteps, a soft smile on her lips. After a moment she dipped her pen and began to write again.

The defeated Union army began trying to pull itself together, without much success. Dread of an attack by the Confederates overshadowed them, though it diminished as the summer days wore on with no attack forthcoming.

Drill, when it was conducted at all, was done in a half-hearted manner. Every day many of the men were missing—gone into Washington to seek distraction in the taverns and brothels. The capital was filled with disillusioned, demoralized soldiers, and their officers were no better; like as not the man shouting orders had brandy fumes on his breath.

Emma sought a different form of reassurance at the prayer meetings still held in the camps. They were larger and more frequent these days, with many new faces of soldiers searching for a way to understand what had happened.

In the face of the army's widespread demoralization, President Lincoln gave command to General George McClellan, who at once began to bring order and discipline out of the chaos that had followed the first great battle of the war. McClellan insisted that camps be kept orderly and clean, and that the soldiers must drill for hours every day. There were grumblings at first, but they subsided as the army realized that McClellan's strictures were intended to improve their effectiveness. Hope and a sense of pride began to grow again among the ranks.

McClellan initiated a series of Grand Reviews to reassure the citizens of Washington that their city would indeed be defended. They served as well to remind the men that they were soldiers, and had a sober duty. Gradually the morale of the army that had been so heartbroken after Bull Run rose. Under their new commander's guidance, the raw volunteers began to hone themselves into a fine military machine.

Emma returned to hospital duty and was assigned to a general hospital in Georgetown, where she cared now for wounded as well as the sick. There were many, many of both —five hundred beds in the Georgetown hospital, and every one of them filled. Measles, dysentery, and typhoid raged among the troops, and still the surgeons continued their grim work, amputating ruined limbs and extracting musket balls and shrapnel from festering wounds.

The patients suffered nightmares and delirium as well, many of them reliving the terrors of the battlefield, and Emma heard their tortured ravings with a grieving heart. She did what she could to ease them, and to reassure those less sorely afflicted who had also to witness these piteous sights.

Summer passed and autumn came, bringing a blaze of color to the trees around Washington. The capital was again filled with martial activity, but there was an earnestness to it now that had been unknown before Bull Run. The frequent reviews reminded everyone, soldier and civilian alike, that the business they were about was serious. General McClellan tolerated no laxity.

In October, Emma returned to duty at the Second's regimental hospital. From brick walls to tents was a change, and Emma felt concern for the patients living in such tenuous shelter, though she herself had no better. She and the other hospital staff worked diligently to improve the conditions in the hospital tents. They dug trenches to divert the runoff from the powerful rainstorms that assailed the camp. They planted evergreens, pitched awnings to provide shade, and in general did all they could to benefit the patients in their care.

One evening while on night watch, Emma sat reading from the Bible to a soldier who had taken a ball in the shoulder while on picket duty. After a time she noticed a private standing nearby, listening. Emma recognized his face, though she could not recall his name. He was in another company of the Second, she thought.

She finished the passage she was reading and checked on her patient, who had fallen asleep under the combined effects of her voice and a generous dose of whiskey. Quietly Emma closed her book and stood, edging her way to the aisle between the rows of beds. The private stepped back to make room for her with a friendly smile.

He had dark hair and earnest dark eyes, and he followed her down the aisle. When they reached the front of the tent, he quietly spoke.

"You have a fine voice."

"Thank you."

"And that is a handsome Bible."

Emma smiled. "I used to sell them. Bibles, and other books."

"I love books," the soldier said, returning her smile. "They are the best solace, and that one the best of them all," he said, gesturing to her Bible.

Emma glanced down the length of the tent to assure herself that no one needed her attention. All was quiet, so she stepped out of the tent, inviting the soldier to join her beneath the awning. The night was calm, disturbed only by the sound of crickets and an occasional voice in the camp below.

"Are you here to visit a friend?" Emma asked.

The private glanced back at the hospital tent. "Yes, Mitchell, but he is sleeping. I came too late."

"I will tell him you were here, if you wish."

"Please do. My name is Robbins. Jerome Robbins."

"Frank Thompson."

Emma held out her hand, and Robbins shook it, smiling. His grip was firm, but without the test of strength she so often encountered.

"It's good of you to come and visit," she said. "It does them so much good to know they are remembered."

"It's the least I can do. Poor Mitchell. He thought the arm would heal."

"The surgeons did everything they could to save it."

Robbins nodded. "I heard."

"Don't worry, he will recover. He bore it well, and his spirits are good." Emma smiled. "That makes all the difference."

"It must be hard for you, seeing them suffer every day."

Emma shrugged. "They are wonderfully patient, most of them. And they respond well to a friendly face, so I try always to be cheerful."

"A noble calling."

His smile was approving, and warmed Emma's heart. She glanced at her Bible, tucked beneath her arm.

"I view it as a ministry, of sorts. I thought once of becoming a missionary. Now God's work is given to me, here at home."

"Does not the chaplain minister to them?"

"He does. Mr. Brown is here every day, he spends many hours comforting the sick. But for some—" she glanced up at Robbins, hoping he would understand. "—for some, it is better coming from an equal than from the chaplain."

Robbins nodded. "They are fortunate to have you here, then, offering both the comfort of the Lord's word and the sympathy of an equal in their time of darkness."

"I can do no less. The simplest things can make a difference. Reading to them, or writing a letter. So many of them are homesick, and when they come here they are separated even from their friends in camp."

Robbins shifted his stance and glanced at the tent once more. "I will come again, then. Tell Mitchell when he wakes that I will come tomorrow to see him."

"Thank you. I will tell him."

They stood gazing at each other for a moment. Emma was smiling, and Robbins smiled back slightly, then offered his hand.

"Well, good night. I'm glad to have met you," he said.

Emma shook his hand. "And I you. Good night."

She watched him stride away toward the camp, thinking it was pleasant to meet a soldier who appreciated God's word and who was aware of the suffering in the hospitals. Most avoided the hospitals if at all possible. Those who did come to visit their friends were the exception.

When Robbins disappeared from view she went back into the tent and walked its length, checking on each patient. She paused beside the bed where Mitchell lay, the stump of his amputated arm swathed in bandages. He slept the deep and silent sleep of exhaustion. Emma stood gazing at him, smiling softly.

"You are lucky," she whispered, though she knew he did not hear. "You have a caring friend."

Washington, D.C., 1883

A caring friend. How ingenuous." Jamie's voice dripped irony.

"Yes, a caring friend," Emma retorted. "I would not expect you to understand such pure and simple feelings."

Spots of red flared high on Jamie's cheeks, and his blue eyes flashed. Emma was pleased with this reaction, though she took care to let nothing show in her face.

She should end this, she knew. It was inappropriate to discuss the past at such length, and in what was becoming such personal detail, before Mr. Glass.

It was Jamie who persisted, however, and Emma was not about to yield her ground. She had come here to petition Congressman Cutcheon, and would not leave without seeing him.

"So that is how it began," Jamie said. "In the hospital."

"That is how our friendship began, yes," Emma replied, "and you know how it ended. What did you say to him, the day you left?"

Jamie glanced at Mr. Glass, who had sat down at his desk with an air of resignation. Emma saw the glint of interest in the secretary's eye, though he feigned indifference.

"He didn't tell you?" Jamie said.

"No, though I wrote to him and asked him to."

Jamie leaned against the front of the secretary's desk, folding his arms. "I think you can guess."

Emma felt a chill in her soul. "You told him all?"

A cold smile. "All. I had an hour to pass before the train arrived. I thought it well spent."

"You had no right."

Jamie laughed aloud. "Right? Was there anything right in it at all?"

"You thought so once," Emma said, her voice tight with anger, "or so you made me believe."

For a moment a look of longing, almost of hunger, crossed Jamie's face. Emma's heart lurched in response, a giddy, sickening sensation she had not felt since those days in the army. Fear combined with hope, and a tingling anticipation. She had not thought she would ever feel that way again.

Jamie turned his head away, scowling. "I thought he should know."

"Thought he should be disillusioned, you mean," Emma said. "You did it for spite. Pure spite!"

"I thought," Jamie said slowly, "that he should know the true nature of his friend."

Emma's anger flared. "Jerome knew my nature better than you ever will! Do you know why? Because we were alike, he and I. We cared about the same things."

"Not all the same things."

"The things that mattered most, we agreed upon."

Jamie's face went white, now. "Thank you," he said in a voice edged with ice. "Now I know exactly where I stand."

"By your own choice," Emma said, gripping her hands in her lap to keep them from trembling. "It was your doing, remember."

He did not answer, but looked away again. Emma saw a swallow move his throat. Suddenly she laughed. How ridiculous, that they should rip at each other so, now that it was long over and past.

"I wish sometimes that I could go back to that time," she said wistfully. At a sharp glance from Jamie she added, "to that time when I served in the hospital. My hours were occupied with the work of God's mercy, and my soul was clean."

"As clean as it could be, living a daily lie."

"The lie gave me freedom to be of service. It harmed no one."

Jamie looked at her wryly. "No?"

"No," Emma said firmly. "I argued that point with myself constantly, you may believe. I was careful to let it harm no one. That is why I had no close friends, why I kept a distance. If I were discovered, I wanted no one to be accused of colluding with me. I kept to myself."

"Until Jerome," Jamie said.

"Yes." Emma nodded. "Until Jerome."

The War: Alexandria, Virginia, 1861

Near dawn, when Emma's shift was ending, she made her rounds one last time and found Private Mitchell drowsing awake. She helped him sit up to drink some water.

"A friend of yours was here last night," she said softly. "Jerome Robbins."

Mitchell's face brightened, then fell. "And I missed him?"

"You were sleeping. He said he would visit again."

Mitchell smiled. "He's a good one."

"Did you know him in Michigan?"

"Not until I joined up. He's a thinking man, likes to debate about politics and such. I think he was in college, before the war."

"And left his studies to volunteer?"

"Well, he's very intent on abolition," Mitchell said, glancing up at her. "Don't raise the subject, or he'll talk you into the ground on it."

Emma smiled. "I'll remember."

She saw Mitchell comfortably settled, finished her rounds, and greeted her counterpart, the male nurse coming in to take the next shift. Yawning, she made her way to her tent, where she found Damon snoring gustily, an empty whiskey bottle lying beside his boots. She crawled under her blanket and soon dropped asleep.

That evening when Emma reported to night duty again, Jerome Robbins was there. She saw him the moment she entered the hospital tent, and though his face was turned away she knew him by his dark curling hair and straight shoulders. He was sitting beside Mitchell's bed, leaning toward his friend, talking quietly.

Emma went about her duties, and when she passed near, Robbins glanced up with a smile. She smiled back, but did not pause to converse. Private Mitchell needed his friend's attention far more than she.

She went her rounds, read a letter from home to one wounded man, gave a dose of medicine to another who was feverish, and brought her Bible to read again to Private Wills, who wanted every night to hear her as he went to sleep. As she read she became conscious of Robbins' gaze on her, though he still sat with his friend. Their voices had fallen quiet, now. Her own was the only voice in the tent.

"Let all bitterness and wrath and anger and clamor and slander be put away from you, along with all malice. Be kind to one another, tenderhearted, forgiving one another, as God in Christ forgave you."

She read on, aware of Robbins listening, aware that the other men nearby listened, too. It comforted them, and she was glad to be the source of that comfort.

She reached a verse that her mouth refused to voice.

Wives, submit yourselves unto your own husbands, as unto the Lord.

Never, answered her heart.

She looked at Wills, who was breathing deeply in peaceful slumber. Closing her Bible, she stood and walked out, taking care not to look toward Robbins, for she did not want him to think her over-anxious though she hoped to converse with him again.

Troubled in her heart, she laid her Bible down on the cot that was provided for the nurses' use. Seldom did its words fail to bring her comfort, but that one verse she could not embrace.

She began her rounds once more, assuring herself that each patient was comfortably settled for the night. When she reached the far end of the tent and turned, she saw that Robbins was gone.

The disappointment that smote her surprised her, and worried her a little. She had no cause to expect Robbins to stay, after all. His friend Mitchell was sleeping, she saw as she came to his bed. She passed onward, glancing at each patient, and when she reached the front of the tent she stepped outside.

He was there, waiting beneath the awning. With a smile that lit his face even in the dim light glowing through the tent's walls, Robbins greeted her.

"Good evening," Emma returned, smiling back. "Thank you for coming to visit. I can see Mitchell's spirits are already improved."

"I am happy to do what I can for him. Poor fellow, he doesn't talk of it, but he's very blue about the arm."

"He'll recover in time. I saw that you brought him a newspaper."

"Yes, I thought it might interest him."

Emma smiled, remembering Mitchell's caution about raising political issues with Robbins. "He told me you are intent on the subject of abolition."

Robbins drew himself up, and his face went serious. "I believe it is the duty of every Christian to oppose slavery."

"I agree. No man should be treated as chattel, no matter his color."

Interest sparked in Robbins's eye. "You support abolition?"

"With all my heart. Slavery is plainly against God's law."

"It is a sin!" Robbins's face lit with passion. "Both a personal sin, and a blot on the honor of our nation!"

Emma nodded. "And the great tragedy of it is that this war is necessary for its removal."

"Yet so many soldiers care nothing about it. Mitchell will not even discuss abolition, he says he volunteered for the Union, not for the sake of the negroes."

"They are afraid, some of them," Emma said. "You can see it in their eyes when they turn away."

"Afraid that they will have to treat the negroes as equals? As men?"

"Or afraid that the negroes will take jobs from white men, and bread from the mouths of their families," Emma said quietly.

Robbins shook his head. "That may be, but still the evil must be ended."

"Yes. The slaves must be freed."

Their gazes met, and in knowing that they were in accord, Emma's heart leapt with happiness. She had never met a man whose ideas agreed so exactly with her own.

A querulous voice rose within the tent, calling for "Frank." Emma glanced toward it, her face growing warm with consciousness of her inattention, though she had only been a moment outside.

"I must go," she told Robbins.

He nodded. "I will wait, if I may. I would like to continue this discussion."

Emma smiled, then ducked into the tent, hastening to the one who called her. As she brought him the water he asked for, her heart was filled with silent gladness.

Robbins stayed late that night, talking with Emma until well past midnight. At last she made him go, pointing out that reveille was only a few hours away. Robbins left, shaking her hand warmly and promising to come again.

He haunted the hospital thereafter, paying frequent visits to Mitchell, and like as not remaining to chat with Emma during her spare moments. They conversed on a variety of subjects, and if they did not always precisely agree, their differences of opinion made for interesting discussion. By the end of a week, they were "Frank" and "Jerome" to one another, and Emma could not remember having a closer friend.

They attended prayer meetings together, and went for long walks when off duty, talking of books, of faith, and of the higher purposes of the war. Jerome continued to visit the hospital every day, sometimes several times in a day.

One afternoon in early November, Jerome appeared in the hospital tent rather earlier than usual. Emma greeted him with a smile as she glanced up from writing a letter for one of the wounded. He nodded in response and wandered down to Mitchell's bed, appearing distracted though he talked to Mitchell with his usual cheer. When Emma had finished the letter and stood, promising to post it at once, Jerome arose as well and followed her out of the tent.

"Frank." His dark eyes were troubled.

"Yes?" Emma said, at once concerned. "What is it?"

"I've been informed I'm being reassigned."

Dismay stabbed her, but she tried not to show it. "Where?"

"Here. To the hospital, as a steward."

Emma could not hide her delight. "But that is wonderful!"

"Did you suggest it?"

Emma blinked in surprise. "No."

His troubled frown persisted. "I thought perhaps...perhaps you had said something to Dr. Bonine."

She shook her head. "No, not a word. But he may have noticed how much time you have been spending here—that is how I came to be assigned to hospital duty."

"Oh."

Jerome paced a few restless steps. Emma watched, regretting his apparent unhappiness though she could not be sorry for his news.

"I am not certain I am best suited for this duty," he said at last.

"Why not?"

He paused and stood looking at her, still frowning. "I wonder if it would not be better that I should remain in the ranks."

"Standing picket duty?"

"It is a combat position, and what I volunteered for. Hospital work is—well. Forgive me, I do not mean to belittle what you do. For you it is different."

Emma bristled. "If you think this work does not require fortitude you are mistaken."

"I know it does, I know. I have watched you. Yours is a different kind of courage, I think." He smiled awkwardly. "And you are well suited to the work. Better than I."

"You mean because I am small." Emma was beginning to be angry now, and knew she was frowning.

"Because you are naturally outgoing, naturally cheerful. I am—it is not so easy for me, to be open with strangers."

Emma could not help a wry laugh. If he knew how much she concealed....

"You need not be open," she said. "You need only be kind. You know how desperate is their situation."

She gestured to the tent, where the sick and wounded lay, so helpless, so vulnerable. Robbins gazed that way and nodded soberly.

"I suppose I am afraid of failing them," he said, his mouth

twisting in a rueful smile.

"You will not fail them."

Emma's anger vanished as quickly as it had come, now that she saw the self-doubt that was at the root of his concern. It was like Jerome to be modest about his own abilities. She took a step closer.

"A steward's duty is to maintain the tents, and keep everything in order," she said. "You will not be called upon to nurse the sick unless one of us is unfit for duty."

He nodded, then gave a sigh of resignation and managed to smile. "I shall rely upon you for advice."

"I am happy to give it. When do you report for duty?"

"Today. That is why I am here."

Emma smiled. "Then let us find Dr. Bonine."

The surgeon welcomed Jerome with brusque friendliness, and set him at once to his duties. For the rest of the day and into the evening, Jerome policed the hospital tents and performed such tasks as the surgeons required of him. Some of the work was menial, and Emma worried that it would displease him, but if so he gave no outward sign of it.

Emma had volunteered for night duty as usual, and she was pleased when Jerome elected to stay as well. He seemed to have set his doubts aside.

Near midnight, when all the men were at last asleep, Emma and Jerome sat down together on the cot provided for the nurses' comfort, and quietly conversed. Jerome seemed tired, though he was as eager as ever to discuss religion. To perfect his faith was his constant endeavor, and he never wearied of the subject.

At length he yawned, and Emma could not help but do so as well. She reached for the blankets folded beside the cot.

"I should let you sleep," Jerome said, standing.

"Stay if you wish. There is room for two."

She said it casually, and did not meet his eye, occupying herself with arranging the blankets. Her heart was beating rather swiftly, though.

"All right," Jerome said, and sat down again to pull off his boots.

They stretched out together on the cot, sharing a blanket. Emma was tired but could not sleep, conscious of Jerome beside her. Her fondness for him kept her awake, listening as his breathing deepened and he fell into slumber.

How precious was this moment, to lie close to one she so esteemed! With a shock she realized that she would never have lain so comfortably with any other man—even Damon, who was kind and a sincere friend. No man had ever enjoyed her trust to the extent that it now reposed in Jerome. She trusted him completely—she would trust him with her life.

The realization was strange for her, having grown up viewing men as her natural enemies, having for so long loathed their demands upon womankind and the sacrifices they assumed belonged to them by right. She had never encountered a man for whom she felt the slightest inclination to give up her freedom.

Not until now. In the silence of deep night, she lay awake, wondering if she could give her heart to a man like Jerome. She had firmly believed it was impossible, but now she was no longer sure. As she lay beside him, breathing in time with his own deep sleep, she thought tentatively of what it would be like to be more than his friend.

Emma closed her eyes, her pulse quickening at the thought of being closer to Jerome. In the past, back in Canada, she had been offered love and spurned it as unworthy of her interest. Later, as Frank Thompson, it had amused her to flirt with young women such as Miss Little. What she contemplated now was something wholly different, something she had never expected to pursue.

And she could not pursue it, not in her present situation. If she did, she would be no better than a prostitute. She would have fallen into exactly the sort of sin she abhorred.

She knew that there were women who entered the army in disguise for just such purposes. She had heard of one who had been revealed and prosecuted. The men guilty of consorting with that woman had been court-martialed.

Never, never would Emma place Jerome in such a position. Neither of them wanted that sort of relationship, she was certain. Jerome was not the sort to descend to such baseness. If he sought a union, it would be under the blessing of holy matrimony.

Emma turned her head to look at him, tender affection filling her heart as she gazed on his face, peaceful in slumber. She would treasure this moment for what it was, and ask no more.

Closing her eyes, she listened to the sounds of the hospital tent. A guy rope creaking under the pressure of a breeze. Patients snoring softly, sighing in sleep or shifting in their beds. Now and then a voice murmuring restlessly as a soldier dreamed of the battlefield.

The warmth of Jerome's body beside Emma filled her with a sense of well-being. Thanking God for the gift of his friendship, she gradually relaxed into sleep.

She woke before dawn, roused by a whimper of distress that she knew presaged a fit of delirium. Jerome still slept beside her. Rising quietly so as not to waken him, she went to the troubled soldier's bed and spoke gently to him, hoping to fend off his nightmares.

He quieted, and she stayed with him, taking his hand and continuing to talk to him. Her gaze strayed to the couch where Jerome lay, and soon she saw him wake and stretch, sitting up and looking about the tent. When his gaze met hers he smiled, and Emma's heart filled with gladness.

She watched Jerome stand and fold the blankets they had shared, then run his hands through his disheveled hair. Her patient then reclaimed her attention for a few minutes, waking with a start. At Emma's invitation he recounted to her what he had been dreaming. She spoke soothingly to him until he was comfortable, then rose to join Jerome.

"Good morning," she said quietly, sitting down on the couch to put on her boots. "I hope you slept well."

"Wonderfully well, thank you," said Jerome, smiling. "I am much refreshed."

"Good."

Emma stood and flung open the front of the tent. The sun had not yet risen, though the river valley was filled with a soft, gray light. The smell of coffee drifted in from the nearby cook-tent.

"Breakfast soon," Emma said. "I will need your help with some of the patients."

Jerome nodded. "Gladly. Just tell me what I must do."

They worked together through the morning, and Jerome's confidence seemed to increase. Over the next few days he settled into his duties and expressed no more doubts. If the work was not glorious, neither was it arduous, and it gave Emma and Jerome even more time to talk.

Their friendship grew, and Emma rejoiced. They spent most of their off-duty hours together as well as their time at work in the hospital. Jerome especially enjoyed discussing the Bible, and they spent many an hour with their heads bent over Emma's book, debating the meaning of a passage.

Emma's days passed happily as the autumn deepened. She enjoyed her work in the hospital even more with the addition of Jerome's company. Now and then she would find him watching her, sometimes with a perplexed expression, though it always gave way to a smile when their gazes met.

One day when they returned to the hospital after a walk, Jerome had three letters waiting. He let out an exclamation of delight when he saw the address on one of them.

"It is from Anna Corey, one of my students," he said, looking up at Emma with a gratified smile.

She smiled in return. "How kind of her to remember you."

"Yes." Jerome glanced at the letters in his hand, then back at Emma. "Do you often receive letters from home?"

She shook her head. "My parents are dead."

It was a small deception—though for all she knew it was true. Easier to pretend that she had no family than to make up excuses for their strange lack of attention to "Frank."

"I am sorry," Jerome said, his brow creasing with concern.

Emma shrugged. "I have been on my own for some years now. I am used to it."

"Have you no sweetheart, back in Michigan?"

"No. Though I do have a young lady friend who writes to me now and again." Emma smiled, thinking of Miss Daphne, whose letters still arrived at erratic intervals and always expressed her dogged determination to execute her duty toward her soldier friend.

"Well, that is something," Jerome said, his face brightening.

"Yes."

Emma left Jerome to enjoy his letters while she made her rounds. Later he showed them to her, generously sharing his news from home. Emma read Miss Corey's letter with a small pang of heartache. There was nothing exceptional in it, but the gentle expressions of affection for Jerome made her wish she was free to offer her own.

Of course, that was unnecessary. Jerome knew she cared for him. Knew "Frank" cared for him, as a friend.

She kept her feelings to herself as she handed his letters back to him, summoning a smile with which to thank him. It was kindness that had made him offer to share, and she was sure he had no idea that reading Miss Corey's sentiments would cause her pain.

November wore on, and soon the news that General McClellan had been given command of the entire army passed through the camp. The Army of the Potomac was now an efficient organization, due to McClellan's careful and exacting guidance. Emma believed he would bring the same qualities to bear in his leadership of all the U.S. Army, and rejoiced in his promotion along with her fellow soldiers.

There were grumblings, political grumblings, as ever in Washington. The city was becoming overwhelmed with supporting the ever-growing military. Cleanliness was an issue, and soon another outbreak of typhus filled beds that had been vacated by wounded who had moved on, either returning to their duties, or to their families, or passing on to a better world.

Some of the grumblers complained that the army had long since been ready to fight, and should move against the Confederates. Emma paid no attention to this. McClellan would decide when and where to attack the Rebels, and she was confident his would be the right choice.

While she felt no trouble over the future of the army, she suffered a growing misgiving about Jerome. He had taken up a regular correspondence with Miss Corey, and often spoke to Emma of her virtues. She knew the resulting pain in her heart for jealousy, and admonished herself for indulging in such folly, but she could not help how she felt.

Jerome no longer showed Emma his letters from Miss Corey. He spoke of them, though, with quiet pleasure and a soft light in his eyes that caused Emma agonies of grief. She began to dread the words, "Miss Corey says."

One afternoon, during one of their customary walks, Jerome was ebullient over his most recent letter from his gentle correspondent. Emma listened in silence to his praise of Miss Corey.

"She is all that a man could look for in a member of the gentler sex. Well worthy of the highest esteem of any who appreciates virtue and true nobility," Jerome said, pausing at the edge of an orchard where they often walked.

The trees were now bare of all but a few leaves, and a scattering of fallen peaches lay shriveled on the ground about their feet. Emma stared glumly at the ruined fruit, regretting its waste, though her farmer's soul knew there would always be deadfalls.

"I wish you could meet her," Jerome went on. "I am sure you would agree with me."

Emma flashed a rueful smile. "I think perhaps no one could appreciate her qualities more than you."

"Well, not more, perhaps, but equally as well." Jerome smiled. "When we return to Michigan, you must come with me and visit Miss Corey."

Emma gazed toward the setting sun. "Michigan is far away."

"Not so far as to be forgotten. Will that not be our ultimate reward, to return home?"

Emma shrugged. "Who is to say which of us will survive to return?"

"Come, now, Frank! It is not like you to be so gloomy! We shall return home, I am sure of it."

"You will go back to college," Emma said, stepping forward among the trees. "Back to teaching."

Jerome strolled along beside her. "And you will return to selling books. You may come and sell textbooks to all of my students."

Emma smiled wanly, but did not meet his gaze. She was watching the sun set, a fiery glow on the horizon, golden-orange cutting through the gathering haze and the web of bare tree branches. It was not enough to warm the chill inside her.

"Or perhaps I will study medicine," Jerome said.

Emma turned to look at him, surprised. Jerome smiled.

"I have acquired a certain curiosity about it," he said. "I've been talking with Dr. Lyster, who says that Dr. Palmer would welcome a student with field hospital experience. I owe that to you," he added. "If not for our friendship, I would never have developed an interest."

Emma swallowed. All at once she saw how tentative was their situation. She had so enjoyed the idyll of the past few weeks, she had almost forgotten that it could not last. Sooner or later the call to arms would come, the surgeons would pack up their equipments, and they all would move forward to battle. Thereafter...only God in Heaven knew what would become of them.

She wanted suddenly to tell Jerome the truth about

herself. She could not bear to think that she might go to her grave without having confessed her deception to him, her closest friend. How dreadful if he were to discover it after her death! If she were carried to the hospital and revealed to be a woman, what a scandal it would be, what a disgrace! Jerome would look a fool—might even be accused of colluding with her—and would hate her for it.

She could not bear to think of that. She turned to look at him, and saw his earnest face frowning in concern.

"Are you all right?" Jerome asked. "You look pale."

Emma glanced down, pressing a hand to her temple. "A headache coming on, I think."

"Perhaps we should go back."

"Yes."

They retraced their steps in silence. Emma was thinking furiously, debating whether to confess her deception to him. Her instinct told her no good could come of it, but still her heart yearned to be clean. She wished to keep nothing from Jerome, her dearest friend. She wondered what he would think, if she told him. Doubt of his reaction sealed her lips.

They reached the camp as dusk was falling. Both being off duty, they parted to go to their respective companies' streets.

"I will see you tomorrow," Jerome said, offering his hand. "You will feel the better for a night's rest."

For once, Emma was hesitant to shake his hand. She made herself do so, however.

"Good night, Jerome."

"Good night."

She turned away, resisting the urge to watch him go. Instead she walked slowly to her tent, where Damon hailed her with cheerful teasing.

"If it isn't our woman, returned to us! And just in time, Frank. Green and Emory are hosting a card game tonight. You should join us!"

Emma shook her head. "No, thank you. I'm tired."

"Running you ragged over at that hospital, eh?"

Emma sat wearily on her bed and sighed. What she wanted was to study the Scripture, seek an answer there to the trouble in her soul, but she had left her Bible up at the hospital.

Damon continued to cajole her and urge her to go to the

card game, but Emma only shook her head. She did not care for such pursuits; in fact she disapproved them. One of the joys of her friendship with Jerome was that he shared her disdain for such things—for card playing, drinking, and coarse language. Common pastimes of many a soldier, but not for the virtuous heart.

At last she lay down on her bed and closed her eyes, hoping Damon would leave her alone. He fell silent at least, for which she was grateful. Not long afterward the company's mess call sounded.

"Are you coming to supper?" Damon asked.

"No, I'm tired. I just want to rest."

"I'll bring you back something."

Emma did not open her eyes. Damon left, returning only briefly to announce he had brought her some food. She thanked him but did not get up, and to her relief, Damon went away at last.

Through the long evening she lay thinking, as the night deepened and the camp settled. Quiet descended, broken occasionally by voices or the music of someone playing a whistle. Emma thought she heard Damon's voice once or twice, amid whoops of laughter from down the street.

How long did she mean to continue? She had never considered the future beyond a year or so. Would she go on as Frank Thompson, eventually to sink into solitary old age, still entrenched in her masquerade?

Until now she had felt no concern over such a fate, but the feelings Jerome had stirred in her would not be stilled. If she ever wished to be close to another—truly close, perhaps even to wed....

She had never considered matrimony. Even when her father had demanded that she marry, she knew she would never submit to that fate. She had hated her father's friend, which had not helped matters, but she had received other, more attractive offers as well. Never had she been tempted to accept.

Would she accept now, if Jerome knew her true identity, and offered her his heart?

Folly. Sheer folly to even think of it.

Yet she could think of nothing else. She lay restless on her bed, tormenting herself with the possibilities, unable to decide what to do.

In the wee hours, Damon stumbled into the tent. She could smell the whiskey on him. Feigning sleep, she waited until he fell into heavy snoring, then sat up in bed.

Dim moonlight shone through the canvas, silhouetting Damon's bulk against the tent wall. The camp was quiet now, save for the heavy breathing of the men.

A hundred men all around her, and none suspected her. Frank Thompson was entirely successful, as he had been for years before the war. It took a great heart and an intelligent mind to make her doubt herself. A soul who was worthy of the highest esteem of any who appreciates virtue and true nobility, she thought with a wry smile.

She would drive herself mad if she continued this. She pulled on her boots and quietly arose, leaving the tent.

The moon struggled to shine through a haze of cloud. The weak light it did cast was enough to illuminate the silent streets of the camp.

She walked down them, each in turn, pretending to herself that it was her whim to walk a circuit of the camp but knowing it was Jerome's tent she sought. She knew which one it was, in the middle of I Company's street. She had gone there with him several times, to fetch a book or a newspaper he wanted to show her. She paused outside it now, listening, trying to discern the sound of Jerome's breathing from amid the others all around.

She had slept next to him often enough, on the nurses' couch up in the hospital. Should she not know his breath?

Folly.

She made herself walk on, through the rest of the camp, then around to A Company's street and onward until she was back in her own street. By now she could see the coming dawn, a dull glow on the eastern horizon. Not wishing to return to her sleepless bed, she walked up to the hospital.

A voice cried out in distress as she approached, and she ran the last few steps to the tent's door, which was closed against the night's chill. She slipped in, and had started down the aisle when she saw that Davidson, the nurse on duty, had already reached the sufferer.

The patient was sitting straight up in his bed, arms flung outward, caught in a nightmare. Davidson had his arm around the man's shoulder and was talking to him in a steady, calm voice. Slowly he quieted, until Davidson induced him to lie down again.

Emma stood watching as Davidson remained by the patient until he was sleeping peacefully. Only then did he rise, and check on the men to either side before coming to the front of the tent.

Emma smiled in greeting. "Well done," she said softly.

Davidson nodded. "You are here early."

"I came for my Bible."

Emma stepped to the couch and picked up her book from the cracker box beside it that served as a table. She hugged it to her, as if she could capture its wisdom if she held it tightly enough.

"Will you watch while I go out for a minute?" Davidson asked.

"Of course."

Emma sat on the couch as Davidson left the tent. A lamp was burning low on the cracker-box table. She turned it up a little, and opened her Bible at random. The page her eye fell upon was in Galatians, and she read at once of freedom, and the words struck a chord in her soul. Eagerly she read, and found verse after verse that rang true.

"—do not use your freedom as an opportunity for the flesh, but through love be servants of one another," she whispered aloud.

And was it not the temptations of the flesh that tormented her? Jealousy, and enmity for Anna Corey whom she did not even know, and even the contemplation of immorality? She winced as she recalled her doubts and torments during the night.

She had lost her way. She must look to faith to restore her.

She read on, seeking comfort in the assurances of the apostle Paul, in his adjuration to follow the Spirit and never falter in her beliefs. At the end of the chapter she closed the book and sat thinking.

She had come near to making a mistake, she believed. She had been tempted to offer herself to Jerome, an offer she was sure he would refuse. If she did not wish him to turn from her in disgust, she must not make that offer.

So, his friend she was and would remain. She still had not decided whether she owed to that friendship her complete honesty. She wanted to confess herself to Jerome, so that she would no longer be guilty of deceiving him, but there were serious consequences to consider.

She heard a footstep outside the tent, and thinking it was Davidson returning, turned to greet him. Instead she saw Jerome step through the door, holding the canvas flap aside.

Her heart stood still at the sight of him. All her feelings leapt within her, her fondness and her wish to explain everything to him. The jealousy and possessiveness, too, though she struggled against them.

He gazed back at her for a moment, then came forward, letting the canvas fall behind him. "Good morning," he said softly.

"You are early," was all she could say.

"I was restless. Are you feeling any better?"

She stared up at him, the truth rising to her lips though she knew she must not speak of it here. She was not in control of herself, she realized with dismay.

"I—no, actually. I feel rather unwell. Would you be willing to take my shift today?"

Concern filled his dark eyes, and compassion. Ah, but he was beautiful!

"Of course," he said. "I am sorry you are unwell. Does your head still trouble you?"

"Yes."

My head. My heart.

"Go and rest, then," Jerome said, nodding. "I'll inform the surgeon."

"Thank you."

She rose from the couch, clutching her Bible, and took a faltering step toward the door. Jerome reached out a hand to steady her. It was all she could do not to flinch from his touch, not because she did not want it, but because she wanted it more than she should.

She cleared her throat, struggling against the tightness in it. "Thank you, Jerome. I am sorry to trouble you."

"No trouble," he said, smiling. "You would do the same for me."

She managed to smile back at him. How kind he was. How

she loved—yes, loved him. She gazed at his face, a good-looking face, though the true beauty of him was in his eyes, through which his soul shone like a beacon.

Footsteps drew her gaze to the tent door. Davidson came through it, carrying a tin cup and the smell of coffee. Emma took a step backward, away from Jerome. With a fleeting smile at him she left the tent, and fled back to the camp.

Damon still lay snoring deeply. In the growing light of morning Emma saw a plate of stew on the cracker-box table at the head of her bead, long since gone cold and filmed over. She set her Bible down beside it and crawled beneath her blanket once more.

She lay still. Though she was weary, sleep was far from her thoughts. She listened to the sounds of the rousing camp, and waited. When Damon had gone at last to report to assembly and his duties of the day, Emma arose and began to pace within the tent.

She thought carefully now, resolutely putting tender feelings aside, trying to cast the cold light of logic onto the choice she must make.

If she told Jerome who she really was, would he betray her?

She could not believe that he would. Even if he disdained her, she did not think he would denounce her. If she reposed a confidence in him, she thought he would keep it.

Well, then. What effect might it have upon him?

It was possible that he would feel betrayed. Certainly she expected him to be angry at having been deceived. Shocked, perhaps, that she would choose to live as a man, and go against her fated role of womanhood.

But Jerome believed in individual freedom as a God-given right. Would he not accept that she had claimed that right for herself? She had been careful to cause no harm to any other.

And if the worst occurred, if she were somehow discovered —not through Jerome, but by some other mischance—what would happen then? Would Jerome be accused of conspiring to hide her identity?

Possibly.

Emma closed her eyes, frowning. The question was which would be worse: to confide in him and thus expose him to a possible accusation in the event she was discovered; or to continue to deceive him, which gave the lie to the very friendship she held so dear?

She wrestled with the problem through the day, going over and over it in her mind. At length, exhaustion dulled her wits, and she lay down atop her blankets and drifted into a restless sleep.

When she woke it was dusk, and the smell of boiled meat filled the tent. Damon was standing over her, a plate in his hand.

"Brought you some supper. Someone said you were sick."

"I—I have not been very well," Emma agreed.

"Here. Try to drink some of the broth, at least."

Damon knelt beside her, careful not to spill the liquid in the plate. Chunks of boiled pork sat in it, unappealing to Emma at the moment, but she smiled and thanked her tentmate as she accepted the food.

"You need to have a care for yourself, and not work so hard," Damon said. "Won't be any good to the wounded if you're half-dead yourself."

Despite her troubles, Emma laughed. "Thank you, Damon. It's very kind of you."

"Well, I said I'd look after you, didn't I?"

"Yes, you did."

Damon stayed beside her, watching until she had sipped a half-dozen spoonfuls of broth. In his own, bluff way, he was as caring as any of the nurses at the hospital, and Emma was sincerely grateful.

"I'll leave you in peace," he said, lumbering to his feet. "You drink the rest of that, hear?"

"Yes, sir!" Emma replied, saluting, which made him grin.

She made good on her promise, finishing the broth and even eating a small piece of the pork, though it tasted like sawdust as she chewed it. Setting the dish aside, she lay back and stared at the canvas overhead.

The tent's poles bristled with a number of nails which Damon had added to serve as hooks for clothing and canteens. He had talked of elevating the tent as some had done—building a low wall of logs around the bottom to make it warmer for winter. Emma was indifferent, having grown up in New Brunswick, whose winters were far more bitter than anything Washington was likely to experience.

Such plans, though, spoke of a permanence which Emma knew was illusory. Though winter was coming on, there were those who would have the army move now, and attack the Confederates. This tent was a temporary home. Like the army.

Perhaps it would be better to continue in her deception. Certainly it would be safer, both for her and Jerome. A wistful sadness filled her as she lay contemplating the future. She and Jerome would continue as friends. The friendship would be safe, though never complete without the total openness and honesty she craved.

This might be the best she could do. Frank Thompson was her way of life, and had been for several years. To change that, to threaten its success, was to take a terrible risk.

Emma woke in the morning, surprised that she had slept the night through. The sun had broken through the haze at last and the day was bright. Damon was up before her, and came back into the tent as she rose from her bed. He was carrying her plate, which he had scraped clean.

"Feeling better?"

"Yes, thank you," Emma said, taking the plate from him.

There was still a hollow soreness in her heart, but she did feel better. The fever of indecision had abated.

She joined Damon at the company's mess, and though she was not hungry she gulped down half a cup of hot coffee and felt the better for it. Doing her best to bid Damon and the others of her company a cheerful farewell, she took her leave and reported to the hospital for duty.

Jerome was there, policing the tents, and she nodded to him in passing. One of the patients had died during the night, and Emma watched Jerome and the ward master carry him out. He had suffered from dysentery, which struck down a great many soldiers. Despite all the efforts toward sanitation, so many men crowded together could not help but pass diseases among them.

Emma went about her duties, summoning a cheer she did not feel as she visited the patients and heard their requests. One wanted her to write letters for him, another to read to him, another made a mournful plea for some fruit. Emma promised to find it for him, an errand that would take her away from the hospital for a time, which did not displease her. Though the sutler charged a high price for such luxuries, Emma often fetched them for the patients, happily paying her own money.

When she and Jerome spoke during the day, as was inevitable during the course of their duties, Emma was glad to find that her voice did not tremble. She thanked him for his kind inquiry after her health, saying that she felt much better.

"Perhaps we can go for a walk this evening," she said. "The weather is fair."

"I would like that," Jerome said, smiling.

They had little leisure for more conversation that day. New patients were coming in—three new cases of typhus—and Jerome was kept busy arranging their beds and seeing them settled. Emma went to the sutler's and returned with a can of peaches for the man who craved fruit, then passed the rest of the afternoon reading and writing for those who had asked it.

Their shift ended after the patients had been given their dinner. Emma and Jerome ate from the hospital kitchen as well, though Emma still had little appetite. She made herself eat some pork and beans, though it sat like lead in her stomach. Coffee helped to wash it down and clear her mind somewhat. She cleaned her mess kit and went outside to breathe the fresh air.

Twilight filled the valley of the Potomac. The evening star shone out above the western horizon. The sky was clear and the night would be cold.

Jerome joined her, gazing over the camp. "Do you still care to walk?"

"Yes, please."

They took their usual route, down a road that ran between orchards in the river bottom. They talked a little of the Trent affair, which was much in the news of late.

The U.S. Navy had seized two Confederate ambassadors from the British packet bound for England and France. Great Britain had naturally taken exception to this, and sabers were heard rattling across the ocean. Neither Emma nor Jerome could see any good coming of the matter, and though it was regrettable, they agreed that Mason and Slidell should be set free.

They reached the peach orchard again and walked into it, strolling beneath the bare-branched trees. They fell silent for a while, then Jerome spoke.

"I have been thinking, since our last conversation."

"Oh?" Emma said foolishly.

"I wonder if I am not dwelling overmuch on Miss Corey's letters to me."

He stopped walking and looked at Emma, and she saw despite the failing light the seriousness of his expression. Her heart sank.

"I would not wish to be guilty of neglecting my duty," he added.

"You have not neglected your duty, Jerome."

"I do not mean merely the duties of my post. I mean my duty to my fellow man. To my comrades. Have I allowed myself to be too much distracted?"

Emma shrugged helplessly. "I cannot say. You must decide that for yourself."

"You are never distracted in this way."

"I do not have such an agreeable correspondent."

Emma turned away, hiding her unhappiness. She wanted to change the subject, but Jerome persisted.

"Her letters are very agreeable," he said. "I find myself reading them over and over again."

"Everyone does that, with their letters from home."

"But not everyone...I find myself wishing to write to her." He began to pace beneath the trees. "Every day. I already send her more letters than she sends to me. Should I not restrain myself?"

"If it eases your heart, then write to her," Emma said miserably. "What harm can it do?"

"I would not wish to appear over-eager. I fear it might give her a distaste for me."

"Jerome, I cannot advise you in this."

"Your mind is clearer than mine, just now. Is it wrong for a man to think so much about a woman?"

Emma gave a hopeless laugh. "I am not a man."

Jerome paused in his restless pacing. "You are young, but no younger than I. You have seen battle. You are more a man than many of the soldiers come to Washington, who are yet to taste of war."

"Jerome—"

"You are a man of sense, and I value your opinion. You always see the right of things. Will you not help me now?"

Emma felt the burden of her deception weighing down upon her. "I cannot help you," she said. "Go to the Scriptures."

"But the Scriptures do not address my particular situation. They are not of this time, of our customs. You might well be in my position, someday."

"I will never be in your position."

"How can you know that? You have a lady friend—"

"A friend. She will never be more."

He smiled, disbelieving. "She might be. Perhaps you will conceive a tender feeling for her."

"No."

"It could happen, Frank."

"No. It could not."

Again the laughing smile. "You know that no sooner one says a thing can never be, than it will come to pass."

"Not in this case."

"How can you be so certain?"

"Because, Jerome," Emma said, dropping her voice low, though there was no one near enough to hear, "I am not a man. I am a woman."

Washington, D.C., 1883

"So you told him," Jamie said, his eyes narrowing.

"Yes."

"He never gave me any indication that he knew. Even when I told him what I knew of you."

"He was a friend," Emma said coldly. "He kept my confidence, though I did not demand his silence."

Jamie's face grew stern; his nostrils flared. "You told him, knowing it would place him in danger," he accused her. "Knowing he could be court-martialed for it!"

"The chance of that was slim."

"But you took it. You took the chance with his freedom!"

Emma tilted her head, regarding him. "Why so bitter, Jamie? I never knew you cared so much for Jerome."

"I didn't," he said in a clipped voice, and strode a few paces away.

He paused before a portrait of President Arthur. The muscles in his back were bunched beneath the fabric of his coat. Still strong, Emma noted.

The door behind Mr. Glass's desk opened, and Emma glanced up. The secretary rose from his desk, went to the door where he conferred quietly for a moment with another gentleman Emma had not seen before, then stepped inside, shutting the door behind him.

Left alone with Jamie, Emma waited. Why was he here, she wondered? What was he doing in Washington, all these years later? Last she knew, he had been bound for Scotland.

"Poor Robbins," Jamie said at last. "The victim of your self-indulgence. He hid it well."

Emma swallowed, angered by his words, but knowing they were true. "Yes," was all she said.

"Weren't you afraid he would betray you?"

"No. I was never afraid of Jerome."

She watched for his reaction, but he gave no sign. Still with his back to her, he stood like a statue. She shifted in her seat, trying to ease the ache in her left foot.

"You feared me," he said at last.

"Yes. With good reason, as it happened."

That stung him, she could tell. He moved, a wince, as if something had struck him between the shoulder blades. Emma allowed herself to smile.

"But Jerome was true to the last. He never betrayed me. I should not have told him, I know." Her smile became wistful. "I knew it the moment the words left my lips."

The War: Alexandria, Virginia, 1861

Jerome stared at her, silent. Even in the gathering darkness, she could see his confusion.

"I am a female," she said, to make certain he understood. "I ran away from home when I was fifteen. I worked as a milliner for a while, then I assumed the name of Frank Thompson and began selling books."

"What are you saying?" Jerome asked, incredulity in his voice.

"I am living a deception, Jerome, but I can no longer deceive you. I honor your friendship too much."

She stood trembling, awaiting his answer. The silence stretched between them, and dread rose in Emma's heart. Never had she shared her secret, entrusted it to another. She had placed herself in Jerome's hands, and doubt now assailed her as to the wisdom of it.

"Why?" he said at last, in an anguished voice.

"I never wished to hurt you, Jerome. I never thought to find such a—such an affinity with a fellow soldier. Your friendship has been the greatest blessing to me, truly, and I tell you this now because I cannot bear to deceive you any longer."

"But why did you run away?" Jerome demanded. She could see his frown, even though shadows darkened his face. "Why did you leave the bosom of your family?"

"I was fifteen, and my father insisted I marry a man I despised. A man more than thrice my own age."

"But—surely your father could not have forced you to marry!"

Emma laughed bitterly. "You do not know my father."

She went on then, and told him everything. How her mother—whose marriage was miserable in every way save for the blessing of her children—had helped Emma escape from her family and go to a milliner friend of her mother's in Salisbury. How Emma feared that her father would find her even there, and moved on to Moncton, where she opened a hat shop with another young lady. How the dread that her father would somehow hunt her down and drag her back to be wed to his elderly friend had prompted her to create a new identity for herself, and find a place in which he would never seek her. A man's place.

Jerome listened in silence as the darkness deepened around them. Emma told him of her success as Frank Thompson, Bible salesman, of her delight in her new-found freedom, and of how she had eventually come to Flint, and there decided to join the Grays.

"The rest you know," she concluded.

A moment passed. She watched him, his face half-turned away from her, frowning in thought. At last he turned to look at her.

"And why do you tell me this now?"

"Because I—"

She stopped, struggling to master herself. Taking a steadying breath, she began again.

"I have told you the main reason. I do not wish any longer to deceive such a valued friend. The cause of my telling you now, at this time, is your confidences to me regarding Miss Corey. You would not have made them, perhaps, had you known I was female."

"I would most certainly not have done!" he replied, and Emma winced.

He began to pace now, stalking back and forth between the rows of peach trees. "How you dared to listen to them is beyond me! You allowed me, under false pretenses, to unburden my heart—"

"Jerome—"

"You took advantage of my trust!"

"I never meant to. I did not ask your confidences."

"Yet you accepted them!"

He was lashing himself into a fury. Emma watched, helpless to prevent it, knowing she deserved every word of his angry accusal.

"If I listened, it was out of friendship," she said.

"Friendship requires honesty!"

"And that is why I have been honest with you now."

"I don't believe you know the meaning of the word! How could you, and act as you did? Every Christian value you claimed was a lie!"

"That is not true—"

"A lie, Frank! Or whoever you are—"

"Emma. My name is Emma."

He stopped and stood staring at her, seething, his chest rising and falling with angry breaths. Emma feared she had lost his goodwill entirely. Danger prickled at the back of her neck, and along her arms.

"Our discussions of faith," she said softly, "of the Scripture, of philosophy—those were all true. I have never deceived you save in this one thing."

"One little thing," he said bitterly.

"I ask your forgiveness, Jerome. I need it. I need it most desperately."

"You want me to countenance this lie. Be a party to it."

Emma swallowed. "You must do as you see fit."

He stared at her again. The moon was rising over his shoulder now, leaving his face shadowed in darkness. Emma gazed at its sullen, gold orb, knowing it illumined her own face for Jerome to see.

"How many others know of this?" Jerome demanded. "Your company? Your captain?"

"No one. No one else knows."

"The man you share a *tent* with? Do you ask me to believe that is innocent?"

"I've lain beside you often enough, and that was innocent!" Emma retorted, her patience strained to breaking. She regretted her tone at once, and added more moderately, "Believe what you wish, I cannot stop you, but Damon knows nothing of this. You will find out if you ask him, though it ruins me."

"They call you their woman," Jerome said doubtfully.

Emma gave a wry smile. "Yes. Ironic, isn't it? A company jest. It began at Fort Wayne, where they teased me because of my small feet."

He turned his back to her then, and stood gazing at the moon. It cast twisted shadows of peach branches across the ground.

"Jerome," she said softly, "I cannot bear to think I have lost your friendship. Please tell me I have not."

"How can I be your friend? I do not know you!"

"You know everything that matters about me. Everything we have discussed is true. That I am female is merely an accident of my birth, it has nothing to do with me."

"This is unnatural," Jerome said, his voice wrought with despair.

"I have never been womanly," Emma said. "No more than a cloistered nun. Less, in fact. Think of me that way, if you will. Unsexed."

Jerome was silent. Emma dared to step up beside him, and turned her head to look at him in the moonlight. His handsome face was frowning, lost in thought.

"You have opened your heart to me," she said. "I will do the same. There is no one in the world for whom I care more than I do you, Jerome. The esteem I feel for you—words cannot express it."

He glanced at her sidelong, then, his dark eyes glinting in the moonlight. Trouble still haunted them, and now a hint of wariness joined it.

He took a backward step, then another, then turned and strode from the orchard, making for the road. Emma watched him go, knowing that to follow, to plead with him further, would be worse than useless. She had placed herself in his hands. Time would reveal her fate.

Her heart ached, and she fought back the tears that started to her eyes. She feared she had said too much, but she had only spoken the truth. She had shriven herself of deception, at least with Jerome.

Would he forgive her? She hoped and prayed that he would.

She gazed about her at the peach trees, their fruitful limbs barren at this season. Barren.

This time tomorrow, if she remained free, she would return to this place and give thanks for it. If she was not free...she would have a new challenge to face.

Closing her eyes, she whispered a prayer for forgiveness, and invoked God's blessing upon Jerome. Whatever the morrow would bring, she loved him still.

Returning to the camp, Emma passed a restless night in her tent. Damon was gone again late into the evening, playing cards and carousing. She feigned sleep when he came in, not wishing to talk.

She lay awake, though, subject to haunting fears, starting at every sound and expecting any moment to hear the heavy tread of the provost guard coming to arrest her. Morning came instead, and no sign of any change.

She reported to the hospital. Jerome was there, but he avoided Emma's gaze, and she in turn avoided meeting him as she went about her duties. When necessity brought them together, they spoke as strangers. Emma was grateful that he had apparently decided not to unmask her, but every cold word or glance they exchanged made her miserable.

She volunteered for night duty that evening, preferring to stay at the hospital where she might at least be of use than to spend another night in camp, agonizing over her fate. Jerome departed at the end of his shift, and Emma was left to the quiet of the night-time hospital. She read in her Bible during every spare moment, seeking consolation.

Remembering her pledge to return to the peach orchard, she did so in the small hours of the night after she was relieved of duty. The sky was cold and filled with glimmering stars. She gazed up at them through the bare branches and thanked God with all her heart for her freedom.

The next two days passed in much the same way as the first. Jerome's manner was distant, and Emma responded in kind. She turned her attention to the patients instead, and took pleasure in giving them comfort. Once, while she was reading a newspaper to one of them, she sensed Jerome watching her and glanced up at him, meeting his gaze. He wore a troubled look, and turned away.

Late on Thursday afternoon, as Emma had just completed a round of the beds preparatory to serving the evening meal, Jerome came up to her. He made a small, formal bow.

"There is a prayer meeting tonight," he said stiffly. "I wondered if you would like to attend."

Emma gazed back at him, gratitude swelling her heat. "I

would like it very much. Thank you."

Jerome nodded, then stepped away. Until the end of their shift he said nothing more to her, but when they stepped out of the tent together, Emma carrying her Bible beneath her arm, she felt almost as if nothing had changed between them. Jerome spoke cordially of the latest news, gave his opinions, and invited Emma to share hers. She did so with slight hesitation, wishing to avoid his displeasure. As they talked, however, she felt more and more at ease.

The prayer meeting lifted her spirits even more. Six other soldiers crowded into Mrs. Brown's tidy parlor, seated upon chairs borrowed from the dining table. The smell of the Browns' supper lingered in the house, making Emma think of her mother and her long-forsaken home. Jerome sat beside her, leaning forward as he listened intently to the Reverend Mr. Brown, the Second's chaplain, reading aloud by lamplight.

"The Lord is merciful and gracious, slow to anger and abounding in steadfast love. He will not always chide, nor will he keep his anger forever. He does not deal with us according to our sins, nor repay us according to our iniquities. For as high as the heavens are above the earth, so great is his steadfast love toward those who fear him; as far as the east is from the west, so far does he remove our transgressions from us."

Emma found comfort in these words, and when the assembled joined together in prayer her heart felt as if a great weight had been lifted from it. She and Jerome walked away together, discussing the meeting as they strolled through the camp toward Emma's tent, which was nearest.

Jerome's manner was much more open, fired with enthusiasm for the subject of their discourse. They found themselves in agreement, as they often did, that it was faith that would be the salvation of all soldiers.

When they reached Emma and Damon's tent they stopped. Emma turned to face her friend.

"Thank you, Jerome. I have very much enjoyed this evening."

He smiled, the first genuine smile she had seen from him since their talk in the peach orchard. "So have I."

"Thank you also," she said, her voice dropping to a near

whisper, "for your discretion."

His smile faded somewhat, and a shadow of trouble returned to his eyes, but he did not turn away. "I have thought long on our conversation," he said quietly. "I have been plagued by many doubts, but always I returned to remembering our discussions of faith. The star of Christian hope must ever bind the links of friendship more firmly between us, I think."

Emma let out a breath she had not realized she was holding. "Yes," she said, smiling. "Yes."

If, in her moments of folly, she had hoped for more, she knew now that this was enough. Indeed, it was a great gift, and she must be duly grateful.

"I shall be true to your confidence in me," Jerome said.

"And I to yours," Emma eagerly agreed.

"And both to our God's." Jerome smiled again, offering his hand. "Good night, Frank."

Emma shook it. "Good night."

She watched him walk away until, recalling herself, she turned and went into her tent. Damon was not there. She sank onto her bed, relief washing cold through her limbs, and gave a quiet sob of gratitude.

From then on, her friendship with Jerome seemed secure, if not quite as intimate as it had once been. Aware that she had bound her heart to him perhaps more closely than was wise, she now took care to spend some time in company with others. If she did not care for the card games Damon liked, she could still enjoy sitting around a campfire with him and others of the company—Ben Shelley and Will McCreery, especially—trading news and stories.

She went to Washington on a pass with several of her company, and enjoyed the day well enough. If she took a greater pleasure in seeing Jerome when she returned that evening, she kept it to herself.

December arrived, and with it winter descended on the army's camps. Orders came to prepare them for winter, and much work went into these efforts. Damon undertook to make their shared tent more comfortable, for Emma's time was still spent largely at the hospital, where disease was now a deadlier enemy in the face of cold weather.

One day she sought the nurses' couch after finishing her rounds, and found Jerome sitting there perusing a letter. He hastily put it in his pocket when he saw Emma, but not before she recognized Miss Corey's handwriting. She turned away again, suddenly assailed by feelings she thought she had set aside. Not wishing to visit her anger upon Jerome, she left the tent abruptly.

The heat of jealousy took Emma's breath away. She fled without knowing where, and was surprised a moment later to find herself standing outside the cook-tent, with snow falling softly onto her face.

"There you are, Thompson! Just the man I'm looking for."

Dr. Bonine's voice roused her from her reverie. He was coming up the path from camp, the shoulders of his overcoat covered in snow.

Emma turned to face him. "Yes, sir?"

"Come in out of the cold," he said, beckoning her toward the dispensary tent.

She followed, welcoming the distraction from her unpleasant feelings, her hands moving automatically to brush the snow from Dr. Bonine's shoulders before they entered the tent. He took off his overcoat and hung it on a peg by the door, then stepped over to the camp stove and rubbed his hands together.

"All quiet in the wards?" the surgeon asked.

"Quiet enough, sir."

"Good. How would you like to go into Alexandria? We are out of quinine, and the quartermaster has none to give me."

"I would be glad to," Emma said.

"I will write you a note to take to Dr. Porter at the Mansion House Hospital. He should have plenty to spare. Or he did the last I spoke to him."

Emma went to fetch her own overcoat from the hospital tent while he wrote. Jerome, who was sweeping snow back from the entrance, looked up as she came in.

"Frank—"

"I am going to Alexandria for Dr. Bonine. Will you keep an eye on them?" She nodded toward the patients as she shrugged into her overcoat.

"Of course," Jerome said.

"Thank you."

She left without saying more, a hard knot of unhappiness still in her gut. The walk into Alexandria served to dispel it somewhat, and also raised her spirits. The cold air was invigorating, and the soft fall of snow left the scene looking quiet and peaceful, even in the city.

Emma made her way to the Mansion House, a fine brick building that had once been a hotel. It was now a military hospital of some seven hundred beds. Emma got a look at the wards as she tracked down the surgeon, and was impressed with their quiet and cleanliness.

The surgeon, Dr. Porter, peered through spectacles at Dr. Bonine's note. "Quinine, eh? Yes, we have some. Not a great amount to spare, but this time of year there is less call for it. Come along, I'll have some packed up for you."

Emma followed him to a large and very well-stocked dispensary, where he set an assistant to measuring out a quantity of quinine. She murmured a compliment on the dispensary's quality, and the surgeon smiled.

"We have the advantage of permanence. You regimental fellows must be ready to move at a moment's notice, and cannot keep such a complete store."

"Hence our need to impose upon you."

"It is no imposition. I get such requests all the time. I take care to have sufficient store to cover them. Now tell me, have you actually had a malaria case?"

"One, but it is not new. A relapse."

"Ah. Well, this should make him more comfortable."

He accepted the package—a bottle wrapped in brown paper against the weather—from the clerk, and handed it to Emma. She received it with a nod.

"Thank you, sir."

"You may tell Dr. Bonine he is welcome."

She followed him out, down the well-lit main corridor to the front of the hospital. She could not help glancing into the wards they passed.

"These men are fortunate, to be indoors out of the cold," she said.

"They are the worst cases, those who would not survive in a field hospital. Many of them will not survive here, either, but we do our best." Dr. Porter raised an eyebrow as he looked at Emma. "Perhaps you would like to be assigned here, instead of working in the cold?"

"Oh, I don't regard the cold," Emma said, watching through an open doorway as a nurse fed broth to a man who was bandaged from head to toe.

Dr. Porter followed her gaze. "Trapped in a tent that caught fire. Badly burned, but he should survive. Have a care to your stoves, private."

She met his gaze. "I will, sir. Thank you."

Upon returning to the regimental hospital, Emma found Jerome building up the fires in the stoves that heated the main tent. She dutifully felt the chimney-pipes to make sure they were not becoming too hot. Jerome watched her with an offended eye, so she told him of the burn victim she had seen at the Mansion House.

"Dear God," he said. "How dreadful!"

"Yes."

She started for the nurses' station. Jerome followed.

"Why did Dr. Bonine send you there?" he asked.

"Quinine," Emma said absently, glancing at the sick roll.

"I could have fetched it."

"I was at hand."

"Frank...."

Emma looked up, raising an eyebrow. Jerome met her gaze.

"Have I somehow offended you?"

"No." She blinked. "I am not offended."

Jealous, angry, mortified—but not offended. Was he upset at her keeping a distance? She was only trying to protect herself. To protect them both.

"Well, I'm going to get some coffee," Jerome said. "Shall I bring you some?"

Thus Jerome, being kind again. It was almost too much to bear.

"No, thank you," Emma said. It was not that she did not appreciate the offer, but that the thought of drinking coffee sent her stomach shrinking into a knot.

Jerome's lips thinned to a line, then he turned and left the tent. Emma allowed herself a sigh, and sought to distract herself with work.

Every day, it seemed, there were moments of awkwardness between her and Jerome. They were offset by moments of happiness, such as the prayer meetings they continued to attend and the walks they still occasionally took when the weather allowed, but there was constraint between them. Emma no longer worried that Jerome would reveal her. It was not that concern that troubled her, but Anna Corey.

Jerome still spoke of his fair correspondent, though with far more reserve than before. Still, every word stung Emma. She listened in silence, and changed the subject as soon as she could, but sometimes all she could do was to walk away.

This puzzled and annoyed Jerome, which in turn irritated Emma the more. She thought he should know that she did not wish to hear about Miss Corey, but apparently he could not help talking of her.

Gradually Emma came to the realization that she must make a change. She loved Jerome, but it hurt her to be near him, to listen to him praise Miss Corey. If he had ever felt an attraction toward Emma, he had chosen against it, and it was folly to remain where hopeless hope tormented her. She must make a change.

On a fine day in mid-December she walked into Alexandria and went to the Mansion House hospital. Seeking out Dr. Porter, she reminded him of his suggestion that she might serve at that hospital, and told him she was now interested.

He smiled. "Cold troubling you after all, young man?"

"Not the cold, sir, but I would like a change of scene."

"Dr. Bonine speaks highly of you. He will be sorry to lose you."

Surprised, Emma felt her cheeks grow warm. "H-he would not be losing me permanently. When the regiment marches again—"

"Which will not be for some months, I imagine." Dr. Jones smiled. "Very well, Private. I will consider your request."

Emma walked back to camp, feeling slightly adrift. Dr.

Jones had promised nothing, but the act of making the request had shaken something free within her. She would leave the regimental hospital, she knew now. If the Mansion House did not come through for her, she would find something else.

Her heart ached with the thought of leaving Jerome, her daily companion of the last several weeks. Yet it ached with being near him as well, and the ache of absence would be the lesser, she thought.

On Christmas Eve, the Second Michigan's camp was filled with a mixture of sadness and cheer. There would be an excellent dinner on the morrow—chicken and turkey for all—but the separation from loved ones made for a melancholy holiday. The mail carrier was eagerly looked for.

Emma went to the hospital tent and volunteered for night duty so that others could spend Christmas Eve with their friends. Jerome was absent on an errand for Dr. Bonine, and the hospital was fairly quiet. Most of the patients at present were sick, rather than wounded, for even the skirmishes between pickets had fallen off with the coming of winter.

The mail carrier came up from the camp, and the patients turned anxious eyes toward him. Whenever he arrived down in the Second's camp a crowd always formed around him, but these men were confined to their beds for the most part. The mail carrier looked to Emma for help. Emma cheerfully accepted the handful of letters and glanced through them to be sure all of the recipients were present in the hospital.

Anna Corey's handwriting leapt out at her. She swallowed and shifted the letter to the back of the stack, looking at the next. She sorted through them, handing a couple of the letters back to the mail carrier and explaining that the recipients had returned to their companies. Two letters addressed to Frank Thompson caught her by surprise; one was in Miss Daphne's handwriting, her dutiful holiday greeting to her soldier friend. The other was from Dr. Jones at the Mansion House. Emma tucked both into her pocket.

She thanked the mail carrier and went around the ward delivering letters to the lucky recipients, knowing she would soon be called upon to read some of them aloud. Jerome's letter from Miss Corey she placed upon the nurses' table. If he did not return to the hospital she would send it down to him at the camp.

Dark thoughts tempted her; she might lose the letter instead. Mail often went astray. For a moment she indulged in imagining tearing up Miss Corey's careful penmanship and disposing of the shreds in the sink, but she would never actually do so. No good could come of it. Her Christian duty was to do the opposite—to make certain Jerome received his letter, and to wish him happiness from it.

Emma returned to the ward and went around to those men who had not received mail, spending time with each of them, reading to them if they wished it, or merely talking. Most were thinking of home and family on this day. Emma listened, smiling and encouraging them to look forward to a brighter future.

She then read letters to those men who were too ill to read themselves, and promised to help write responses. One man, who was so weak from dysentery that he could hardly keep his eyes open, listened in silence. When Emma finished reading his wife's letter his lips formed the words, "Thank you."

"You are most welcome," Emma said. "I will read it to you again later if you wish."

He nodded slightly, then closed his eyes and sighed, his expression peaceful. Emma smiled, slid the letter under his hand, then went on to the next patient.

It was late afternoon by the time she had a moment to peruse her own letters. She opened the note from Dr. Jones first, and discovered it to be an order to report to Mansion House hospital for duty on the morrow.

Her heart staggered slightly. She glanced out at the patients, feeling a strange reluctance to leave them. They would be cared for, she knew, but it was strange to think it would not be by her.

She stood up, and feeling restless, walked out to the cook tent to get herself some coffee. Dr. Bonine was there and Emma showed him her orders from Dr. Jones.

"Ah, yes. He sent me a note as well. We shall miss you, Frank."

"I—thank you, sir. It is only temporary." She glanced at the cook, a new man recently assigned to the duty, whom she disliked.

"It will be good experience for you," Dr. Bonine said, smiling. "You will learn a thing or two there, I expect."

Emma smiled back and returned the letter to her pocket before pouring herself a cup of coffee. She went back to the hospital tent and sat on the nurses' couch, sipping gingerly at the brew. It was strong and tasted slightly burned, but she did not care. At least it was hot.

Setting the cup aside, she took out Miss Daphne's letter, and was soon smiling at a description of the Ladies' Afternoon organized by Mrs. Joslin for the purpose of sending Christmas cheer to every soldier in the Grays. This was a formidable task, and while Miss Daphne did not complain, exactly, she did congratulate herself on her fortitude at committing to write *eight letters* all in an afternoon, which made Emma chuckle.

Daphne had been highly amused by a story Emma had written to her of catching an eel for a patient who craved fish. Unable to extract the hook from its mouth, Emma had resorted to dragging the eel back to the Second's camp by the fishing line. Miss Daphne wanted to know if "Frank" had ever retrieved his fishhook. Her letter concluded shortly thereafter (Emma had no doubt she was conserving her resources for the labor to which she had set herself), with kind wishes for a Merry Christmas and a Happy New Year.

Smiling softly, Emma was folding the letter when she heard a step outside the tent and glanced up to see Jerome coming in. A tumble of emotions went though her upon seeing him, knowing she would no longer be constantly near him.

His gaze went past her to the letter lying on the table, and his eyes lit with happiness. Emma glanced away, and busied herself with putting her letter from Miss Daphne in her pocket.

She stood up, then, and taking up writing-board, paper, pen and ink, went back into the hospital ward to write letters for those unable to hold a pen. This kept her busy until it was time for the patients' supper, when she must of necessity work with Jerome to help some of the men who could not feed themselves.

They moved in accord, having little need to speak as they both knew what needed to be done. Emma felt the harmony between them, the understanding that enabled them to communicate with a glance or a nod. She treasured that understanding still, and her heart was heavy with the thought of parting from Jerome.

She knew, though, that she must, and in any case, it was already done. All that remained was to make her farewells, but she was strangely reluctant to do so.

Perhaps she feared his taking offense, or demanding an explanation. Certainly she had no wish to discuss her reasons for leaving; if he did not understand them at once and by instinct, then he was better off not knowing them.

The patients having been fed, Emma and Jerome retired to the couch with their own supper. They talked a little of the day, the progress of the patients, and the latest Washington newspaper, which had already been passed around the ward so much that it was beginning to fall apart.

"Chaplain Brown has invited a few of us to his tent for prayer this evening," Jerome said. "Do you join us?"

Emma shook her head. "I have taken the night duty. Please give the chaplain my regards."

"You are always taking night duty."

"I like the quiet."

Emma smiled, thinking of the evening they had first met. Jerome met her gaze, and Emma felt again the kinship she treasured, along with a pang of sorrow at leaving. Jerome seemed to sense this, for his brow creased slightly.

"Is everything well with you, Frank?"

"Quite well, thank you."

Jerome gazed at her a little longer, then looked away. "It is hard to believe Christmas is here already."

"Yes. The autumn passed quickly. I have enjoyed your friendship, Jerome."

He looked at her again, a slight puzzlement in his expression. "And I yours."

"I have a present for you."

Emma set aside her plate and took a small, silver watch and chain from her coat pocket. She placed them in Jerome's hand and squeezed it briefly.

"Th-thank you," Jerome said, looking astonished. "I didn't...I haven't—"

Emma shook her head. "Merry Christmas, Jerome."

He gazed at her, then smiled the smile that lit his face with happiness. "Merry Christmas."

Emma smiled back, and feeling a lump begin to form in her throat, made haste to stand up and carry her plate away. Jerome took his leave shortly thereafter. She bade him good night and watched him walk down the hill to the camp, hoping he would understand when he arrived for duty on the morrow and learned that she was gone.

Mansion House was an agreeable place to work, and Emma quickly adjusted to her new situation. Dr. Jones was kind, if also strict, and appreciated her ability to cheer the sick and wounded men who came to Mansion House hospital.

As the winter wore on and spring approached, Emma felt herself regaining her balance. If she still missed Jerome, at least she no longer thought of him day and night. She made other friends, good friends and good company, if not so close as she had been with Jerome. She continued well in health, and often attended prayer meetings, though not always in the Second Michigan's camp.

Still, she felt a lingering sadness that she could not seem to shake. At times she would leave her shift at the hospital in a state close to despair, and would seek comfort in the Scripture. At others she knew a heavy reluctance to return to the hospital, though once there she became caught up in answering the needs of the unfortunate men who were wounded or sick.

She found it harder and harder to bear the demise of those who were beyond recovering. Each death seemed to tear a small piece from her heart. She prayed for the strength to endure.

March arrived, and with it a renewal of murmurs from the discontented in Washington. General McClellan had brought the Army of the Potomac into fine shape, and was now being pressured to make use of it. Scouting missions and skirmishes increased, and the hospital began to receive an increase of wounded along with the sick.

One morning Emma was summoned to attend upon Colonel Poe, the Second Michigan's commander ever since Colonel Richardson had been given command of the entire brigade. Emma presented herself at the Headquarters tent, and after a short wait, was duly ushered into Colonel Poe's presence.

Colonel Orlando Poe had wildly curling hair, a dimpled chin beneath a fierce mustache, and sharp eyes that often as not suggested an ironic outlook on life. His eyebrows rose as Emma stood at attention before the Colonel's desk.

"Thompson," he said, though the assistant adjutant had announced Emma a moment before.

"Yes, sir."

"You have been serving hospital duty for six months."

"Y-yes, sir," Emma replied, though she had not paid attention to how long she had been serving as a nurse.

Colonel Poe stood up and walked around his desk, looking Emma over. He was several inches taller, and gazed down at her with eyebrows still quirked. He walked in a slow circle, around Emma, and she began to fear that he suspected her.

She struggled to maintain her calm. Had Jerome had a change of heart, and decided to reveal her after all? But if that were so she would have been arrested, she thought. She gazed straight ahead, remaining at attention while her heart pounded painfully, and hoping that the heat in her cheeks was not enough to show.

At last Colonel Poe stood before her again, then leaned back against his desk.

"How would you like a change of pace?"

Emma swallowed. "Sir?"

"I need a new mail carrier. Someone agile, who can handle a horse. You can ride?"

"Oh—yes, sir."

"You would be in the saddle a good deal."

Emma had never considered leaving the hospital, but now her heart seemed to lift at this offer. To ride every day, in the fresh air, to be able to come and go as she pleased, and not stifle in the hospital with the sick and dying. It seemed the answer to her prayer—an unexpected answer, but one that would allow her a respite from the gloom of nursing duty. Let her spend some time away from the hospital, recover her spirits, and then she would be able to return.

"I would not mind, sir," she said. "I have been accustomed to riding daily." Early in her bookselling career, before she had set up her carriage, she had ridden all of her routes.

"Good," said Colonel Poe, flashing a smile. "I will issue your assignment at once. Report to the quartermaster for a horse."

Thus Emma's transformation from nurse to mail carrier, a change that agreed with her even more than she expected. She had a great deal more freedom. As long as the regiment's mail was picked up and delivered in a timely fashion, she might otherwise do as she pleased. The one shadow that fell on her happiness in the first week of her new duty was the appearance of a letter in Miss Corey's handwriting.

She had already made a habit of bringing the regimental hospital's mail to the dispensary tent and giving it over to Dr. Bonine or his assistant. In this way she avoided seeing Jerome directly. She buried Miss Corey's letter within the stack of mail and left all with the assistant surgeon, escaping as quickly as she could down to the Second's camp.

She had become the most looked-for member of the regiment, and was usually greeted by cheers as she visited each company in turn. In addition to the mail, she often picked up newspapers in Washington for those who requested them. Her natural turn for sales asserted itself, and she began to make a little extra money selling conveniences that the sutlers did not carry, watches and the like. No one remarked at her keeping a supply of pocket handkerchiefs on hand. Colonel Poe turned a benignly blind eye to this activity, and Emma prospered.

In mid-March, General McClellan issued an announcement that the Army of the Potomac would soon move against the enemy. Speculation abounded, but when the Second received marching orders a few days later, they were astonished to learn they were to travel by steamer to Fortress Monroe, at the extreme of the Virginia Peninsula. In a drizzling rain the regiment boarded the *Vanderbilt* at the Alexandria wharf, and late in the evening commenced a slow and dreary trip southward.

The steamer was crammed full of soldiers. The entire brigade was aboard, or so it seemed, and there was scarcely room to move. Emma glimpsed Jerome once—he had found a good seat on the upper deck—but she went another way and did not speak to him.

The river was filled with transports, all making their way to Fort Monroe in the worst weather. Storms soaked the soldiers and churned up the water enough to make a number of them ill, which added to everyone's discomfort.

Upon arrival at Fort Monroe the *Vanderbilt* languished for two more days in the river before its unhappy passengers were allowed to disembark. Despite the continuing rain, which turned their new camping ground to mud, the men of the Second were happy to be ashore.

Their camp was several miles from the fort, which could not accommodate the entire Army of the Potomac. The fort's commissary did issue soft bread to all the new arrivals, a great comfort. The Second pitched their camp and settled in as best it could in the rain and mud.

Before a week had passed, many of the soldiers were laid low by a miasma. Emma did not escape, and lay in her tent for several days, shivering and sweating by turns. When at last she felt well enough to rise and return to her duties, she had to fight her way through near-chaos to find the mail depot and collect the regiment's letters.

Returning to the camp with several days' worth of mail in her bags, she felt like Father Christmas. The men, weary of mud and the cold, incessant rain, gathered eagerly around her horse. She handed out letters and reaped the reward of delighted smiles from their recipients.

The field hospital had not been set up yet, hence Jerome was with his company. Emma gave him two letters, neither from Miss Corey, and received a brief smile in return. Thanks enough, she supposed. Perhaps he had been hurt more than she expected by her unannounced departure from the hospital. She had tried to prepare him for it, at least. She had said goodbye in her own way, wishing him a Merry Christmas.

Folly to dwell upon it. She turned her expectations to the future instead. General McClellan had moved his vast army here, and soon they would march up the Peninsula toward Richmond.

One night a commotion roused Emma from sleep, and she and Damon both got up to see what was happening. Most of the Second turned out as well, gathering around a group of negroes whose shouts of "Glory, glory!" had awakened the regiment.

They were all dressed in humble clothing, much soiled and tattered. A campfire was quickly built up, and food and coffee provided to the negroes, whose gratitude was touching. The eldest among them eagerly told their story, and the soldiers listened in wonder.

They were contrabands, runaway slaves. Hearing of the Federal army's approach, they had dared to make their escape from bondage, and had spent ten harrowing days hiding in the forest, seeking an opportunity to reach McClellan's army. In that time they had eaten nothing but what they could find in the woods.

They had been fired upon by Confederate pickets, one of their number killed and another badly wounded. This night they had come to the water's edge, and been seen by Dr. Bonine, who at first had thought them enemies and had summoned a handful of guards from the Second's camp.

The good doctor, who was not now present, for he had taken the wounded man to be cared for, had realized upon his return to the river that the men he had seen were not pickets, but refugees. Their attempts to cross the creek were unsuccessful, for the water was too deep to wade and it was apparent that they could not swim. With the help of the soldiers, Dr. Bonine constructed a raft and tied a rope to it, and had by that means brought the escapees across the river to safety and freedom.

Emma was fascinated by this story. She had not previously met any contrabands, but now she spoke with them and listened to their stories, and was struck by their dedication to find freedom at any cost. She was also impressed by their knowledge of the Scripture, for though they could not read or write, they yet knew the substance of the Bible well and were devoted to Christ Jesus.

She wished she could teach them. They were eager to learn, and if her obligations had not prevented her, she would have undertaken their education.

It was not to be, however. Orders went out for the army to march, and with two days' rations in their haversacks, and in a driving rain, they slogged their way up the peninsula to arrive before Yorktown, where they bivouacked on ground over which the water was running like a flood.

Emma had her horse, a sturdy bay gelding whom she named Samuel, to look after as well as she could. She found room with the headquarters horses, in a shed near the farmhouse that Colonel Poe and his staff had taken for their use, and received the adjutant's permission to house her mount there. After seeing to his needs, she prepared to return, cold and wet, to the Second's temporary camp, but she was distracted by the sight of Chaplain Brown coming out of a smaller house adjacent to the farmhouse. She hastened over to him, discovered that he was engaged in bringing in firewood, and offered to help.

The house had but one room and looked to have been that of a foreman, perhaps. Scarcely any furnishings remained, its occupant having retreated from the Federal advance. The chaplain and Emma brought in three loads of wood, then dragged in a couple of stumps from the yard for seats. The stumps were wet from the rain, but as Emma was wet herself, she gladly sat down on one, rubbing her hands before a sputtering fire.

"Thank you, Frank!" the chaplain said, rather out of breath, as he fed wood to the feeble flames. "We have not seen you much at our meetings of late," he added gently.

"No, well, I have sometimes gone to meetings in Alexandria," Emma said.

"Are things well with you?"

Emma blinked, reminded suddenly of Jerome. "Yes, of course," she said, managing to smile. "I quite like serving as mail carrier. I had not realized how much my spirits were oppressed by being constantly among the sick."

Chaplain Brown nodded, watching her with a slight look of concern. "Your spirits are recovered now?"

"Well, apart from being soaked through," she said, with an attempt to laugh. The jest fell flat, and she gazed at the flames. "I have been somewhat restless, I suppose."

"So have we all. Perhaps this move will cure that."

"Except that we still are not doing anything." Surprised at how petulant her own voice sounded, she looked at the chaplain with a rueful shrug. "I am too impatient for action. I have always been one to seize the day, and think later of consequences. But I know it takes time to shift an army, and that General McClellan will advance when the time is best."

Chaplain Brown looked at her with a somewhat curious expression. "There may be opportunities for action quite soon —for some."

Emma raised her eyebrows. "Some?"

The chaplain added another log to the fire, and spent some moments adjusting its position. As there were no tools in the house, he used his fingers, and flinched back when they came too near the coals.

"A man named Webster was captured lately by the Confederates," he said. "They intend to hang him as a spy."

Emma blinked. "That is dreadful."

"Yes."

The chaplain gazed at her earnestly for some moments, until Emma was beginning to be uncomfortable with the silence. He then looked at the fire, and absently shifted a log with a fingertip.

"I know of a situation that might be available, for one who seeks action and has sufficient moral courage."

Emma caught her breath. Did he mean the unfortunate Webster's position? Then the man truly had been a spy?

"It is a situation of great danger and vast responsibility," the chaplain said, meeting her gaze.

Cold washed through her veins; a different cold than the chill inflicted by the weather. It was part fear, and part excitement.

"Tell me," she said, leaning forward.

Washington, D.C., 1883

"So the good chaplain invited you to become a spy?" Jamie's sneer was somewhat less pronounced.

Emma paused before answering, seeing a young man about to enter from the hallway. He took two steps in, glanced at Jamie, then Emma, then the closed door behind Mr. Glass's desk, and retreated again.

"Yes," Emma said when he had gone. "Colonel Poe had asked him to think about which men in the regiment were of good character and unquestionable loyalty."

"Colonel Poe? I thought McClellan had Pinkerton for that."

"He did, but Colonel Poe was a friend of McClellan's, and had done such work for him before. When we arrived on the peninsula the urgent need was to determine how many men the enemy had ranged against us. McClellan sought as many sources of information as he could find."

"And you applied."

"I did." Emma smiled, remembering. "I could not resist. I was already living one disguise. The prospect of living a disguise within a disguise intrigued me."

Jamie shook his head. "Madness." He paced to the door, looked out into the hall, and returned. "You could easily have been discovered. Did they not examine you before taking you into the secret service?"

Emma's smile broadened. "Oh, yes, but the only physical examination was phrenological. Fortunately the bumps on my head were deemed favorable."

"That was all the examination you received?"

"No, I was questioned at length—exhaustive length, by two different committees—about my views of the rebellion and my reasons for desiring the work. I was also required to demonstrate my competence with firearms. They were satisfied."

Again, Jamie shook his head. "It would never happen today."

"We are not at war today," Emma said softly. "Many of the things we did then would not happen today."

Jamie looked sharply at her and a handful of emotions crossed his face in quick succession. She could not read them all, but the last of them lingered, a look of mournfulness, of loss.

"Perhaps you are right, and I was mad," Emma said. "If so it was a successful madness. I was given three days to prepare, at the end of which I was to venture into Yorktown to learn how many Confederates were there."

"And what form did your preparations take?" Jamie said somewhat absently, gazing past Emma.

"I acquired a suit of plantation clothing and a negro wig, had my hair sheared close to my head, and colored my skin with silver nitrate," Emma said, grinning at the memory. "I became a contraband."

The War: Near Yorktown, Virginia, 1862

Emma stood in the shadow of the dispensary tent, waiting for her heart to slow to a normal pace. Her scalp itched beneath the woolen wig, and her eyes stung a little from the proximity of silver nitrate.

She had walked through the Second's camp without being recognized—a good test, since as mail carrier most of the men knew her by sight—but she wanted a further assurance. Her disguise had to sustain more than a cursory glance if she were to succeed in her mission.

With the afternoon fading, she had made her way to the hospital, hoping to find Dr. Bonine there. She knew he would not take her for one of the contrabands he had helped to rescue, but she thought she could rely upon his taking an interest in a stray negro.

She hovered near the dispensary tent until she was certain no one was within. Dusk was coming early, aided by a heavy layer of clouds, and the campfires and lanterns were already lit. Inside the dispensary tent a dim light emanated from a lamp burning low. The tent's door was tied closed, and Emma concluded it was unoccupied.

Stepping out from behind the canvas, she made her way up to the main hospital tent. If Dr. Bonine was not there, she would try his private quarters.

The door here was closed as well against the chill and damp, but not tied. As Emma came near she heard footsteps approaching. The canvas door was flung back, and Jerome stepped out, a dirty plate in his hand.

Emma's heart caught and for a moment she could only gaze at him. He paused, looking back without recognition, and said, "What do you want?"

Emma lowered her gaze and made a stooping bow. "Beg pardon, Massa, I be looking for the doctor."

"I am not your master." Jerome's voice was sharp, but he softened it with his next words. "Are you sick?"

"No, sir. I heard mebbe he could use a boy take care of his horse."

She glanced up at Jerome, not needing to feign hopefulness. He peered at her, frowning slightly, and she began to quail.

"Well, the doctor is not here," Jerome said at last. "Come back in the morning."

"Yes sir. Thank you, sir."

Jerome brushed past Emma on his way to the cook tent. She watched him go, feeling a mixture of jubilance and disappointment. Either her disguise was a complete success, or Jerome had put her so thoroughly out of his mind that he no longer knew her.

He was returning, and Emma realized she should have left, but it was now too late. She watched him cross the few strides back to where she stood.

"Well? What is it?" he said.

"B-beg pardon, Massa—sir. I be awful hungry."

Jerome pressed his lips together in the thin line she knew so well. It marked his impatience, but it softened again almost as once.

"Come with me, then."

She followed him back to the cook tent, and waited outside while he went in. In a moment he was back, pressing two pieces of hardtack into her hand.

"Thank you, sir," Emma said, bowing again. "Thank you!"

Having said she was hungry, she raised a cracker to her lips, and was suddenly assailed by fears. Her teeth were too good for a contraband's, so she hid them, and as she started to bite the cracker she remembered at the last moment that she should probably not show familiarity with hardtack. She bit it as she would a piece of bread, uttered an exclamation of surprise, and gnawed at it sideways until she broke off one corner.

Smiling as she chewed, she saluted Jerome with the cracker, then turned and slouched away. She could feel his gaze upon her, watching her.

As he did not hail her again, she concluded she had succeeded in deceiving him, and that this was a sufficient test of her incognito. She slid the crackers with which he had provisioned her into a pocket, then checked the rest of her supply. A small bottle of silver nitrate, a pocket mirror, two sheets of paper and a pencil, were hidden inside her shirt. She also had some money in the waistband of her trousers, and a loaded revolver at the small of her back beneath her clothing, its solid weight a comfort.

She was as ready as she could be. With excitement beating in her veins, she started toward Yorktown.

Leaving the Federal camp was not difficult; no one seemed to care where a lone contraband was headed. Passing through the Confederate picket line would be less simple, and Emma approached it cautiously, leaving the road and keeping under cover of the woods.

She had been walking for some time by now, and decided it must be near midnight. Darkness aided her as she eased her way forward until she saw a Rebel picket ahead and to her right. He was standing at attention, musket in hand, facing the Federal camp. Emma crept cautiously through the woods, passing within ten yards of where he stood and never drawing his notice.

Separated now from her own people, she felt terribly alone and somewhat uncertain what to do. She determined to wait until morning and find her way into the Rebel camp by daylight. Continuing into the woods until she felt she was a safe distance from the pickets, she lay down and tried to rest.

Reaction set her trembling, and the night's chill only increased her shivering. She wondered if she would ever return to the Federal camp. She might be discovered and hanged like poor Webster, or worse, she might die undiscovered, the victim of some cruel Confederate whim. The guise she wore made her feel terribly vulnerable. Even in her own army's camp, where folk were tolerant toward runaway slaves, she had not received much friendly treatment.

Jerome had been kind, though compared to what she knew of his generosity and kind-heartedness, his manner had been cold. She had taken on a role far different than Frank

Thompson, who was popular, prosperous, and independent. In the cold dark of the Virginia night, she began to doubt her courage.

Dawn brought a sense of calm, if not a complete renewal of confidence. Emma arose from where she lay and looked about her, wondering if she might be able to discern the number of the Rebels' cannon from there.

A road passed through the woods not far away—the same road she had walked upon from the Federal camp, and left when she came near the Rebels. She made her way to it and walked up to the top of the next hill. Ahead she saw only trees; the woods were too thick and she was still too far from the Rebel lines. If she was to learn anything of value, she must penetrate further into the Rebels' camp.

Voices reached her, causing her to duck out of sight behind the trees. The lilt rang familiar; she had heard it among the contrabands who had come to the Second's camp. Daring to look out from her hiding place, she saw a half-dozen negroes coming along the road carrying buckets in either hand. They were talking cheerfully among themselves, laughing now and then. For men suffering under the yoke of bondage, they seemed carefree.

Emma came to the edge of the road and showed herself. The smell of coffee reached her as the negroes came near, and her stomach rumbled.

"M-morning," she said as the men reached her. "What you got in them buckets?"

"Breakfast for the pickets," said a tall, lanky man. "You look like you slep' in the woods."

"True 'nough," Emma said, peering toward the buckets. "I did."

"Have you some," said a smaller, round-faced man, smiling kindly. He set down his bucket and unwrapped a napkin from a heap of cornbread, then handed Emma a piece.

"Thank you! Much obliged," she said, cupping the warm bread in her cold hands.

Another of the negroes poured coffee into a tin cup for her, then they all left, heading for the picket line. Emma sat in the road and ate her breakfast, grateful for this small bit of good fortune. She felt much better presently, and when the negroes returned, she joined them, offering to carry some of the buckets.

"Sure, now you gonna carry them," said the tall man. "Now that they's empty!"

Emma laughed along with them all and took a bucket from the tall one, who seemed to be the leader. The bucket contained a jumble of empty pitchers and cups. Emma added her cup to it and walked along with the others, her burden clanking gently. In this way she walked straight into the Confederate camp, unchallenged.

By this time she knew the names of her new friends, and had told them her own was "Ned." At a large open-air kitchen she yielded up her bucket, and the others of her party dispersed to report to their foremen for the day's work, leaving Emma standing alone and somewhat at a loss.

Yorktown had been a fortress during the revolution, and the Rebels were hastily enhancing its fortification. Emma gazed at the nearest earthwork, which was completed and housed two three-inch rifled cannon in embrasures. She raised her gaze beyond to more distant works, trying to discern the type and number of guns.

"You there!"

Emma jumped and turned. A Rebel officer mounted on a bay horse came toward her, his face reddened from exposure to sun, his expression belligerent.

"Who do you belong to, and why are you not at work?"

The horse tossed its head as its rider urged it right up to Emma. She took a step back from the restless hooves and ducked her head.

"Oh, I..."

A smart slap stung her back across her shoulder blades. Astonished, she managed to keep from looking up in indignation at the man who had laid his whip to her. She ducked her head, seething.

His voice sneered. "Take that black rascal and set him to work, and if he don't work well tie him up and give him twenty lashes."

Wheeling his horse, the officer rode away, leaving Emma breathless with fear. A whipping, which it seemed she might be given at a moment's whim, would reveal her for certain. She might never feel the lash, but her fate would undoubtedly be even worse. She looked at the man the officer had spoken to, who wore civilian clothes and a broad-brimmed hat, and stood smiling mirthlessly.

"Better get to workin', boy," he drawled. "Thisaway."

He led Emma to where a new breastwork was being built, gave her a wheelbarrow and a pickaxe, and set her to work at once. The threat of whipping soon faded in her mind, replaced by a numbness that was the consequence of backbreaking toil, as she joined the crew of slaves taking gravel up the breastwork by means of wheelbarrows.

The barrows were pushed up a single plank laid from the foot of the work to its top. Emma was not the only one who needed assistance to get her barrow up the wobbling plank. By the end of the day her hands were raw with blisters, and she had a more literal appreciation of the bondsman's hardship.

At last darkness put an end to the work, and Emma shuffled along with the others to get her supper rations, which consisted of more cornbread and a generous dollop of whiskey, which as it did not interest her she gave to another. Neither meat nor coffee was given to the negroes. Emma began to see the advantage of being on the detail that took breakfast to the pickets, and made up her mind to seek out

Joe, the tall lanky man who was boss of that crew.

Finally at liberty to walk the camp, Emma did so, taking note of the number and placement of guns, and the extent of the earthworks. No one paid her any heed as she wandered the full length of the works. She found a sheltered place to make notes of what she had seen and draw a rough sketch of the works, which she hid beneath the sole of her shoe.

By now she was weary enough to be near dropping asleep. The prospect of another day laboring on the works sobered her, however. She knew that another such day would leave her hands bleeding, if she suffered no worse fate.

She returned to the negro quarters, which were simply an open field on which the slaves lay upon the ground or huddled around campfires. All were men; she had seen a few female slaves in the camp, but apparently they were quartered elsewhere. She took her place at one of the fires and listened to the desultory conversation of the men.

"You all working on the forticashuns?" she asked.

Most of the men around the fire nodded, save for one smaller fellow, about Emma's size. The man next to him cuffed him.

"Deezer's on the water detail, ain't ya?"

"Carry water all day, water to the whole brigade," Deezer answered. "Not so much different than carryin' rock."

"Ho," said one of the others, and a pithy comparison of the demands of the two duties followed. Emma listened, nodding her head in agreement with her fellow gravel-haulers. When the subject shifted she got up and stretched, and moved away as if to go to bed. She moved only as far as to get out of the firelight, however, and sat down again to wait.

The group around the fire broke into a song. Emma listened, amazed. Even in their plight, these people could make joyful music.

The song ended and another was taken up, accompanied by clapping and exclamations of praise. Perhaps half an hour had passed when a pause occurred. Deezer stood up, announced he needed to piss, and walked off. Emma rose and followed him toward the sinks.

"Say there, Deezer," she said when they were far enough from the fire not to be overheard, "you think you might trade work with me tomorrow?"

He stopped and looked at her. "Why'd I want to do that?"

"Look how my hands is all blistered."

Emma showed her hands, and Deezer peered at them in the dim light. "Shoot, looks like you never done a day's work before!"

"Not this kind of work, no," Emma said. "Listen, I'll give you some money if you switch with me. Let me carry water for a day or two while my hands get better."

"You got money? Yankee money?"

Emma nodded. "Give you five dollars," she said.

The man's sudden stillness told her she had made a mistake, had offered too much. No help for it now, though. From her pocket she brought out five coins, which she had moved there earlier from the waistband of her trousers, and showed them to Deezer.

"Five dollars!" he said, and gave a low whistle. "I ain't never had five whole dollars in my life! Where you get that money?"

Emma put a finger to her lips and smiled slyly. "Never you mind. I give you two now and three tomorrow night. We got a deal?"

Deezer licked his lips, staring at the money. "Three now and two tomorrow."

"Done."

They shook hands on it, and Emma handed over three dollars, slipping the other two coins back in her pocket. Deezer's gaze followed, speculative. She would have to watch her back, she decided.

Parting from him, she returned to the camp and strolled past the campfires until she spotted Joe from the breakfast detail. She sat down beside him and struck up a conversation, hoping that Deezer, if he saw her there, would think twice about trying to rob someone who had such a large friend.

At length she stretched out on the ground and slept the dreamless sleep of the bone-weary. Before she knew it, morning had dawned gray and chill, and the men around her were groaning and griping as they got to their feet.

Emma met Deezer in the breakfast line. True to his word, he showed her the cans she must use to haul water to the troops, and directed her to the well.

The day being cool, and the well not very far from where the brigade she was serving was posted, Emma found the labor far from strenuous. She took a long time filling canteens at each place she stopped, and listened to the soldiers' conversations. Large portions of the discourse consisted of cursing the Yankees, an activity at which the soldiers were as well-versed as their officers. At times, though, the talk turned to reinforcements, how many troops had come and from where, and how many more were expected. Emma listened avidly, though she hid her interest as she sat quietly filling canteens.

"General Johnson should arrive today, I hear," said one soldier, a sunny-faced man no older than Emma who looked like he belonged on a farm, carrying a hoe instead of a musket.

"I heard he was expected yesterday," said another around a wad of tobacco in his cheek. He spat a stream of dark juice onto the ground.

"Bad weather, bad roads. We'll see him soon, and ten thousand men with him. See that old fellow there with the white beard?" The first soldier pointed along the line. "That's General Lee."

"General Lee? Who is he?" asked another.

"Only the best engineer in the Confederacy, that's who! He's come to inspect the fortifications."

Emma paused in her work to watch Lee for a moment. He was talking to another officer—a colonel, Emma thought, though it was hard to tell at this distance. General Lee pointed toward the Federal lines, then waved a hand at the Rebel earthworks in a gesture of dismissal. Having toiled over them all the previous day, Emma found herself feeling resentful. She hid a smile, and wondered what the general's gesture really meant.

Her cans being empty, she made her way back to the well to refill them. As the morning wore on she heard much the same gossip from all of the men to whom she carried water. Come afternoon, though, the news shifted. General Johnston had arrived, and a council of war had been called. General Lee was in attendance.

Emma continued carrying water and listening. Late in the afternoon a fresh buzz of gossip began to be heard—Yorktown was to be evacuated! General Lee had declared that the fortifications could not be held once McClellan brought his siege guns to bear.

When would the order come, and to where would the army fall back? These questions were debated endlessly among the men. Emma wished she knew the answers, or even just that the evacuation was certain. That would be news of value enough to make her expedition worthwhile.

Finding herself with a little time to spare, she carried some water to her fellow laborers of yesterday. They received it with gratitude, and after one man drank a dipperful of cool water, he looked at Emma with a puzzled expression, then nudged his neighbor.

"Jim, I'll be darned if that feller ain't turning white!"

Washington, D.C., 1883

"Y ou walked away unchallenged?" Jamie's eyes glinted with interest. Emma had told him of her work as a spy, back when they were acquainted during the war, but never in such detail.

"Yes," she said, unable to help smiling. "I dared not approach our picket line. I went as close as I could and waited until morning, then hoisted my handkerchief as a signal of peace, and so returned to our camp."

"And to the waiting arms of General McClellan."

Emma glanced sharply at him, but decided to ignore his snide tone. "I made out my report to the general, yes."

"Yet he did not act on the news of Yorktown's impending evacuation."

"He had been given what he called positive intelligence that the Confederates meant to hold Yorktown at all costs."

"But they didn't."

"No. They didn't."

Jamie came closer, and sat in a chair opposite Emma. The way he leaned toward her, casually resting his elbows upon his thighs and clasping his hands between them, made her think of the old times. He had been used to sit just so in camp, bending near the warmth of the fire, leaning forward to murmur some tidbit of gossip. She recalled him in uniform, firelight playing in his pale hair, gleaming on the bars of his shoulder straps.

"There are some who question whether you were ever in the secret service at all," he said softly.

Emma stiffened. "I am aware."

"They say you made it all up for your book."

"People make any number of ridiculous accusations against authors."

"Do you claim every word in your memoir is true?"

His voice was soft, the prowl of a hunter. Emma drew herself up.

"No, I do not!"

She stood and began to pace, walking stiffly for her left foot was slightly numb. "Of course it is not entirely true," she continued. "I never stated in it that I was enlisted in the army, for one thing. My publisher wished to preserve the illusion that I served as a female nurse."

She paused and looked back at Jamie, who was watching her feet. Sensing her regard, he looked up at her face.

"I was young when I wrote it," she said. "Some of the incidents I mentioned were told to me by others. I included them because I thought they would capture the interest of the reader."

"Such as that touching scene you described at Antietam, when the Second Michigan was nowhere near the battle."

Jamie smiled in quiet triumph. Emma felt her ire rising, but kept her voice level.

"I did not know you had read my little book."

"I didn't. I heard about it from friends."

"Perhaps you should not rely wholly upon their judgment."

His eyes narrowed and his lips curved slyly. "Are you saying I should read it? Will I find myself flatteringly depicted?"

Emma shot him an irritated glance. "No. I do not care if you read it. In truth, I did not expect it to receive the attention it did."

Jamie leaned back, grinning. "Now, that I find hard to believe. You were never averse to attention."

Emma did not deign to answer this. She glanced at the closed door into Congressman Cutcheon's office, wishing Mr. Glass would return.

"You must have made a tidy sum from that book," Jamie said. "I know it was all the rage for a time. It cannot be money that brings you here."

Emma fixed him with a cold gaze. "I gave every penny of my profits from that book to the relief of wounded soldiers."

Jamie's brows flew up in genuine surprise. "I had not heard that."

"It is true. I have a letter from my publisher to that effect."

"May I see it?"

She stared at him, angry at his disbelief, and disinclined to humor his request. "I brought it to show Congressman Cutcheon."

"You fear my regard will damage it?"

Pressing her lips together, she withdrew the precious packet of letters she had brought with her from her pocket. These were her best hope of winning support for her claim. She leafed through them until she found Mr. Hurlbert's letter, then handed it to Jamie and stood over him while he read it.

"W. S. Williams—is that not the company whose books you sold before the war?"

"It is."

He quirked an eyebrow at her, then looked back at the letter. His face softened as he read, the irony leaving it, creases fading from his brow.

"Your book sold almost two hundred thousand copies?"

"Perhaps a hundred and eighty thousand."

Jamie stood quietly for a moment, gazing at the letter, then he folded it and handed it back to her. "That is quite a testimonial."

Emma put the letter with the others and returned all to her pocket. Jamie was regarding her thoughtfully.

"Thousands of dollars to the Sanitary Commission and other causes," he said. "Five thousand for the sick and wounded at Harper's Ferry. I had no idea."

"I made no parade of it," she said, somewhat defiantly.

Her leg was troubling her, so she returned to her seat. She avoided Jamie's gaze, looking once more to the closed door instead.

"That was a noble deed, Emma," Jamie said softly.

Something shivered inside her. He had not called her by her name...in twenty years and more. He had rarely done it at all. It should not have affected her so profoundly, but she could not deny that it did.

She swallowed, suddenly weary, suddenly wishing she were elsewhere. She felt Jamie's presence as a danger in more ways than one.

"So your efforts at Yorktown went unappreciated," he said, reverting to their earlier subject.

His tone implied no irony; was he seeking to make

amends? She did feel somewhat mollified. He believed her, or wished her to think that he did.

It was not that she wanted praise for what she had done in the service of her country. The very nature of her service had prohibited it, at the time.

She recalled how she had gone to Chaplain Brown upon her return to camp, enlisting his help to resume her normal guise. He had fetched her uniform while she scrubbed herself with soap to remove the coloring as much as possible. She had remained a nice maroon color for several days, and her skin had peeled a bit from its mistreatment, but it had all been worthwhile in her view.

"My efforts were not entirely wasted," she said. "I saw to it that the spying peddler never plagued us again."

"But the Confederates evacuated Yorktown after all."

"Yes...."

Emma frowned at the memories that arose, memories of her first true moments of terror. Even now her heart raced at the thought of that time.

"And we followed."

The War: Williamsburg, Virginia, 1862

The roads were a sea of mud and the rain fell in torrents. Thunder roared, but it was the thunder of cannon, and the flashes of fire were of musketry, not of lightning. The retreating Confederates had taken a stand in an earthworks near Williamsburg dubbed Fort Magruder after their commanding general. By the time the Second Michigan brought up the rear of the pursuit, the battle was fully involved.

The sounds reverberated through the woods and over the plain. Emma flinched despite herself when a minie ball whined past her head.

She rode her faithful Samuel, trailing in the wake of Colonel Poe and his staff. As one of the few in the regiment who were mounted, she felt she made rather too large a target, and was glad when Colonel Poe chose a position at the rear of an open field and pitched his colors. The regiment arrayed itself on the field, arms in hand, staring nervously at the chaos before them, into which they would soon plunge.

"Report to your company, Thompson," the colonel shouted over the din.

Emma nodded, dismounted, and left her horse on a hastily-established picket line at the edge of the field with those belonging to some of the other officers. Taking her musket in hand, she hastened along the line to her company. Damon greeted her with a flashing smile as she took her place beside him. So many times they had stood so, drilling in the camp. It was familiar and at the same time, vastly different.

The taste of gunpowder was on the air, even through the rain. Flashes of light from cannon or musket fire revealed timber felled in all directions, making cover for hundreds of Rebels who poured a deadly fire into the advancing Federal troops.

The Second joined the advance, slogging through mud and mire. In the face of a continuous hail of bullets from hundreds of rifle pits, the Federals grimly moved forward.

Emma heard a voice calling above the din, "Thompson! Frank Thompson!"

Following the sound, she saw Colonel Poe standing on a slight rise ahead of the regiment, beckoning to her. She left the ranks and ran to join him.

"Get your horse and carry this to General Kearny," the Colonel said breathlessly, holding out a scrap of paper torn from a pocket notebook. "Hurry!"

"Yes, sir!"

Emma stuffed the note into her breast pocket and scrambled back over the broken ground toward the woods. No longer surrounded by her fellows, she was suddenly more aware of the bullets flying all around her. She dared not look back, but ran with her heart pounding and her lungs aching, hoping her mount would still be where she had left it.

She passed a soldier lying face down in the mud. Unable to leave him so, she pulled him onto his side, and saw that half his head had been blown away. With a small, mournful cry she left him and hastened on.

Samuel was where she had left him, all his limbs tensed nervously at the sound of battle. He shied from her when she first came near, but she spoke to him and petted him to soothe him. She secured her musket to the saddle and mounted, then rode to the edge of the woods.

The field over which the Second had passed looked less harrowing from here, though she could see two other men who had fallen, apart from the one she had touched. She watched the dark line of the Second slowly continuing toward the enemy, only separated from her by a field yet in a sense far distant.

Turning her horse, she sought the road and pressed forward. Her regiment had been the last to come this way, but couriers still hastened to and from the battlefield, and a line of stretcher bearers was already trudging grimly to the rear. Emma asked everyone she passed where to find General Kearny, and was soon directed to his position.

Bullets sang around her ears again. Already she was becoming accustomed to them, and flinched only when one came particularly close. She saw General Kearny surrounded by a clot of officers, and rode up to them.

From here the full battle was visible, and Emma caught her breath in awe at the terrible scene. Cannon belched fire from redoubts in the Rebel earthwork, and she could see the force of their brutal discharge mowing swaths in the Federal ranks. Men struggled forward over fallen trees, across muddy fields, and through tangled undergrowth. Some suddenly ceased in their efforts and instead sank slowly to the earth, or dropped swiftly senseless, felled by enemy bullets.

Tearing her gaze from the battle, Emma dismounted and made her way to where General Kearny stood with his staff, observing the battle. She presented him with Colonel Poe's note, and on his order stayed to carry his reply. While she waited, her gaze drifted back to the battlefield.

"First engagement?" asked a voice nearby.

Emma turned her head and saw a wry fellow with sandy hair and lazy eyes in a lieutenant's uniform watching her. A member of someone's staff, no telling whose. There were several commanders gathered here.

She mutely nodded. It was not the Second's first engagement; technically that had been at Blackburn's Ford, at Bull Run, but there they had just been pinned by enemy fire. It had not been like this. Nothing like this.

She had seen the results of battle, in the hospitals where she had labored. She had not previously seen how the dreadful wounds occurred. She had known, but knowing at a distance was not the same.

"Take that back to your Colonel, Private."

Emma accepted a folded piece of paper from General Kearny's adjutant. The General himself had already moved away, talking with another general and gesturing toward the field.

"To Colonel Poe," she repeated, confirming that she had not been confused with another.

"Yes," said the adjutant. "Make haste."

She led her horse away from the command post and mounted, riding back to her regiment as swiftly as she could. They had advanced somewhat from where she had left them, and she moved farther forward in the woods before looping Samuel's reins around a tree branch. She gave him a pat and a few words of reassurance, then unlashed her musket from the saddle and started across the field once more.

A minie ball passed so close to her cheek she could feel the breeze of it, and paused, gasping, before moving on. She broke into a trot, thinking she would notice the bullets less that way, and perhaps be a less promising target.

Colonel Poe welcomed her with a harried glance and snatched the message from her hand before she had finished her salute. He scanned the page, then glanced up at her.

"Well done. Lend a hand to Filbert with that stretcher, now. Sergeant Monroe's been wounded."

Emma followed his gesture to where the sergeant sat, blood streaming down his face from a wound on his brow, and one arm cradled limply in his lap. Private Filbert, a strapping fellow, was trying to coax him onto a stretcher that lay beside him.

"I'm all right," Monroe said over and over. "I'm all right."

"No, you ain't," Filbert said gruffly. "You've been shot. Twice."

"My arm wasn't shot," he insisted. "I hurt it when I fell. I'm all right."

Emma knelt by Monroe and wiped the blood from his eyes with her handkerchief. "Let us take you to the surgeon," she said gently. "He'll bandage you up, and then you can return to duty."

She glanced sidelong at Filbert, silently adjuring him to follow her lead. He raised an eyebrow but said nothing.

"I-I can do my duty," Monroe said fretfully.

"Not with blood all over your face. You'll terrify the men. Come, let us get you cleaned up first."

At her gentle urging, he allowed himself to be moved onto the stretcher. Emma and Filbert picked it up and hurried toward the rear, bullets flying around them as thick as ever.

When they got off the battlefield and the hail of bullets decreased to an occasional whine, Emma gave a small sigh of relief. Now she had only to contend with the mud in the road, which went up to their knees.

The rain had lessened somewhat. A field hospital had been set up behind the lines, and Emma and Filbert turned their charge over to one of the nurses there. They returned at once to the front, where Emma spent the better part of the afternoon as a stretcher bearer.

The labor was grueling, especially as the mud worsened with each passing hour, but she would rather carry wounded than create them. She did not fear death, nor to face the hail of bullets at the very front of the battle, but even now she disliked the thought of firing a musket at her fellow man. Her heart resisted that act of destruction, though her opponent be ever so determined an enemy and ready to kill her without a moment's thought.

Filbert was wounded and himself dismissed to the rear; another took his place. Emma was exhausted, but labored on. On one occasion she and her partner returned to the field and, happening to find herself near her own company, she looked anxiously for the faces of her friends. She saw Lieutenant Turver bending over someone sitting on the ground. Peering harder through the rain, she realized that it was Captain Morse.

With a small cry of dismay she started toward him, stretcher still in hand. Her fellow bearer followed.

The captain sat on the ground, his face pale and set in a grim expression. One leg was stretched before him, and Emma disliked the way it lay—the boot was still on it, but seemed slightly askew.

"Sir!" She knelt beside him and reached toward his leg, but he shook his head.

"It is broken," he said. "Shattered, I think," he added, smiling grimly.

"Oh, Captain! I am so sorry!"

Morse looked up at the lieutenant. "Go on, Turver. You are in command. Thompson will look after me."

Turver shot Emma a glance, then hastened away, calling out an order. Emma touched the captain's arm.

"Let us take you to the surgeon," she said.

"Just carry me out of range of the guns, then go back and look after the boys. McCreery and Lyman have fallen, and perhaps they are worse off than I am."

Emma's heart filled with admiration for his courage and his thoughtfulness toward his men. She and her partner tenderly laid him on the stretcher and carried him to the rear, then returned to the field at his insistence.

McCreery had indeed been wounded. Emma took him to

the hospital and returned to hunt for Lyman, but did not find him.

The afternoon was lengthening, and Emma saw to her dismay that the Federals were now losing ground, being pressed back by the vicious persistence of the Rebels who had the advantage of better cover. Reinforcements had been looked for all afternoon, but as the shadows lengthened hope had faded.

The ground between the two forces was covered with dead and dying men and horses. The smell of death was everywhere. Emma had never seen anything so hellish, and if it were not for the work that kept her constantly moving, she would have wept.

Suddenly a shout went up from the Federal line behind her. Emma turned, and her heart lifted up in hope as the whole army took up the cry.

"Kearney!"

Fresh troops streamed forward onto the field. Leading them was General Kearney on horseback, his color-bearer beside him, the flags whipping in the wind-blown rain. The weary Federals continued to cheer as their comrades pressed the Confederates back into their works. Charge after charge was made against the Rebels, and their batteries were taken from them one by one, until Fort Magruder was silenced at last. The Confederates fled the field, sped on by Yankee bullets.

Night came swiftly, and with it the rain fell the harder, as if the cold sheets could douse the blood from the ravaged field. Emma snatched a moment to attend to Samuel's needs, finding him a patch of grass near a little rill. She labored on, buoyed up by the excitement of victory, though soon the tragedy of losses overwhelmed that happiness.

A truce was called to allow both armies to withdraw their wounded. Rebel and Yankee surgeons worked side by side, regardless of their allegiance or that of their patients.

Hundreds of casualties lay on the field. The agonized cries of the wounded rose up in the night, piteous, heartbreaking. Emma and others brought torches to the sodden field and continued their grim work, searching through the mud and felled timber and tangled undergrowth, following the desperate cries of the wounded.

All night long Emma and her partner trudged back and forth between the hospital and the battleground with their stretcher. The yellow flames of the torches fluttered over the field, restless and searching, dipping now and again to illuminate the face of one fallen, endlessly following the voices calling for help.

Once Emma and another searcher came to a wounded man at the same time, and she looked up to see Jerome's face regarding her, pale in the flickering torchlight. Emma stepped back as Jerome knelt beside the sufferer. She watched him tenderly take the man's hand, then turned to seek someone else who needed help.

As the night wore on the cries of the wounded grew weaker. Many had already been carried from the field. Others, the "goners" who were beyond help—with wounds to the head or the belly—were left to die where they were, even though they might be lucid. Emma's heart ached for them; one of her hardest duties was to pass them by.

She worried that there were still others who might be saved but who had given up hope, or lost the strength to call out. She searched on, though her arms ached as if they would fall from their sockets.

Toward dawn the rain stopped. Emma was grateful, though little more comfortable, as she was already wet through. She and her partner trudged over the field in silence, passing the dead and the dying in search of the living.

She saw a man moving feebly and hastened to him. He was large, and lay on his side, half-drenched in blood from a wound through his thigh. Emma and her partner laid the stretcher beside him and made ready to move him onto it. As she rolled him onto his back she saw his face and gasped.

"Damon!"

Damon was too weak to hear her. His face was terribly pale and she knew a stab of dread. He had lost so much blood, and had lain in the cold rain all night—

She refused to allow herself to think in that way. Glancing up at her partner, she lifted Damon's shoulders and together they shifted him onto the stretcher. They carried him to the hospital, where Emma saw to it he received immediate attention. The surgeons were all busy with the grim work of amputations, but Emma found a nurse she had known at Mansion House and helped him clean and bind up Damon's wound, then begged him to look after Damon carefully.

There was little more to be done for Damon besides keeping him warm and giving him as much water as he could drink. He roused a little as Emma tucked a blanket around him, and gazed up at her.

"Frank?"

"Yes." She smiled down at him, struggling for the cheer she had always maintained in the hospitals.

"Is it over?"

"Yes. A victory. The Rebels have fled."

"Oh." Damon closed his eyes and smiled. "Good."

She would have lain beside him, lending him the warmth of her body, but there were wounded still on the field. Instead she squeezed his hand and left him to return to her labors.

Morning came and still the field was littered with wounded as well as the dead. Daylight brought the awful task of identifying those who were killed, and laying them to rest. The dead were laid out in rows, their faces covered, awaiting burial in the long trenches that were being dug.

Emma worked on until, too exhausted to walk another step, she stumbled to the woods outside the hospital and collapsed, sleeping like the dead. When she woke she smelled coffee, and followed the aroma to a field kitchen that had been set up to feed the hundreds of wounded. A cup of strong coffee and a hard biscuit restored her enough to return to work.

She sought out Damon and almost cried aloud with relief when she found him sitting up with the aid of a nurse, sipping gingerly at a cup of hot broth. He looked weak, but alive, and he grinned as Emma came up to him.

"Here's our woman, come to fuss over me."

Emma smiled. "I'm glad to see you looking a little better."

"Hmph," Damon said, and took another sip. "My head is spinning."

"You lost a lot of blood. We didn't find you until almost dawn."

"How's the captain? I heard he was wounded."

Emma nodded. "I last saw him a few hours ago. He was well enough, considering."

"Did they take off the leg?"

"No."

Emma did not say what she feared, that Captain Morse eventually would lose his leg. It was quite badly broken, as she understood, though she had not examined him herself. Still, men of courage often recovered from worse wounds, and she had no doubt of the captain's courage.

For the next several days Emma worked in the hospitals, helping tend the wounded of both armies. When she first visited a group of Rebel wounded, she was startled to see familiar faces from Yorktown among them, one the sergeant of the picket guard who had given her a shake and threatened to shoot her if she fell asleep while on duty.

A sharp tingle went through her upon seeing him, but he showed no sign of recognition and thanked her kindly for the water she offered. The coloring had now faded from her skin, and in her normal guise she little resembled the contraband she had been in Yorktown.

She moved on, and soon came to where a negro lay groaning on the floor. Kneeling beside him, she spoke to him gently.

"Can you drink some water?"

He turned his head and opened his eyes, and Emma caught her breath. He was Deezer, the young water carrier whom she had paid to exchange work with her. His face was now contorted in pain, and he gazed at her unseeing. Emma lifted his head and held her canteen to his lips. He swallowed a few sips of water, then lay back exhausted and let out another groan.

Emma continued dispensing water until her canteen was empty, then sought out the surgeon. "That man," she said, pointing to Deezer, "is his wound mortal?"

The surgeon glanced at him and shrugged. "Likely not."

"Will you see that he is well cared for? I owe him a favor."

The surgeon gazed at her strangely, but gave another shrug and a nod. Emma watched him walk over to where Deezer lay and squat down to examine him. There was no more she could do—she could not explain to the surgeon her reasons for wanting to help Deezer—so she filled her canteen and moved on.

As the days passed and the crisis of battle had ended, Emma returned to her duties as mail carrier, but the loss of many of her friends was a blow. Captain Morse and Damon were both sent home to Michigan to recover from their injuries. The Second had been hit hard at Williamsburg, with seventeen killed and nearly forty wounded.

The rest carried on, and Emma sought distraction from loneliness in long talks with Chaplain Brown, attending prayer meetings when they occurred, and visiting the Second's wounded still recovering in the hospitals.

One day when Emma stopped at the Second's headquarters after fetching the regiment's mail, she was asked by the Assistant Adjutant General to stay. Colonel Poe wanted to speak to her.

Ushered into the colonel's presence, she wondered in trepidation if he was now going to relieve her of her mail duties. This would be hard to bear, for she loved the freedom it allowed her.

Colonel Poe sat behind his camp desk, glancing through the mail she had just delivered. At last he set the stack aside, folded his hands, and looked up at her.

"Your work at Yorktown was successful," he said.

Surprised, Emma blinked. "Yes, sir."

"A pity the information you gained was not put to better use."

Emma made no reply. The colonel straightened one of the papers beneath his hands and cleared his throat, then spoke quietly.

"I have been given to understand that General McClellan would welcome any intelligence from behind Rebel lines. He wants to know what we will face when we cross the Chickahominy."

Emma drew a breath as understanding dawned within her. She was being offered another opportunity to go spying.

She knew that McClellan was building bridges across the Chickahominy to replace those the Rebels had torn down. When the new bridges were complete, he would send his siege guns over them to hammer Richmond.

"I see," she said. "Has the General given specific instructions?"

"No. Look for an opportunity. When you are ready, come to me and I will write orders placing you on detached duty."

Emma swallowed. She would get no help, then; she must rely upon her own resources if she were to go at all.

"Have you any other questions, Thompson?" said the colonel, his voice unusually gentle.

"No, sir," Emma said slowly.

"Then you are dismissed." He took up his correspondence again and started to look through it, though he glanced once at her, frowning slightly in concern, as if to express his understanding should she choose not to pursue another foray behind enemy lines.

Emma left, and spent the rest of the afternoon in a state of distraction as she handed out the regiment's mail. Contemplating McClellan's request, she knew a hesitation she had not previously felt. To go again behind enemy lines, to risk her life to gain whatever information she might gather, possibly to have these efforts go for naught once more, gave her pause.

Perhaps it was Williamsburg that had changed her view. The horrors of the battlefield remained with her, a reminder of the seriousness of the effort in which they were engaged. Her thoughts confused, she set out to visit the hospitals hoping it would give her opportunity to reflect and resolve her conflicting feelings.

She certainly could not use her contraband disguise again.

It would be too dangerous. If anyone among the Rebels recognized and remembered "Ned," she would undoubtedly be shot for deserting her post on the picket line.

No, if she went, she would have to come up with a different disguise, one that did not put her in danger of betraying herself by her unsuitedness, as her blistered hands had done after a day's labor.

The hospitals were quieter now. The crisis of battle being over, now the silent struggle to survive was underway—to survive the wounds, the sickness, the despair and the nightmares that followed battle. Emma visited all the Second's casualties, and many from the other regiments in her brigade. She accepted messages, wrote letters, and most of all listened.

The stories the men told of how they were wounded and what they had faced on the battlefield were similar to what she had heard before, but having now been on the field herself she heard them with increased appreciation. She, too, suffered nightmares from time to time.

As she listened to the patients' deepest fears, often told in a whisper so that she had to bend close to hear, the conviction grew in her heart that she must do everything she could to minimize the casualties borne by the Federal army in the future. If she must go behind enemy lines to do so, practice deception and risk her own life, she was willing.

The nurses gave her silent, grateful glances, for they knew that a new face, a visitor, did much to cheer the men. Emma spent several hours at the hospital, and by the time she departed, burdened with messages and requests, the day was ending.

She walked toward the regiment's camp, passing the town square of Williamsburg on her way. In the market there she saw a tinker hawking his wares, and several peddlers with carts or baskets full of goods. Reminded of the traitorous peddler in Yorktown, she at first bristled, then felt a dawning comprehension.

This could be her next disguise. Peddlers came and went among the armies—there was always demand for the comforts they sold. She would be in no danger of conscription to hard labor. She could pass through the enemy lines unquestioned, a refugee fleeing the Federal advance.

An old woman in a drab dress and a red woolen shawl noticed Emma staring and came up to her. She hefted a large wicker basket and pulled back a calico cloth from its contents.

"Buy a pie, me darlin'? Fresh, swate berry pies!"

She was Irish. She peered up at Emma through dusty spectacles, her gray hair curling beneath the shawl. Fascinated, Emma took out her wallet.

"How much?"

"Ten cents for one, twenty-five for three."

"How many have you in the basket?"

"I've two dozen in all, just come from the oven this hour."

"I'll give you three dollars for all of them and the basket."

The woman's brows flew upward. "Bless you, me boy! Three dollars for all!" Emma could see her greedily calculating the total. "But the basket cost me two dollars, it did."

"Four dollars, then."

"Done! And may the dear lord bless your kind heart!"

Emma handed her the money and took the basket, turning to start back to the hospital. "Will you walk with me a little, ma'am, and tell me about yourself?"

"Now, what could the likes of you be wanting with the company of an auld woman?"

"I am curious about the people of this town. Have you lived long in Williamsburg?"

"Oh, aye! Twenty years, I have. If it's gossip you want, I'll oblige you, though I'd welcome a pint of ale to moisten me throat." She glanced toward the public house with a hint of longing in her eye.

"I'll give you the price of a pint if you'll accompany me," Emma said. "I haven't the time to sit, I'm afraid."

"Well enough."

With a shrug and the tiniest of sighs, the old woman turned away from the square and hobbled along beside Emma as she walked back to the hospital. Her name was Bridget O'Rooney, she said, and she told several colorful stories along the way, Emma prompting her for information about herself whenever she paused.

Mrs. O'Rooney's life had been varied, gypsy-like, and filled with adventure. She had three grown children, one of whom had baked the pies. Emma drank in every word, including the odd turns of phrase and the lilt of her voice.

When they reached the hospital Emma thanked the peddler woman, gave her some coins, and bade her farewell. Flashing a grin, Mrs. O'Rooney darted away with surprising liveliness, no doubt to repair to the public house for her pint.

Emma went into the hospital, distributed the pies to the delighted patients, then returned to the square with her empty basket. Evening was coming on and the peddlers were packing up their wares, but Emma was able to purchase a dress, a shawl much like the pie-seller's, and several trinkets that might be amusing to soldiers. She put all in the basket and carried it back to her regiment's camp. It seemed she had acquired a new vocation.

General McClellan celebrated the victory at Williamsburg by moving his army closer to Richmond; first to West Point, then to White House Landing, where he seized control of the railroad terminus. Emma was often there, where she picked up news and gossip along with the mail. Word of the Monitor's victory over the Merrimac and the Rebels' subsequent abandonment of the Norfolk naval yards was celebrated throughout the army, and did much to raise the spirit of hopefulness in the hearts of the men.

Meanwhile Emma continued to collect her peddler's costume and the wares she would carry as evidence of her trade. She added a couple of the watches she often sold in camp to the basket to augment her store of trinkets, and hired one of the Second's more talented cooks to bake several cakes and pies.

She bought an old pair of shoes and a tattered petticoat from one of the regiment's laundresses, and acquired a surplus patchwork quilt from the hospital. She obtained another wig, this one a steely gray, which she intended to cover with a matronly cap.

At last she was ready. She visited Colonel Poe, who duly wrote our her orders for detached duty. These she tucked into her Bible and left in her writing desk; it would never do to carry them on her person.

With fresh pies and cakes tucked in amongst her other

goods and the pieces of her disguise, the whole wrapped in the patchwork quilt and tied into her basket, she rode toward the Chickahominy River in the company of Private Shelley, who had agreed to accompany her to the shore and look after her horse. She had told him she would be back in camp by sundown. In fact, she had no idea when she would return, if at all.

"Why are you crossing the river?" Shelley asked.

"A lark," Emma said. "I want to see if I can get a look at the Rebels."

"Why not just volunteer for picket duty?"

"Too easy. And too many bullets in the air. I'd rather catch them unawares."

Shelley shook his head. "You've gone mad, Frank."

"You're probably right." Emma laughed, feeling a wild recklessness. It was indeed mad to do this, but she was determined.

Was this what the gambler felt, when he staked all he owned on a throw of the dice or the turn of a card? If so, she could begin to understand the attraction of sin.

Reaching the river's edge, Emma paused and with the Shelley's help tied the basket onto her back to keep it out of the water. She then shook hands with her friend and urged Samuel into the water. A few strides across the swampy, sucking shore, and they were into the current.

The river was cold, and Emma clenched her teeth together to keep them from chattering as Samuel swam across. He lurched up onto the opposite bank, grunting with the effort, and stamped into the swamp as if seeking dry land. Emma halted him and dismounted, led him back to the shore, and with a friendly pat sent him back to where Shelley was waiting. Waving farewell, she turned and went into the swamp.

She strode well away from the shore, still shivering with cold from her dunking in the river. When she judged she was well out of sight among the dismal, moss-draped trees of the swamp, she untied her basket from her back and made an unpleasant discovery.

The basket and everything in it was soaked. It had gotten wet after all, and the pies and cakes were ruined. Disgusted, Emma threw them on the ground, but she was determined to go on. She changed from her wet uniform into her wet peddler's costume, then buried the uniform near a quaintly twisted tree. All of this took considerable time, and by the time she was ready, night was approaching.

She had no intention of trying to slip past the Confederate pickets again. In this guise, she might walk up to them and request passage, but she should best do that in daylight. She must spend the night in the swamp, she concluded. Resigning herself to an uncomfortable night, she wrapped herself in the quilt and tried to find a bit of ground that was not too sodden to lie down upon.

Chills soon shook her. An ague overtook her, and with it the most violent, dreadful shivering, so severe that she thought she would freeze solid. Later in the night, the chills were followed by their opposite—a fever so high she became delirious, and imagined herself beset with all manner of horrors. Fiends tormented her, and the horrors of a thousand deaths seemed to be concentrated around her.

The boom of cannon-fire and the screaming of shell through the woods jarred her awake. It was morning, and she was under attack.

Chickahominy Swamp, Virginia, 1862

Sitting up against the tree under which she had slept, Emma tried to quell the panic that arose in her. The roar of the cannon continued, frighteningly near and intense. Had she been discovered? Did it merit the deployment of a battery to subdue her?

She knew McClellan had sent a corps across the river to ensure that the engineers rebuilding the bridges would not be harassed. Perhaps ill chance had placed her between them and the Rebels.

Her head swam, and her ears rang. She was weak as a kitten, and could no more rise and escape the cannonade than she could fly. She sat waiting for fate to overtake her.

Glancing down at the dress she wore, she laughed aloud at the irony of it. All her years of avoiding the traps and restrictions of feminine life, and now look at her. Would she die in her proper costume, then? Not that this guise was especially proper.

All the trouble she had gone to—assembling this costume, learning the Irish phrases and copying the brogue of good Mrs. O'Rooney—would it all go to waste? The ludicrousness of her situation made her burst out in uncontrolled laughter, but soon her mood sobered.

Her mind wandered to the battlefield at Williamsburg, then to the hospitals there, where she had carried the wounded and tended their hurts. In her confusion Jerome was there, her friend and companion as he had once been. She thought back through all the events of her life, and indulged in the hopeless contemplation of what might have been if she had not chosen this particular path.

She might have encountered Jerome in other circumstances, in the guise of a woman, and been able to win his heart as well as his friendship. She might have become a wife. In the delirium and discomfort of her present situation, that fate seemed less dreadful to her than it once had.

The cannonade ceased after a time, and she concluded she

had not been its object after all, but still she was too weak to rise. Chills and fevers continued to assail her by turns, and she lay for two more days and nights in the dismal Chickahominy swamp. Mosquitoes tormented her, and delirious visions robbed her of sleep. She imagined herself discovered, hauled before a tribunal, court-martialed. Helplessly, she wept.

On the morning of the third day after crossing the river she felt somewhat better. She got to her feet without too much dizziness, and stood looking about her. Deciding she preferred any fate, even to be shot by Rebel pickets, to that of rotting away in the swamp, she arranged her costume as best she was able, picked up her basket, and started toward where she hoped she would find the enemy lines.

By late afternoon she was deeper in the swamp than ever, and realized she must have mistaken her direction. She had neither sun nor compass to guide her. Grimly she struggled on, dreading the thought of spending another night in the swamp.

The roar of cannon began again abruptly, though not so near as it had been in the morning. To Emma at that moment it was the sweetest music she could have hoped to hear. She followed the sound, and in a short time was infinitely relieved to stumble out of the swamp and onto a road.

From the grass growing in the ruts she concluded the road was little used, but still it must lead somewhere. She took up the march along it, and soon spied a small white house in the distance.

She paused, setting down her basket, and adjusted her attire. The hem of her dress was damp and muddied, as were her shoes. She took off her wig and gave it a good shaking-out, then put it back on, pulled her cap over it, and brushed the leaves and twigs from her shawl before settling it over her shoulders again. The mud she could do little about, and she suspected her face was a fright, but she must proceed or she would surely die here.

Drawing a breath, she picked up her basket and made her way to the house, hoping to trade some of her trinkets for something to eat. She knocked on the door and waited, but no one answered.

"Hello?" she called, knocking again more firmly.

Listening for a footstep, she heard none, though she thought she heard a small sound from within. She tried the door and found it unlocked, and cautiously pushed it open.

"Hello?"

The house looked abandoned, save for a man—a Rebel soldier—lying on a straw tick on the floor beside the hearth. What fire had been there had long since gone out, and the soldier did not answer her save to stir feebly and let out a small moan.

Emma set down her basket and knelt beside him, taking his hand in hers. Thinking it best to maintain her chosen role, she spoke in the Irish brogue she had practiced.

"Ah, ye poor lad! How came ye to be here all alone?"

He looked at her with mournful hazel eyes, answering in a feeble whisper. "I was sick with typhoid and could not keep up with my company. Had to fall out, and found my way here. The family left soon after I came. They were afraid."

"Afraid of the Yankees, aye."

Emma nodded, then gazed at him. He appeared to be about thirty years of age, with dark hair and a sober countenance, handsome though drawn by his illness.

"Is there anythin' I can do for ye, swate boy?"

"I'm hungry," he said humbly. "I haven't eaten since we left camp a few days ago."

Reminded that it had been equally as long since she herself had eaten, Emma glanced at her basket, sharply regretting the loss of her pies. "I wish I had something to feed ye, lad, but the truth is I've nothing meself."

"The family left some corn meal and flour," said the soldier. "They didn't want to take the time to cook it for me, and I haven't been strong enough—"

"Say no more, me boy! I'll have you some corncake in two shakes of a lamb's tail!"

Emma got up and hastened to the kitchen, where she did indeed find some flour and meal. She built up the fire and put a saucepan of water over it to heat, for she could find no kettle. In short order she had made a large hoe-cake and set it before the fire to bake.

While the cake cooked she scrounged in the kitchen and found a small basket the family had forgotten to take with them. It was packed with earthenware and several small items including a tin of tea, which Emma seized with triumph.

The water being hot, she made tea for herself and the Rebel, and when the cake was done she helped him to sit up a little and fed him, as she had so often done for the sick in the hospitals. For this he thanked her with a grave courtesy that touched Emma's heart. When his appetite was appeased she ate her own portion, grateful beyond measure for the simple sustenance.

He seemed somewhat stronger, and Emma conversed with him. He told her his story in greater detail. She found that he was thoroughly dedicated to the Confederacy, though he seemed not to harbor the bitter hatred of Yankees she had so often witnessed. He seemed sober and gentlemanly, and at length she asked him if he considered himself a Soldier of the Cross.

"Yes, thank God!" he said, his eyes lighting with enthusiasm. "I have fought longer under the Captain of my Salvation than I have yet done under Jeff Davis."

"Can you, as a disciple of Christ, conscientiously and consistently uphold the institution of Slavery?" Emma asked gently.

He fixed his mournful gaze on her, and though he said nothing, his eyes seemed to show that she had touched the trouble in his heart. Emma held his gaze, feeling a deep sympathy for him.

All at once she realized she had let her brogue fall away in the course of their conversation. She knew a moment's alarm, then decided she had little to fear from this man, who was still very sick. She knelt beside him and felt his pulse, finding it terribly weak. The strength he had seemed to gain from the food was all but spent, and he lay gazing at her as if pondering whether hers would be the last face he saw.

"Will you pray with me?" he asked after a few moments.

Emma nodded, unable to refuse him. Nor did she dare to address her Maker in an assumed accent, so it was in her normal voice that she prayed for the soldier, beseeching God to grant him grace to sustain him in this trying hour, and hoping for the triumph of truth and right.

As she made to rise the Rebel grasped her hand. "Please tell me who you are. I cannot, if I would, betray you, for I shall very soon be standing before that God whom you have just addressed."

Emma's heart went out to him. She dared not answer him truthfully, and would not tell him a lie.

"I will tell you when you are stronger," she said.

He smiled, the lids drooping over his beautiful eyes, then falling closed. Emma suspected he understood her exactly.

The day was ending. Emma knew she was not far from the Rebel lines, but she still felt weak herself, and decided to remain in the house overnight with the Rebel. She had not the heart to abandon him, leaving him to suffer alone once more.

She made some corn gruel for her patient and tenderly fed it to him, but she could see that he was not strong. After making him as comfortable as she could, she went around the house, secured the doors, and covered the windows so that no light would be seen from outside. Thus settled, she sat beside the soldier again and took his hand.

His pulse was very weak, his brow damp with perspiration. Emma wiped it away, and his eyes thanked her silently. She was certain now that he would not recover, and could not help but weep for the death of one so nobly cast, be he her enemy or not. Seeing her tears, he looked startled.

"Am I really dying?" he whispered.

Emma nodded. "Yes, you are dying, my friend. Is your peace made with God?"

He paled, and swallowed. "My trust is in Christ. He will not forsake me."

Some moments passed, as the soldier seemed to gaze beyond the room into some unseen realm. Emma held his hand gently, and watched him. At length he looked at her again.

"I have a last request to make. If ever you pass through the Confederate camp between here and Richmond, inquire for Major McKee, of General Ewell's staff, and give him a gold watch which you will find in my pocket. He will know what to do with it. And tell him I died happy, peacefully."

Emma blinked back more tears, and nodded. "I will."

"My name is Allen Hall."

He took a ring from his finger and tried to put it on Emma's, but his strength failed him. "Keep that ring in memory of one whose sufferings you have alleviated," he said after a moment, "and whose soul has been refreshed by your prayers in the hour of dissolution."

He then folded his hands as if to pray, and smiled. Emma prayed again, softly, her throat tightened by tears.

Suddenly he lifted his head, struggling up, and cried, "Glory to God! I am almost home!"

Emma knew it was true; she could see that death was near. She gave him some water, and opened the window that he might breathe easier. He put his hand in hers and signed that he wished her to hold him. She took his head in her arms and cradled him, and a few moments later he died, his hand gripping hers with the last of his strength.

Emma gently laid him down, closed his eyes, and folded his arms across his breast. His face was beautiful and calm. When she had arranged his blanket and could do no more for him, she returned to an awareness of her situation.

It was midnight, and profound silence reigned. There was naught to chase away the darkness of that gloomy hour save the consciousness that God was there.

Emma sat beside the soldier, grateful now that she had been detained in the swamp so that she would have the opportunity to attend this man's death. She meditated for a time, and imagined she felt the presence of happy spirits come to gather up the soldier's soul and welcome him to heaven. At last she wrapped herself in her patchwork quilt, lay down beside the fire, and slept.

She awoke much refreshed, and after spending some moments regarding her late charge, in whom she already saw the changes of death, she cut a lock of his hair, retrieved the watch and a packet of letters from his pocket, and tenderly replaced the blanket.

"Farewell, my friend," she said softly, then got to her feet.

In preparation for her foray into the Rebel camp, she searched the house and appropriated anything that might add to her wares. In the basket in which she had found the tea there were also pepper, mustard, an old pair of green spectacles, and a bottle of red ink. She used these to enhance her disguise, making a mustard plaster to blister one cheek and painting the red ink around her eyes, though she imagined they were already reddened with weeping. Setting the spectacles on the end of her nose where she could look over them, for looking through them made her head ache, she felt ready to face the Rebels.

She packed her two baskets, said a last farewell to her former charge, and left the house, following the road toward Richmond. She walked some five miles before she saw a picket in the distance.

Sitting down to prepare herself before approaching, she poured some of the pepper into her pocket handkerchief and held it to her eyes, which commenced to watering at once. She had borrowed a bit of white curtain from the house, and she now displayed it as a flag of truce as she approached the picket.

The soldier on guard was large and burly, with a belly that spoke of many a good meal enjoyed in the past. He watched Emma's approach with wary curiosity, and smiled broadly as she came near, no doubt amused by her appearance, swamp-bedraggled and burdened with her two baskets.

"Well, now," he said in a booming voice, "what 'ave we 'ere?"

Emma froze, the words of her assumed accent dying on her lips. The man was an Englishman.

Near Richmond, Virginia, 1862

E mma hastily applied her peppered handkerchief to her eyes beneath the spectacles. It was too late to change the approach she had practiced so carefully, so she carried on.

"Ah, such a sad day 'tis," she cried, "though the sun be shinin' ever so bright."

"Sad day, is it?" said the picket. "Wot's the matter then, Biddy?"

With tears streaming down her face, Emma blurted out her doleful tale in broken phrases, hoping her brogue would pass muster with one who had no doubt heard true Irish voices far more often than she. She told of the Rebel soldier whose death she had attended, and of his dying request that she carry a message to Major McKee. The picket listened attentively, and when she had no more to say and subsided into sniffling into her kerchief, he straightened.

"Well, now, that's a sad enough tale, 'tis, and all the sadder for you being so far from your 'omeland. You pass along and go just wherever you please, ma'am." He leaned toward Emma, a sorrowful expression in his pale eyes. "I wish I was at 'ome with my family, and that's the truth. Jeff Davis and the Confederacy can go to 'ell for all of me. Englishmen 'ave no business 'ere."

"Oh, indeed I wish ye was all at home with yer families," Emma said, "and sure it's we poor creatures of wimmen that's heartbroken entirely, and nearly killed with this unnatural war!"

The picket nodded sagely, then added, "Go on along then, Biddy, but you'll not want to spend the night in camp. We've 'ad word that McClellan's finished 'is bridges, and the Yanks will attack soon."

"Oh, bless me! Now I wish even more ye was at home and not here!"

The picket grinned. "Don't you worry 'bout me, ma'am. Made of iron, I am! And Jackson and Lee are ready for them Yankees. Got masked batteries all along our front to welcome

155

'em. There's one just there," he said, pointing to a large heap of brush not far from the road. "That will give 'em fits if they come this way!"

Emma looked at the brush heap and saw the gleam of a cannon's barrel beneath the branches. Her heart jumped in alarm at the thought of the guns firing at her own comrades. A sense of urgency filled her, and after thanking the picket for his kindness, she hastened into the camp.

She inquired at once after Major McKee, and was told he was away from camp and would not return until evening. Thinking she had best make good use of her time, Emma first found a shanty where some negro women were cooking, and begged a little food, which they kindly gave her. She then wandered the camp, taking note of all she saw and heard.

She had no trouble finding out the strength of the Confederate forces or their plans for the coming battle. Everyone she spoke to seemed to want to talk of nothing else. She committed the details to memory against her future report, thinking grimly that she would prevent the Rebels' success if she could.

When five o'clock came she again sought Major McKee, and this time was rewarded by finding him present at his tent. He was tall and gruff, and looked at her sternly as she curtsied.

"What is your business with me?" he demanded.

"Ah, a sad business," said Emma, bringing out Allen Hall's watch and letters, "and it fair breaks me heart to tell ye."

She had no need to resort to her peppered handkerchief to start the flow of tears, for the watch and letters awoke her memories of the noble young man's death. She wept freely as she described the event to the Major, who listened, then put his face in his hands and sobbed like a heartbroken child.

At length they both grew calmer, and the major stood up.

"You are a faithful woman, and you shall be rewarded. Can you go direct to that house, and show my men where Allen's body is?"

"I can."

The major took an eagle from his pocket and held it out to Emma. "If you succeed in finding the house, I will give you as much more."

"Oh, thank you, sir, but no. I couldn'a take your money."

The major looked at her strangely, and Emma realized with a stab of fear that it was out of character for a poor Irishwoman to refuse money. She sought refuge in her handkerchief and a fresh bout of tears.

"Oh, General, forgive me, but me conscience would never give me peace in this world or the next, if I would take money for carryin' the dyin' message of that swate boy that's dead and gone, God rest his soul!"

The major seemed satisfied, and asked Emma to wait while he fetched a detachment of his men. He soon returned with twenty-four men, a sergeant and corporal, and a stretcher on which to carry Allen Hall's body. Emma approached the major, wringing her kerchief in her hands.

"General, I've been sick several days, and slept little last night. I think I cannot walk so far again so soon. Could you let me have a horse for the journey?"

Without question, the major turned at once and ordered a horse saddled. Emma felt a pang of conscience as she mounted it with the assistance of the colored boy who brought it, for she knew she was about to violate the Major's trust in her. His confidence had led him to give her the very means of her escape, and for the first time in her spying adventures, she felt truly mean.

His next words dissipated that feeling, however, for as he sent his men forward he told them, "Now, boys, bring back Captain Hall's body if you have to walk through Yankee blood to the knees."

Emma rode away with the soldiers, surprised to learn that Allen Hall was a captain, for there had been no insignia of rank on his uniform and she had assumed he was a private soldier. When they passed the Confederate picket line Emma took the lead, riding at a walk and very nervous of encountering a Federal scouting party, for surely she would be shot and killed if that occurred.

Luck was with them, however, and they proceeded without encountering any Yankees. The sun had set and dusk was falling as they came in sight of the little white house. The sergeant in command of the detachment halted them before approaching it, and assigned one squad to bring out Captain Hall's body, while the rest would guard the approaches to the house.

"It's a pity we didn't bring an ambulance," the sergeant said aloud, gazing along the shadowed road toward Federal lines.

"Oh, aye!" Emma agreed, though she was secretly glad she had the only horse in the party.

"Ma'am, would you be so kind as to ride down the road a little way, and if you see or hear any sign of the Yankees, ride back as fast as you can and tell us?"

"Sure, and I'd be happy to," Emma said.

She rode ahead, pleased to comply at least with the first part of the sergeant's request. As she did not immediately see any sign of the Yankees, she decided she had better ride on until she did.

Once out of sight she whipped up the horse to a gallop, and made for the Federal lines as fast as she could. She managed to locate her buried uniform and hastily donned it. On nearing the picket line she took out her white flag of truce, waving it above her head in the darkness as she answered the picket's challenge.

She was passed through the lines and at once sought out General Keyes, the commander of the corps guarding the bridges. She made her report to him, leaving out only the detail about the party sent to recover Captain Hall's body, for she had no desire to see that little escort captured.

Keyes nodded as he listened. "You've done well, Private...?"

"Thompson, sir."

"Excellent work, Thompson. I shall write you a pass to cross the bridge. General McClellan will want to hear your report."

The result of Emma's foray was an immediate alertness among the Federals, who were ordered to be prepared for battle at a moment's notice. Battle soon came, for the Confederates took advantage of a terrible storm that swelled the Chickahominy, washed away one of the new bridges, and made the other unsafe. The Rebels fell upon the two Federal corps that were subsequently stranded on their side of the river. Emma served as an acting orderly during the fighting, and carried General Kearney's desperate plea for reinforcements.

Later she tended the dozens of wounded who had crawled to an abandoned sawmill for shelter, with only the help of two men who were somewhat less disabled than the rest, for the surgeons had all been sent forward. Busy with the immediate needs of the men around her, she did not learn until much later what had transpired in the battle.

The reinforcements sent to Kearney had turned the tide of what became known as the Battle of Fair Oaks, but the victory had come at a terrible cost: almost 3,500 wounded, and nearly 800 killed. Emma's heart ached as she saw the wounded lying upon the blood-soaked ground in rank upon rank, awaiting the attention of the surgeons.

She spent hours and hours helping to carry the most severely wounded to the railroad cars bound for White House Landing, to be shipped north from there on hospital boats. She knew many of them would not reach their destination alive.

For the first week of June it rained steadily, then a dull, numbing heat settled in. The pickets of both armies agreed not to fire upon one another, for it did no good. Everyone was waiting for a move, but the move was not forthcoming. General McClellan was hesitant to risk his men again, a sentiment of which the army approved if the President did not.

Emma returned to her duties as mail carrier, spending hours in the saddle, often at night, always alone. She rode to Fort Monroe and back on a road where rumor told that another mail carrier had been attacked by bushwhackers. She knew the truth of the rumor by the fragments of letters that crackled beneath her horse's hooves in the darkness.

In mid-June, both armies were electrified by the audacity of Confederate General Jeb Stuart, who with 1,400 cavalrymen rode completely around the Army of the Potomac in a raid. The result among McClellan's army was a restlessness in which the men began to wonder openly when they would move against Richmond.

The move came at the end of June, beginning with a push

to capture an oak grove in front of the Federal line. Oak Grove was but the first in seven days of battles, during which time General McClellan concluded it was necessary to shift his base of operations from White House Landing to Harrison's Landing on the James River.

While General Porter's men fought desperately to hold off an advance of the Confederates at Gaines' Mill, Emma was sent to ride among the hospitals remote from the lines of communication and inform them of the impending retreat to the James. She spurred her horse from place to place, not pausing to rest as she carried the warning.

At a small field hospital at Talleysville, not far from White House Landing, she dismounted and called for the commanding officer. Cannon fire could be heard from the front not far distant. Curious men emerged from the tents, and Emma's heart skipped when she saw Jerome among them.

"Frank!" He hesitated, then hastened to her side. "What is the matter?"

"The army is retreating," Emma said somewhat breathlessly. She caught sight of the surgeon approaching and addressed herself to him. "I am sent to warn you all that any who can walk should fall back, for no ambulances can reach you."

"We have wounded here who cannot walk," Jerome said.

"Then I fear they will fall into the hands of the enemy," Emma told him.

Jerome's face hardened. The surgeon stepped forward. "How long do we have, do you think?"

Emma shrugged helplessly. "General Porter is ordered to hold his ground, but with no hope of reinforcement. I think he cannot stand much longer. The rest of the army is falling back to the James."

The surgeon exchanged a glance with Jerome, then turned and went back into one of the tents. Emma looked at her friend.

"You must come away."

Jerome shook his head. "I cannot abandon these men. You know I cannot."

"But you will be captured!"

"So be it."

Fear for her friend and anger at his stubbornness warred within her. "Jerome—"

"Hey, Thompson!" called a familiar voice, in somewhat feeble tone.

Emma turned and saw Captain Lawson, with whom she was acquainted, and three lieutenants of her brigade emerging from one of the tents. They all looked weak, as though just recovering from fever.

"We're to fall back to the James, is that it?" Lawson demanded. "Well, give me your horse."

"I-I am expected to report back to the chief of the ambulance corps," she said.

"You may report to him on foot," the captain replied. "You are in good health, and can bear the journey better than I."

"Hey, let *me* have the horse, Thompson," said one of the lieutenants. "Remember how I loaned you the money for newspapers?"

"No, I should have it!"

The four of them commenced to arguing over Emma's horse, which she had not agreed to give up. Jerome watched with a wry expression. At length the captain, who had the advantage of rank as well as a gift for argument, made so strong a case that Emma felt resigned, at least, to relinquishing her poor Samuel. She looked at the four men, who should be able to reach the James, she thought, though they would any of them do better mounted than on foot.

"You must share the horse, then," she said.

"That would put you at risk of capture," Jerome said to her, suddenly stepping into the discussion.

Emma gazed at him for a moment but made no answer, turning back to the convalescents instead. "Two of you shall ride at a time, and shall go no faster than the other two can walk."

Captain Lawson looked sourly at her, but was not so mean as to deprive the lieutenants of their chance at riding. Emma made them draw lots to see who would ride first. The captain, being unlucky in this lottery, looked even more sourly than before.

Emma decided to ensure he would not appropriate Samuel to his own use by promising, most generously, to inform headquarters of their arrangement. She saw them off, then turned to find Jerome still standing near.

"You should not have done that," he said, though there was a hint of softness in his gaze, as if he admired the gesture despite its possible consequences.

"I saw some horses and mules at a farm nearby," Emma told him. "I mean to go and catch one of them."

Jerome nodded. "Good. You must get away from here. It would not do for you to be captured."

A rumble of cannon fire punctuated his statement. Emma glanced toward the front, then back at Jerome.

"Come with me," she said urgently, lowering her voice.

He only shook his head. Her heart sank. She knew she would not convince him to leave, and that remaining meant his inevitable capture.

"Jerome—"

"Good luck, Frank. You had better hurry and catch that horse."

He turned and walked away, back toward the hospital tents. Emma watched him go, miserable in the knowledge that he would soon be taken prisoner by the Confederates. With a soft, strangled cry, she turned away, picking up a run as she made for the farm, feeling the shadow of the Rebel army drawing near.

Washington, D.C., 1883

"Did you catch a horse?" Jamie asked.

Emma glanced up at him, shaken from her reverie. "Yes. I made it back to our lines, with some little difficulty."

"But Jerome was captured."

Even now the thought of it made her heart ache. She shifted in her chair.

"Yes. It was inevitable. He made a noble decision."

Jamie's huff of scornful laughter annoyed her. "Noble Jerome," he said. "Why not Saint Jerome?"

"What right have you to mock him? You never made such a sacrifice!"

His smile vanished and his face went very still. "No?" he said quietly. "You forget the circumstances under which I left the army."

Emma felt a flush of indignation, old feelings returning in full force, as if they had never faded. "That was different."

"It was no different."

"Jerome had no connection with those men—"

"It was no different."

The bitter look on Jamie's face slew her arguments. For the first time she wondered if he might possibly have been as unhappy as she at the way things had fallen out, back during the war. She had always assumed he was happy. She gazed at him thoughtfully.

"How is your—"

The door into Congressman Cutcheon's office opened, and Mr. Glass stepped out. "You are still here?" he said in a tone of surprise, peering at Emma through his spectacles. "The Congressman will certainly not be able to see you today."

"I will wait," Emma said calmly, earning a grimace from the young man.

He caught up a pencil and a handful of paper from the desk, and retreated to the inner sanctum once more, shutting the door behind him with a snap. Emma sighed.

"The wheels of government grind slowly," Jamie said.

Emma smiled wryly, and laughed a little. "That is one thing we all learned in the army. Poor Jerome spent months at Camp Parole, waiting to be exchanged."

"At least he was there and not in a Confederate prison."

Emma glanced up at Jamie, remembering that he had been less fortunate. He'd spent six months in a Rebel prison camp, longer even than Jerome had kicked his heels at Camp Parole, which being operated by the Union was far more comfortable than any prison could be.

"In a way Jerome's capture was a blessing for me," she said. "When I learned that he was at Camp Parole I sent him five dollars in a letter. After that all our disagreement was forgotten."

"All forgiven, for the price of a half-eagle."

Emma ignored Jamie's sarcastic tone. He had always tended to be cynical, but now she thought she sensed hurt, and possibly even jealousy, behind the bitter words.

Perhaps it was because she was older now, and could observe him through the filter of her own many experiences of life since the war. Jamie had lived in her memory as somewhat larger than life, but she saw now that he was merely human after all. There were gray hairs among the gold at his temples, and an air of loss about him that did not fit with her memories.

"That was a bad summer," he said quietly.

A smile touched Emma's lips briefly. "Yes. We lost little Mac, for the first time."

The Peninsular campaign had failed, and a wrathful President Lincoln had ordered General McClellan to support General Pope in defending the capital, which the Rebels were now actively threatening. McClellan was furious, and his demoralized army applied themselves to the task with less than complete enthusiasm.

Jamie nodded. "The echoes of woe reached us, even in the Carolinas."

Emma glanced up at him. "Well, Pope was a disaster!"

"Hm."

She remembered that Jamie had been serving under General Burnside at the time, who was later to prove himself even more a disaster. So many lives wasted. She shook her head.

"Whatever else may be said of him," she said, "McClellan took care of his army."

"Too great care, some say."

"Perhaps so, but it gained him one thing—the unshakable loyalty of his men."

Jamie gave a wan smile, then looked away. "Even now."

How strange to see Jamie in this somber mood. He was usually—or had been usually—all fire.

Emma's limbs were growing stiff again. She stood, and walked to the hall and back, trying to work the ache out of her left leg. She wished she could remove her boot, but this was not the place. How ironic it would be if the wretched leg drove her away from here when nothing else could displace her.

"You still limp," Jamie observed.

Emma bit back a sharp retort, and chose calmer words. "I have always limped. Why do you think I am here?"

He looked genuinely surprised. "Is that it? Your old injury?"

She paced away again, struggling against a rising anger. "I was injured in my country's service. Should I not be compensated?"

"Medical costs?" he said softly. "Surely you can find help with that. You never lacked for friends—"

"It is the principle of it," she said, turning abruptly. So doing, she stepped badly and her left leg crumpled.

"Emma!"

He was at her side instantly, catching her in his arms, lifting her up. The pain in her foot left her speechless for a moment, unable to protest as Jamie unceremoniously picked her up and carried her to a chair.

"I am all right," she said, and tried to pull away.

He ignored this, and kept tight hold as he carefully set her down. His arms were strong as they had ever been, and the smell of him brought back a rush of memories she had tried to bury.

"Let me go, Jamie."

Her voice trembled on the words, a weakness she silently cursed. Jamie obeyed, dropping his arms from around her, but he remained on his knees beside her, gazing at her in concern. All mockery was gone from his blue eyes now. He looked at her with an expression she very much suspected was tenderness.

"You know, you never told me how it happened," he said.

She shook her head, exasperated. "It was the stupidest thing. I made a fundamental mistake."

One eyebrow rose in a quirk she well remembered, and suddenly she felt much better. She laughed, then closed her eyes. It had not been funny at the time.

"I thought you were injured during the battle," he said.

Emma nodded. "At Second Bull Run. It was the first day of the battle, yes. I was riding courier."

"What was your mistake?"

She looked at Jamie and sighed. "I asked a mule to do what could only be expected of a horse."

The War: Manassas, Virginia, 1862

Matters had come to a head at the end of August, and all signs pointed to a second battle at Bull Run, on almost exactly the same ground as where the first had been fought more than a year earlier. Emma rode toward the front as the day began, carrying messages and mail, hurrying in the hope of delivering her messages before the battle commenced.

Samuel had not been returned to her, and a succession of other horses had followed him. Her current mount was an army mule, a creature of great strength and good heart. Emma took him cross-country, making him leap hedges, fences, and whatever else lay in their way. Coming to a wide ditch she urged him to jump it, but the mule could not make the leap, and instead tumbled headlong into the ditch.

Emma flew off his back and slammed against the far side with a force that stunned her. She slid down, ending in the mud and water at the bottom of the ditch. The mule, struggling to escape the sucking mud, lost its balance and fell on top of her, crushing her left side.

Pain shot through her leg, driving all other thoughts from her head. The mule, struggling to get out of the ditch, trampled her. At last it succeeded in scrambling up the bank.

Emma lay still, dazed, drifting in a cloud of pain. She did not know how long she lay before the boom of cannon fire startled her back to awareness.

The mail!

Emma stirred, and looked up. The sky was overcast, glowing a little as the sun's light strove to break through. Painfully she dragged herself out of the ditch, spurred by desperate anxiety for the messages that were her responsibility. If the mule had run off, mail and messages alike could fall into enemy hands.

Reaching the top of the ditch bank, she saw to her relief

that her mount was standing a few yards away, quietly cropping grass. She rolled herself onto the bank and assessed her injuries.

Her left leg was useless below the knee; broken, she thought with a grimace. Her left side ached terribly and a sharp pain stabbed at her when she moved, making her sick to her stomach.

Move she must, though. She had to deliver the mail.

Holding that imperative in her mind, and squeezing her eyes shut against the pain, she crawled toward the mule. When she was only a couple of paces away she struggled to stand, but her left leg would not bear her weight. She limped to the mule and leaned against its flank. The animal turned its head and lipped her hand, as if in apology.

The mail bags and saddle had slipped and were now hanging below the mule's belly, covered in mud. Emma struggled to put them to rights, and at last managed to get them back where they belonged.

Her next object was to mount, which proved more difficult. After several unsuccessful attempts she paused to rest, her leg now throbbing, pain accompanying every breath. She could not mount in the normal way, with her leg as it was. She looked about her for a tree stump or boulder that she could use as a block, but there were none.

She opened her saddle bags and took out a rope halter. She tied several loops in it, hooked one over the pommel of her saddle, and used the others to climb onto the mule's back.

She slid her right foot into its stirrup and used her hands to situate her useless left, finding the support of the stirrup to be less painful than leaving the leg dangling. After stowing away the halter and checking that the mail bags were yet secure, she urged the mule forward.

Cannon fire continued, but it was the occasional fire preliminary to battle, not the continuous roar of engagement. The gunners of both sides were finding their ranges, preparatory to unleashing true hell.

Emma rode as fast as she could stand to, not as fast as she would have liked. Still she managed to reach the front before the battle had begun, and, gritting her teeth against the pain, delivered her messages and mail. Duty served, she turned her mule toward the rear again and rode in a daze of exhaustion for the field hospital.

She did not dare to report the injury. Instead she rode up to the tent, and remaining in the saddle, called out to the nearest surgeon.

"Dr. Vickery! Will you do me a favor?"

He came forward, a look of inquiry on his face. "Has the battle begun?"

"Not yet." The mule jibbed, and Emma winced. "I have hurt my leg. Could you give me something for the pain?"

"Come down and let me look at it."

Emma shook her head. "No time. I am on courier duty."

The surgeon frowned, then shrugged and went into a tent. He returned a moment later with a small bottle. Emma almost cried with relief as she accepted it.

"A spoonful in a cup of water," he said. "And come back and have it looked at when you have time."

"Thank you." Emma slid the bottle into her pocket, managed a smile and a wave of farewell, and started her mule toward headquarters.

She did not stop there, but went on to the Second's camp, now abandoned with the regiment away on the battlefield, a ghost town of white tents. Emma rode her mule up to her own, slid from the saddle, and stumbled inside.

With shaking hands she poured water from her canteen into her tin cup, then put a splash of the medicine into it. She gulped it down and sat gasping, fighting nausea. After a moment she lay down on her bedroll.

She shared the tent with three other men: Halsted, Houlton, and Bostwick. They would be on the field now, muskets in hand, ready to face the enemy. As she lay awaiting the release of sleep, she sent up a silent prayer for them.

As if in answer, a single boom of cannon sounded in the distance, followed by the rolling rumble of many more. The sharp crackle of musketry overlay the deeper echoes. The battle had begun.

For two days Emma lay alone in her tent, listening to the

sound of warfare. Occasionally she would sit up to take more of the medicine, and once she ate part of a cracker, but mostly she lay drifting in and out of sleep, praying for the pain to fade.

The sounds of battle ceased at the end of the first day, and the sounds of night closed about her—crickets and cicadas, the occasional hoofbeats of a horse passing in the distance. Her mule must by now have wandered off in search of food. She regretted she was unable to care for it, but she could not really even care for herself.

Cannon and musketry woke her on the second morning. As she lay listening, she wondered about the fate of her friends. How many would the Second lose in this battle? How many would be sent home to Michigan to recuperate, and how many to be buried by their grieving families?

Darkness came again, bringing silence once more. Emma lay waiting. It hurt to breathe; she knew she had broken a rib, and now suspected it had punctured a lung, for she coughed now and then which hurt even more.

She could not possibly submit to an examination of her lungs. The immediate result would be her discovery. She frowned and squeezed her eyes shut at the thought of being escorted under guard away from her beloved regiment, a criminal, dishonored. She would bear any pain rather than submit to that.

A murmuring roused her. At first she thought it some fantasy of her delirium, but gradually she realized it was the sound of voices and shuffling feet. The Second Michigan were returning to camp.

Moments later the door of her tent was pulled aside, and a dark shape came in, speaking in Bostwick's voice. "Hey, here's Frank! We thought you'd been killed when we didn't see you any more."

Her other tentmates crowded in behind him, joking wearily, teasing Emma about missing the battle. One of them lit a candle and stuck it in his bayonet, stabbed into the ground. Emma smiled feebly up at them but made no reply.

Halsted's bedroll lay next to hers, and he sat on it now, his dirt-smeared face showing concern. "Say, you look pale, Frank. Are you sick?"

Emma shook her head slightly, and tried to clear her

throat. She had drunk the last of her water in the afternoon, and been unable to drag herself up and look for more.

"Took a fall from my mule," she said in a cracked voice. "Hurt my leg."

"You should be in the hospital, then," said Houlton. "You of all people should know that!"

"Can't," Emma said, then paused as a stab of pain struck her. She wanted to cough, and resisted.

"Well, we can carry you," Halsted offered, frowning as he leaned over her. "You look like hell, Frank."

The cough came, and she winced, squeezing her eyes shut in agony. After a moment she opened them again. They were all gathered around her now, her tentmates, peering down at her.

"Water?" she croaked.

Bostwick pushed a canteen into her hands. She gulped a few swallows, then lay back, exhausted.

"Thank you. I'll be all right. Just need to rest."

"You should have the surgeon look at that leg," Halsted said. "Boys, go fetch a stretcher."

"No! No, it's just a sprain!"

Bostwick and Houlton were already out of the tent. Terror swept through Emma, more nauseating than the pain. Halsted leaned over her and gently brushed her hair out of her eyes.

"You'll feel better up at the hospital. Have someone waiting on you hand and foot for a change."

Emma stared at him, desperate. "Please, Richard, no."

He smiled. "You always were a stubborn one."

She caught his wrist. "I *can't!*"

He looked at her hand gripping his arm, then gazed back at her in confusion. "Why not?"

Fairfax Station, Virginia, 1862

Emma stared up at Halsted's kind, weary face, and knew she had reached a crisis. His very kindness would betray her unless she could convince him to leave her alone.

She struggled up onto her right elbow, the better to face him. "Richard, I cannot go to the hospital. If I am examined they will find me unfit for service, and discharge me."

"Why would they...?"

He stopped, mouth hanging open, suspicion dawning on his face. Emma did not know if he had guessed aright. In truth she did not care, as long as he allowed her to stay here instead of going to the hospital.

"Please," she whispered.

He stared at her for a long moment, then got up and left the tent. Emma closed her eyes, exhausted. She almost did not care any longer. In a sense, discovery would be a relief, for it would end her struggles. She hated the thought of it, though. Hated the shame it would mean, the loss of her friendships. Perhaps she had just lost Halsted's; she could not tell.

Voices outside the tent, Halsted and the others. Emma could not make out the words. Pain was numbing her thoughts.

She reached for her cup and poured some water into it from the canteen, sloshing a little. Added a dollop of medicine from the little bottle. It was almost empty.

Halsted came back in the tent and sat down beside her, resting his hands on his knees as he gazed at her. "I've sent them back with the stretcher. Now, will you explain to me why you fear the surgeons?"

Emma thought of making some jest to the effect that she didn't want her leg amputated, but she had heard such words in earnest too many times to speak them lightly. Instead she gazed steadily back at Halsted.

"I'd rather not."

He looked perplexed, and annoyed, and perhaps a little

worried. "Frank, we're your friends."

"And I prefer that you remain so. Just let me rest here a day or two longer. I'll be better, you will see. Anyway, the surgeons must all be busy just now. Is the battle ended?"

"Yes." Halsted's face grew grim. "Pope was flanked by the Rebels. We've fallen back to Centreville, and may pull back farther."

Emma grimaced, then lifted her cup with a shaking hand. Halsted steadied it for her and helped her to drink. She gulped down the water greedily, eager for the medicine's effect.

"Thank you." She let her hand and the empty cup drop. "There is one thing you can do for me."

"Yes?"

"If you can, find the mule I was riding. A roan, with the empty mail bags on him. Someone may already have found him. I need the mail bags."

"You aren't going to ride for the mail like this!"

"Not tonight. Tomorrow I should be better."

Halsted shook his head. "You are stubborn as a..."

"Mule?"

Emma tried to smile, though she feared she must still look rather desperate. Halsted gazed at her a moment longer, then stood up.

"Give me your plate. I'll bring you some supper."

Emma found it and handed it to him, then lay back, her head swimming as the medicine began to take effect. She had no idea how she would ride the next day, but she was determined to fulfill her duty with regard to the mail.

Already it had gone two days undelivered, though since the army was engaged in battle that was not unusual. If she failed to resume her duties, though, the post would be taken away from her, and her life in the army would become much more difficult and dangerous.

The next morning, amid the protests of her tentmates, Emma bound up her leg with a scarf, and mounted the self-same mule that had thrown her, which Bostwick had found wandering in the woods and brought back to camp. Under her friends' worried gaze she hauled herself into the saddle and rode off to collect the mail.

Her leg hurt with the mule's every jarring step, as did her sore rib, but she endured. She stopped at a field hospital—a different one—and persuaded a nurse she knew to give her more medicine.

By the time she had brought the mail back to camp she was exhausted and aching with pain. She rode to her tent in a weary daze, thinking she could not possibly do this again another day. Halsted and Houlton came out to meet her, Halsted catching her as she slid from the saddle.

"The mail—"

"I'll bring it," said Houlton.

Halsted still held her. Her breaths came short, from both pain and a blossoming fear, then he pulled her arm roughly around his shoulder and helped her into the tent. Houlton brought in the mail bags and set them beside Emma's bedroll, then went away to take care of the mule.

Emma sank onto her bed with a grateful sigh. She put a hand to her aching leg and felt the bones grind inside it as she stretched it out before her. She must bind it more tightly, perhaps find something with which to splint it. She closed her eyes until the pain faded, then reached for the mail bags.

"You're completely mad," said Halsted.

Emma looked up at him and grinned wearily. "I can't deny that."

She opened the bags and began to sort the mail by company, laying the letters in piles on her bed, with a separate stack for the headquarters staff. Halsted sat watching.

"How you intend to deliver it? You can't walk."

"Then I'll ride."

He frowned. "Parade around the camp on your mule? That'll be a show."

Emma pressed her lips together. In truth she was not sure how she would manage to deliver the mail, but she had no choice. The alternative was unacceptable.

Bostwick came in, grinning as he entered the tent. "Miller wants to know if you still have watches, Frank. His was struck by a minie ball. Gave its little mechanical life to save him a wound. Can you believe it?"

Emma took a small leather box from beneath her cracker-box table. "Here they are. Would you mind taking it to him? You can keep the money."

Bostwick and Halstead exchanged a glance. "I wouldn't take your money, Frank," Bostwick said, then left the tent.

Emma went back to sorting the mail, certain now that her tentmates had discussed her situation in her absence. What they had concluded she was uncertain. She dared not raise the subject herself, for fear that they would demand what she could not do.

Instead, she pretended nothing was amiss. She would carry on as always, until either she was no longer able or was prevented by the actions of others.

"Shall I help you sort it?" Halsted said after a while.

"If you like. Thank you. There's one for you here—I think it's from your mother."

Emma handed him a letter. Their gazes met as he took it, and the look on his face made her heart freeze.

"Why?" he said quietly. "Why are you here?"

Emma glanced away and swallowed. "For the same reason as everyone else, to serve my country."

"But why would you go to such trouble, and lie about—"

"My age?"

Emma glanced toward the door of the tent and the sound of others passing in the street. They were surrounded by soldiers, any of whom could hear. She let her eyes plead for Halsted to keep silent.

"I wanted to serve the Union," she said again. "I had to serve, my conscience would give me no choice. That is the only reason."

Halsted frowned down at the letter in his hands, turned it over, then set it aside on his own bedroll. He reached into the mail bag for a handful of mail, and began sorting it into Emma's stacks.

By the time they had finished, Houlton was back from tending the mule. Emma looked up at him with a grateful smile.

"Did he give you trouble?"

"No, none. He's as gentle a beast as I've handled. How did you come to part company with him?"

"Tried to make him jump a ditch," Emma said. "It was my

fault. I was hurrying to deliver the mail."

She looked at the stacks of letters on her bed. She had no idea how she was going to deliver them. Walking was out of the question, and she knew Halsted was right—riding her mule about the camp would attract just the kind of notice she did not want.

She gathered up the mail, keeping the stacks in order by company, and put them back into the mail bags. The headquarters mail she kept out, as its delivery was the most urgent. She picked it up and looked at Halsted.

"Could I ask you to take this up to headquarters for me? Tell them I'm not feeling well?"

Halsted nodded and reached for the letters. Emma put them in his hand, her throat tightening with gratitude.

Houlton gestured toward the bulging mail bags. "Shall I pass out the rest of that for you?"

Relief washed through her. "Yes, if you don't mind."

"I just go to each company's street, right? Do I call them together?"

"They'll see the mail bags and come, or hear you calling out names. If any letters are unclaimed just bring them back."

"All right."

Houlton hefted the mail bags onto his shoulders. Halsted stood up and joined him, starting out of the tent.

"Thank you. God bless you both," Emma said.

Houlton smiled and Halsted gave a nod as they left. Emma reached for her canteen and cup, fixed herself a dose of medicine and drank it, and lay down.

All through September Emma's tentmates silently helped her. She insisted on fetching the mail, but it was they who delivered it, especially at first. Gradually her pain subsided and she was able to do more herself, but there were often days when she could not set her left foot to the ground.

Bostwick sold her watches for her and brought her meals to her. Halsted looked after her mule and continued to help with the mail on days when Emma felt too poorly. Houlton brought her an endless string of remedies for her hurts, his faith in the latest of them never failing.

The Second Michigan participated in the battle at South Mountain on September 14, but Emma did not go onto the field. She had intended to volunteer for courier duty, but Halsted persuaded her to stay behind at camp, with the nearest thing to a threat that he had uttered. Emma meekly obeyed, more out of a sense of obligation to her kindhearted friends than from any true fear of betrayal.

Slowly the pain of her injury faded and she regained her mobility. She occupied her idle hours in reading and writing letters, especially to Jerome, with whom she maintained a frequent and enthusiastic correspondence.

All constraint between them seemed forgotten. Jerome wrote to her of his boredom in Camp Parole, where he was not allowed to do anything beyond tending the few sick in the hospital, a task that came nowhere near occupying all his time. Emma, kept to her bed by her injury, could sympathize.

She told him a little about her recuperation, which elicited a long response full of very flattering expressions of concern. Jerome wished he were there to take care of her himself, and railed against the fate that kept him idle at Camp Parole instead. Emma assured him she was all right, and that her tentmates gave her all the help she needed.

They exchanged long letters on the subject of the President's proclamation of emancipation, issued shortly after the grim battle of Antietam, in which the Second Michigan did not take part. Both agreed that the step, which had roused a great deal of ire in certain quarters, was the only possible course that would save the country's honor.

Come October Emma was back in the saddle and eager to prove herself capable once more. She was particularly anxious that Colonel Poe would see how fit she was. The colonel was temporarily in command of the entire brigade, a command it was rumored might become permanent.

Technically the Third Brigade was under General Berry's command, but the general had been absent for some weeks, and the brigade had conducted itself well under Colonel Poe's guidance. Emma, who liked and admired her colonel, could only hope the rumored promotion would come through.

Changes were taking place everywhere. In early November General McClellan was yet again relieved of his command, to the indignation and sorrow of the army. General Burnside was the Army of the Potomac's new commander, one who by his own admission was not fit for the post.

Along with these changes came one of more immediate interest to Emma. The army was being reorganized, and Colonel Poe was at last to be given his own brigade, a new one, in expectation of his promotion to Brigadier General. The Second Michigan was transferred from Berry's Brigade to Poe's new Brigade, along with the 17th Michigan, the 20th Michigan, and the 79th New York.

Emma was at brigade headquarters one afternoon to collect the mail, and stopped in to say hello to the Colonel. Headquarters was housed in several buildings near the ferry at Edwards Landing, Colonel Poe's office being in a small house with a pleasant front garden, somewhat neglected. Waved into the office by an aide, Emma did not realize at first that the Colonel had company as she dug in her pockets.

"I brought you some apples, sir. They're a little green yet, but—oh, I beg your pardon!"

She stopped, apples in both hands, and stood gaping at the man sitting with Colonel Poe, who wore an infantry uniform with sergeant's stripes on the sleeves. He was tall and slender of frame, with blond hair just tinged with a hint of red. He raised blue eyes to Emma's and quirked an eyebrow that was darker and redder than his hair.

"It's all right, Thompson," said Colonel Poe. "Frank Thompson, mail carrier," he added to his guest. "Frank, this is Lieutenant James Reid, Acting AAG of the brigade."

Edwards Ferry, Virginia, 1862

O h!" Emma felt a rush of heat in her cheeks, and stuffed the apples back into her pockets. She looked at Lieutenant Reid again, thinking his face familiar.

"I believe we may have met—weren't you a sergeant in the 79th New York?"

"Very observant, Thompson," said Colonel Poe, lounging back in his chair. "He was indeed, until about fifteen minutes ago. I just signed his promotion."

Reid flashed a grin at the colonel, who smiled back. Poe must have liked him, to promote him to the brigade's staff as Assistant Adjutant General, a position of considerable responsibility.

"Congratulations," Emma said.

Reid glanced at her, still smiling. "Thank you."

"What was that about apples?" said the Colonel.

"Oh." Emma stepped to his desk and emptied her pockets onto it. "I passed an orchard on the way in, where there were still a few clinging to the trees. I thought you might like some."

"Ah! Thank you. Most observant indeed, and most resourceful."

Emma felt Reid's gaze upon her and glanced at him, apple in hand. "Would you like one?"

He smiled ironically as he leaned forward to accept the apple. His fingers—long, elegant fingers—brushed Emma's as he took the fruit.

"Thank you."

She felt unnerved by him, by his casual touch and his apparent wry amusement. She was suddenly aware of all her inadequacies: her small size, her disability, and the awkwardness of having blundered in upon Reid and the Colonel's conversation. Instinct told her to flee.

"Well, pardon my interrupting," she said, taking a shuffling step backward, then another.

Colonel Poe smiled and polished an apple on his sleeve.

"Not at all, Thompson. Thank you for the apples."

"You're welcome." Emma felt the doorjamb against her back, and stopped, still gazing at Lieutenant Reid. "Congratulations again."

Reid nodded, the red eyebrow rising. Emma turned and hastened from the room.

She collected the mail and with the heavy bags slung over her shoulder, limped out to where she had left her mule. Riding back to the Second's camp, she tried to find a new direction for her thoughts, but kept returning to the meeting in the colonel's office. She had recognized Reid, but did not really know him. Perhaps that was about to change.

Soon thereafter, Colonel Poe sent her to Washington to deliver mail to the Second's wounded who were in hospitals there. She had leisure to make some visits of her own, to points of interest in the capital, as well as to replenish her supply of handkerchiefs. She also had time to rest and recuperate further from her injury, and by the time she returned to Edwards Ferry she was feeling quite nearly herself again.

From that time on Colonel Poe kept Emma busy carrying his official dispatches as well as the mail. She was often in the saddle, like as not riding to Washington and back once a week or more.

Returning to Poe's headquarters on one such occasion, Emma found Lieutenant Reid sitting behind the colonel's desk, writing a letter. He glanced up at Emma, who stood holding her leather dispatch pouch.

"Frank Thompson," Reid said, breaking into a grin.

"Y-yes. I'm surprised you remember."

"How could I forget the first person to congratulate me on my promotion?" Emma had not heard him speak much before, and now noticed the slight lilt to his voice. "The colonel's out," he added. "Shall I take that for you?"

He set his pen in the standish and held out his hand. Emma hesitated. Ordinarily she insisted on placing dispatches directly into the colonel's hands, but there was nothing urgent in the pouch today, and certainly the adjutant held a position of high trust and responsibility. He was, in many ways, the commander's right hand.

She handed him the pouch, and watched him open it and glance through the messages inside. He took them out, laid them aside on the desk, and gave back the empty pouch.

"Thank you, Thompson."

Reid's smile remained and his gaze lingered, making Emma uncomfortable. She shifted, leaning most of her weight on her good foot.

"Please tell the colonel I'm sorry I missed him."

"I will."

Emma turned away, heading for the door. Reid's voice called her back.

"Thompson."

She turned, remaining by the door. "Yes?"

Reid leaned his elbows on the desk, watching her with slightly narrowed eyes. "How do you like being a regimental mail carrier?"

Emma blinked. "I like it very well."

"Long hours in the saddle."

"I enjoy riding."

"Mm. Colonel Poe says you're good at it."

Emma shifted her left foot to ease a cramp. "Usually."

"Usually?"

Was that too arrogant? Yet it was true. She was a good rider, and saw no reason to deny it.

Reid tilted his head to one side. "How did you hurt your leg?"

"An unfortunate accident."

"Ah." He smiled and his eyes narrowed a little more. "That is why you say 'usually'?"

Emma made no answer. After a moment Reid's smile widened. He picked up his pen and carefully scraped the excess ink from the nib.

"Thank you, Thompson."

She watched him begin to write, pen scratching on paper. Thus dismissed, she turned to go. As she went out to her horse, she wondered about Reid's curiosity. Perhaps he was merely familiarizing himself with all the Colonel's staff, even down to the mail carrier for a regiment not his own.

The next time Emma reported to Colonel Poe he gave her a fat pouch of dispatches and an unexpected surprise. Lieutenant Reid was again in his office, and the colonel gestured to him.

"Lieutenant Reid will accompany you to Washington."

Astonished, Emma glanced at Reid, then back at the colonel. "Sir?"

"He has some business to conduct on behalf of the brigade," said Colonel Poe. "You may as well ride together, and keep each other company."

Emma looked at Reid, who returned a friendly smile. "I am leaving directly," she said.

Reid stood up and took his overcoat from a peg by the door. "My horse is ready."

He gestured for Emma to precede him. Having little choice, she stepped out of the office and passed through to the yard, where her horse stood by the fence where she had left it.

Several others were there as well; usually there were a number of horses tied outside headquarters. Emma watched Reid go to the head of a magnificent bay gelding.

Her own mount, a former cart-horse named Ben, recently acquired in place of the mule, could better be described as a sturdy animal. His coat was an unremarkable brown for which the word "sorrel" was almost too rich. She liked Ben for his sure-footedness and stamina, but he was not much to look at. She hauled herself into the saddle, settled her left foot in the stirrup as comfortably as she could, and turned to the road.

Reid fell in beside her, and for the first mile or so kept silent. Emma set a brisk pace once they were away from the village, but in fairness to Ben she could not maintain it indefinitely. She dropped to a walk to let him rest, and Reid, whose horse seemed not to have noticed any exertion, kept pace.

"The colonel tells me you are also a foreigner," he said.

Emma nodded. "I am from Canada originally, but I have been living in America for some time."

"Selling books, I hear."

Emma felt a prickling at the back of her neck. She turned her head to look at him.

"You take quite an interest in a lowly mail carrier."

Reid smiled. "Ah, well, there is a reason."

He said no more, and Emma did not press him. She felt any show of curiosity about his purpose could only make her appear unconfident, and that she could not risk. She looked forward rather grimly to the end of this journey.

To her surprise, Reid shifted the subject. "What do you think of Burnside?"

"I have not seen him," Emma said.

"That never stops one from having an opinion."

Emma shrugged. "My opinion cannot matter much. I had rather have McClellan, but the government seems set against him."

"We had all rather have McClellan."

Reid gave her a description of Burnside, whom he had seen twice when he had gone to army headquarters on Colonel Poe's business. "He is about to make a move, you know."

Emma glanced up in surprise. "Now? I had thought we were about to go into winter quarters."

"Lincoln wants action."

Emma shook her head. "That is all very well for him. It is not the President who will be stuck in mud up to the knees."

Reid smiled. "I am curious to see some of those old battlegrounds. I missed some of the earliest battles."

"We will pass a number of the other battlefields, if you care to stop and look."

"I would like that. Will you be my guide?"

Emma glanced at him and saw him smiling. She gave a shrug. "If you like. I doubt there is much to see."

There was, in fact, quite a lot to see, especially at Bull Run, where the second fight had taken place not many months since. The battlefield was still covered with carnage, men and horses thrown in heaps and a little clay thrown over them, others lying where they had fallen, their limbs bleaching in the sun.

"Look at that," Reid said, pointing off to one side as they crossed the field. He dismounted, leaving his horse to stand as he gazed at a cavalryman and his horse lying together.

Nothing was left of them but bones, scraps of hide, and the cavalryman's clothing. One of his arms stood straight up in the air.

"He's lost his hand," Emma said, dismounting.

"Here it is."

Reid knelt beside the cavalryman and pointed to where his hand lay on the ground where it had dropped off, white bones in perfect order, nothing missing or displaced.

"Shall we take it?" he asked, looking up at Emma.

She glanced dubiously at the man's uniform, hanging on his bones. "We have no way of knowing who he was."

Reid gazed at her for a moment, then a corner of his mouth twitched upward. He stood, leaving the hand where it was, and went back to his horse.

They rode on to Centreville, where they paused again. It was here that Emma had served in the stone church. It was in ruins now, abandoned. Emma stood within its crumbling walls, gazing at the sky and remembering the horrors she had first witnessed here.

Reid joined her, but kept a polite distance and remained silent, as if sensing that her mood was not for conversation. Emma walked along the center of the church to the back, where the surgeons' tables had stood.

"This was a hospital," she said. "I had my first taste of battlefield nursing here."

"I had heard you were formerly a nurse," Reid said, coming to join her.

"In Washington, in the regimental hospital. It was different here."

She stepped to the back door, which hung by one hinge, rotting. Looking out across fields that had since been swept by fire, she remembered her flight from the Rebels and wondered what had become of the wounded she had been forced to abandon.

Jerome had been captured rather than leave the men who were in his care. Emma was suddenly smitten by guilt, wishing she had done the same, but that was folly. She could not have risked capture, which would certainly have led to her discovery.

Sensing Reid's gaze upon her, she looked at him. The wry smile he often wore was gone, leaving his face unusually sober. She felt a strange attraction to him, as if he needed some comfort that she could offer.

She turned away, shaking her head. It was the memories of this place, no doubt—of the desperate need of the wounded, and her anxiety to ease them. Always she responded to that need, to a call for water, or the simple desire for a sympathetic ear.

She missed the work, she realized. Missed the satisfaction of helping others. It had borne her spirits down, once, being every day among the sick and dying, but now she thought she could return to it if only she had the strength. At present, her leg was too weak to enable her to lift and carry patients.

"What is it?" Reid asked, his voice gentle.

Emma glanced at him, saying nothing. He gave a rueful smile.

"You look a little haunted."

Emma gazed at the ruined walls again. They were falling in upon the floor. This place, which had once sheltered the wounded, was itself now dying.

"We are all haunted, are we not?"

She stepped across a tumbled wall as if to break free of the church's shadow, and walked back to where the horses waited. Reid followed, and in silence they resumed their journey.

They rode on, visiting the battlefield at Chantilly, then riding on until dusk. They found lodging at a farmhouse for the price of four dollars and listening to the farmer's endless stream of complaints against the army. Emma was inclined to be offended, but Lieutenant Reid seemed to be more amused than anything, and she held her peace.

In the morning they continued to Washington, where they were greeted with the news that Burnside was moving the army, shifting his base from Warrenton to Falmouth, a move that had begun shortly after their departure. Emma, surprised by the swiftness of the change, had to acknowledge that Reid had been right.

"Well, I had seen clues of it," Reid said. "No matter, we shall manage."

They parted to pursue their separate duties, and after bidding Reid farewell, Emma watched him trot his bay up the avenue toward the Capitol. When he was out of sight, she made haste to attend to her deliveries.

Washington was as full of life and color as ever. Emma had long since become inured to the sight of generals in plumed hats and gold-fringed epaulets, a costume which would never be seen on the field. Washington had its own values, some of which had little to do with the army's actual efforts on behalf of the country.

As evening approached, she began to think of her dinner. She often dined at Willard's when she was in the capital, if she had funds enough, for it was the most elegant place in the city and she had always been fond of elegance. As her stomach was now grumbling at her, she started thither.

Willard's Hotel was the center of military color in the city. It was here that visiting generals stayed, and made sure to be seen hobnobbing with the political elite.

She entered the lobby a few minutes before five and looked about at a panoply of ornate plumage, interspersed occasionally by sober civilian attire. A shock of pale hair caught her notice.

Lieutenant Reid was standing in an alcove, talking with an older man in sober civilian attire, whose black beard was peppered with gray. Reid's expression was earnest. After a moment the man took out a purse and gave him a handful of coins, which Reid tucked into his pocket.

Emma stepped back, then turned and walked toward the hotel's front desk, certain that Reid would not have wished her to see that transaction. She wondered briefly what it was about, but in Washington there was no way of knowing.

The man could be a lobbyist, or a person who had some reason to bribe Reid though she could not imagine what that would accomplish. Reid might be selling information, but in Willard's Hotel he would not likely be selling it to an agent of the Confederacy. Perhaps it was something else altogether. Perhaps the man was sending money to a relative in the army, through Reid's agency.

Concluding that it was useless to speculate, Emma strolled toward the desk intending to look in the register to see if any of her acquaintances were staying at Willard's. She was prevented by a hand upon her arm.

"Thompson! Are you here to dine?"

"Yes," Emma said, turning to face him.

Reid grinned. "I've bespoken a table. Have you?"

"Not yet."

"Then share mine. You won't get another before ten o'clock."

As she allowed herself to be led across the lobby and into the dining room, she wondered fleetingly whether the gentleman with the peppered beard would also join them. She saw no sign of him. Several other gentlemen who were waiting outside the restaurant cast dark looks at her and Reid as they were ushered at once to a table.

Reid summoned the sommelier and after some discussion selected a bottle of French wine. Emma mentally counted the money she had brought with her. She had enough for dinner, even an elegant dinner at Willard's, but not enough for extravagance.

"Well," said Reid, looking pleased with the world, "at last we may relax! I trust your errands went well?"

Emma murmured agreement, not thinking it worthwhile to complain of being detained for two hours at one general's office while she awaited his reply to Colonel Poe's message.

She had not finished quite all of her errands, though she had managed to deliver all the colonel's dispatches.

"My tasks were made hideous by this change of base," Reid said, "but it's all straightened out now. Oh, and I've booked passage for us and our horses on a steamer to Aquia tomorrow. We should be able to find the brigade from there."

"That is most kind of you," Emma said. "Thank you, Lieutenant."

"Jamie, please," Reid said, flashing a smile. "No need to stand on ceremony, eh?"

Emma summoned a smile in return, but it was a somewhat stiff one. Officers did not fraternize with enlisted men. Perhaps the lieutenant was merely indulging in a bit of laxity inspired by the heady environment of Washington. Why, then, did she feel suspicious?

Reid leaned forward, speaking in conspiratorial tones a he cast a glance around the dining room. "Now, Frank, which of these generals is the greatest buffoon, d'ye think?"

Surprised into laughter, Emma turned it into a cough. "None of them," she answered sotto voce. "It is that naval officer over there, with the hat like Lord Nelson's."

The conversation continued in this vein until the wine arrived, which did nothing to sober their tone. Reid had a wicked sense of humor and took great delight in lampooning the Preeners of Columbia, as he called them. Emma laughed until her sides ached, and kept laughing until their dinner was served.

Reid then shifted the conversation. "You came from Canada." he said, cutting a bite off his chop. "Nova Scotia, I think. How did you come to enlist in Michigan?"

"I was there selling books, as you've heard."

"Why Michigan, though? A bit far from your home, isn't it?"

"That is exactly what made it attractive."

Reid laughed, and Emma glanced up from cutting her own meat. His face shone with amusement, a good-hearted amusement as opposed to the wicked mirth of a few moments before. Emma was fascinated at the difference.

"Well, I left home myself," Reid said, "though 'twas in the hope of making my fortune."

"In the land of opportunity," Emma added.

"Well, it is."

"It is indeed. I was quite serious. I certainly owe my fortunes to this country."

Reid polished off the wine in his glass and filled it again, emptying the bottle. Emma watched in trepidation as he summoned the sommelier.

"Another of the same, my man," Reid said, handing him the bottle.

Emma pressed her lips together, silently recalculating her finances. She looked at Reid when the sommelier had gone.

"And did you?"

Reid glanced up at her. "Did I what?"

"Make your fortune. In New York, I presume."

"Ah." Reid chuckled. "Yes, I did, after a fashion."

He drank again, rather deeply, then set down his glass. "You must have made more selling books than you do as a private soldier. Why enlist, then?"

"To serve the Union, of course. Is that not why you enlisted?"

"To serve...yes, that is one of the reasons."

He gazed at Emma, all the laughter now gone from his face. She wondered if he were becoming drunk, and if he were the sort who turned nasty in such a condition.

She took a sip of her own wine, holding it in her mouth a moment to enjoy the bouquet. She never touched strong spirits, and drank wine seldom enough that even one glass had a noticeable effect on her.

Reid was gazing into the distance now, no longer seeing Emma or anyone in the room. A frown had settled on his brow. She had begun to wonder if indeed he was drunk, when suddenly he fixed his gaze on her, eyes sharp and clear as ever.

"Freedom, that's the important thing," he said. "Nothing else matters."

"I agree."

He picked up his knife and fork again, cutting rather savagely at his meat. Emma watched him for a moment, then took her courage in hand.

"What do you think of Lincoln's proclamation?"

Reid's brows rose. "Which?"

"Freeing the slaves. What do you think?"

She half expected him to grumble. She had heard many in the army complain that free negroes would take jobs away from honest white men. Reid, however, seemed not to care.

"Slavery is wrong, I suppose."

"I am certain it is wrong."

Reid glanced up at her. "An abolitionist, are you?"

"Yes."

"You'll want to be careful how you talk about it. Could be a disadvantage in certain circles."

"Circles in which I am not likely to travel," Emma said.

"Don't be so certain of that."

She watched him eat a bite of meat, wondering what he meant. After a moment he glanced up at her and grinned.

"Anything can happen. Look at me—I enlisted as a private, worked my way up to sergeant, and now I'm on a brigadier's staff."

"Through your own merits."

"That had something to do with it. Friends make a difference, too." Reid's eyes narrowed in calculation. "You're well-liked, and well-known in your regiment. Colonel Poe likes you, too."

"Does he? I have never been certain."

"Oh, he does. Only wait and see how well."

Emma sipped her wine. She did not like being baited, as she felt Reid was doing. If he wanted her to beg him for more information, he was bound to be disappointed.

Reid seemed to sense her reticence and began to talk of Burnside's plans instead. "He's sent for pontoons from Harper's Ferry. We'll be crossing the Rappahannock."

Emma pushed a potato around her plate with her fork. "On to Richmond, yet again."

"Come, now! Where's your patriotism? Where's that Union spirit?"

She smiled faintly. "Still here. Only dampened a bit."

"It'll be damper yet in a day or two, once we're back camping in Virginia mud."

"I fear you are right."

"Do you mean to eat that, or are you just going to chase it around your plate all the evening?"

Emma sighed and pushed the plate away. "I've had enough."

Reid stabbed the potato with his own fork and ate it. "You enjoyed the meal, I hope?"

"Oh, yes. Willard's is always excellent."

"You're a man of taste, Frank."

Emma found that amusing, and looked back at Reid with a dry smile. He summoned the sommelier again, which chased her amusement away.

"A bottle of your best brandy," Reid said. "Send it to my room, if you please."

The sommelier bowed gravely as he accepted the coin Reid pressed into his hand. "Yes, sir."

"You'll join me?" Reid said when he had gone, his brows rising as he smiled.

Emma laid her napkin beside her plate. "Thank you, but I intend to visit the hospitals this evening. I have mail yet to deliver."

"Ah. Afterward, perhaps?"

"Best not. I shall be out rather late."

"All the more reason for a little fortification."

Emma felt a small shiver of danger, which gave her pause. She did not think Reid offered any true threat, so whence came her fear?

She stood up and took out her wallet, extracting the majority of her funds. Reid pressed back her hand.

"No, no, lad. Let me get this."

"Sir, I—"

"As thanks for your company."

He smiled, the engaging smile that was so disarming. Emma began to think that this was the most dangerous of his smiles.

"Thank you, sir. That is most kind indeed."

"This would have been a dull trip without you."

She met his gaze. "Dull for me as well."

His smile brightened into an expression of delight, and Emma felt her guard slip a little. Reid was quite charming, really. Too charming. She liked him.

"I will return here in the morning," she said.

"Unless you change your mind about the brandy."

Laughing a little, she shook her head and stepped away from the table. Reid reached for the wine bottle, and the last she saw of him he was making sure none of it went to waste.

Stepping into the sharp evening air, Emma felt her head clear a little. It was not the wine, but rather the decadent atmosphere of Willard's that had clouded her thoughts. Washington was a city of decadence, of course, but it had other sides as well. She now turned her attention to one of these.

She went to her lodging—in a much more modest establishment—and fetched the small satchel in which she'd brought letters to be delivered to members of the Second who were recuperating in Washington. They were scattered among several different hospitals, and she made a point to stay and visit with each man unless he was sleeping, so that it was past midnight by the time she sought her bed.

She woke with the sun shining in her window. Hastening to dress, she settled her bill and hurried to Willard's, not stopping for breakfast. If there was time she would take a meal at the hotel, but she was not certain how early they would have to board the steamer for Aquia.

The lobby was less busy at this hour, though there were still plenty of important-looking people there. Emma searched in vain for Reid. She was about to go to the desk to learn his room number when she noticed the civilian gentlemen she had seen giving Reid money the previous evening. He was sitting on a sofa, reading a newspaper.

Emma hesitated, then decided to approach him. He would be a more reliable source of information than the desk clerk, and besides, she was curious about him.

She came closer, and saw that the gentleman's clothing was of the finest quality. Beside him on the sofa lay an elegant beaver hat and an ivory-handled walking stick.

Emma gently cleared her throat, and smiled an apology as the gentleman looked up. "Please excuse me. I happened to notice you talking with Lieutenant Reid yesterday evening. I am to meet him this morning, and wondered if you could tell me whether he is here?"

"I haven't seen Jamie today, no," the gentleman said. There was a burr to his voice, and when he spoke he seemed older than Emma had first thought. "Are you a friend of his?"

"I am in his brigade. We traveled here together."

Movement on the staircase caught Emma's eye, and she looked up to see Reid hastening toward them. He looked rather concerned, and she wondered fleetingly if his association with this gentleman was indeed clandestine. If so, the gentleman showed no sign of it, for he caught sight of Reid and folded his newspaper.

"Ah, here he is. Good morning, Jamie. This young lad is looking for you."

"Morning, sir." Reid gave the gentleman a deferential bow. He seemed a little pale; the effect of the brandy perhaps. He turned to Emma and nodded. "Private Thompson."

"Good morning, sir," Emma said crisply, following his lead of formality.

The civilian gentleman looked expectantly at Reid, who flushed slightly. "This is Private Frank Thompson of the Second Michigan, sir. Private Thompson, this is Mr. William Woods, my father-in-law."

Emma hid her momentary surprise, and managed to make a creditable bow. "How do you do, sir?"

"Not verra well, to be honest," said Mr. Woods. "The climate of this place disagrees with me."

"Well, you'll be back in New York soon enough," Reid said pleasantly. "Shall I escort you to the station?"

"Thank you, no. I have a bit more business to conduct yet today. I'll be taking the afternoon train."

Mr. Woods stood up with the aide of his walking stick, and Emma realized he was more frail than he appeared. He turned to Reid, who reached into his coat pocket and brought out a letter which he pressed into Mr. Woods's hands.

"Thank you, lad. Mary'll be glad to receive it. She was right sorry she couldn't come with me."

"Take her my love, and tell her to get well. Has she seen the doctor lately?"

"Ach, doctors. They're a tribe of murderers, if you ask me."

Emma, who had seen surgeons up to their elbows in blood, standing for hours at a time over the grisly tables where they amputated limbs until their hands were too cramped to hold the saws, kept silent. Mr. Woods picked up his hat and started toward the door, leaning heavily on his stick. Reid accompanied him as far as the front steps.

Emma had not expected her speculations about the gentleman's identity to be answered in quite this way. She had not known Reid was married; she had assumed not, in fact, as he seemed just a bit wild. He must be more settled when at home, she reflected. The army had a liberating effect. Knowing Reid had a wife at home, something to anchor him, however far away, made Emma feel a little less suspicious of him.

"Pardon me for making you wait," Reid said, returning.

Emma shook her head. "Family obligations. I quite understand."

Reid smiled crookedly. "He's a bit tetchy, but he has a kind soul."

Emma nodded. "When must we be at the docks?"

"Not for a couple of hours yet. Have you eaten?"

"No."

"Breakfast, then!"

They returned to the dining room, and were soon discussing a hearty breakfast of eggs, ham, and toast. Emma dug in with enthusiasm. One advantage of traveling frequently to Washington was the opportunity to eat much better than army rations. She considered it well worth the expense.

"A pity your wife could not visit you," she said, spreading orange marmalade on a slice of toast.

Reid glanced up. "She's been unwell."

"How long is it since you last saw her?"

"Nearly a year. I went to New York on furlough after I was released."

"Released?"

Reid put down his fork and took a swallow of coffee. "From prison. I was captured by the Rebels at First Bull Run."

Emma drew an involuntary breath. "I didn't know. I'm sorry."

A fleeting smile crossed his face. "Just as soon forget it, myself. I was sick six ways from Sunday when I got out."

Emma's heart went out to him. How dreadful, to spend months in a prison camp! She cut a bite of ham, silently giving thanks that she had been fortunate in this regard.

"I have a good friend who was taken prisoner, but he was paroled," she said.

"Lucky for him."

"He's still at Camp Parole, waiting to be exchanged."

"Mm." Reid ate a large bite of toast. "Did you get all your letters delivered?"

Emma answered, letting the subject drop as she perceived this to be Reid's wish. He seemed somewhat introspective, so for the rest of the meal she chattered about the hospitals and the men she had visited. Reid nodded politely now and again, but his thoughts appeared to be elsewhere.

When they had finished breakfast, Emma insisted upon paying for her share. Reid did not argue, but merely gave a wan smile. The morning being now well advanced, they retrieved their horses and repaired to the docks, where they boarded a government steamer bound for Aquia.

They arrived to a drizzling rain and the familiar chaos of

an army in the throes of relocation. Retrieving their mounts, she and Reid set off in the rain for Falmouth, where they were told headquarters had been established. They talked little on the journey, both being occupied with their own thoughts, and rather more interested in making good time than in making conversation.

Soon they began to see row upon row of white tents pitched in the mud. The road was a sticky, gooey mess, and before long they passed an abandoned ambulance, up to its hubs in mud.

"It is worse than the Peninsula!" Emma remarked.

They found the brigade's headquarters camped on a hilltop some miles from the town. Emma collected the Second's mail, then turned to Reid.

"I have some messages for the Colonel."

"I can take them to him if you wish."

She looked at him, rain dripping off the brim of his cap. She no longer felt hesitation about trusting him.

"Thank you. Tell him I will be there shortly, once I sort out the regiment's mail."

"Tireless lad." Reid smiled as he accepted the dispatch pouch, then held out a hand. "Thanks for your company, Thompson."

Emma shook his hand, surprised at how warm it was despite the rain. She could not help but return his smile.

"My pleasure," she said, and turned her horse toward camp.

Though Burnside had succeeded in moving his army quickly, he was less successful in getting it across the Rappahannock. The pontoons were delayed, first by an order gone astray, then by the rains that turned the roads into sucking mud.

As the days passed, the army's spirits waned, for they knew General Lee would soon move to counter Burnside. Before long, Confederate batteries were seen on the heights above Fredericksburg, just across the river, and still the pontoon bridges were not built.

Emma found herself spending more and more time at headquarters, partly because Colonel Poe called upon her to act as his courier with increasing frequency. She also lingered for the sake of Lieutenant Reid's company, which she continued to enjoy.

Reid—or Jamie as he insisted she call him—was intelligent, clever, and liked to laugh at the world. She began to spend the occasional evening with him, though she declined to become his drinking partner. He seemed to understand her dislike of spirits, for he soon ceased to offer her brandy, and then ceased to drink it in her presence. Emma could only appreciate this considerateness.

Returning from another trip to Washington on a bitter day early in December, she sought out Colonel Poe and handed him a pouch full of dispatches, along with a pocketful of apples, doughnuts, and a very nice orange. The colonel turned the orange over in his hands, admiring it before putting it away in his camp desk.

"Thank you, Thompson." He looked through the dispatches, pulling one from the stack and dropping the rest on his desk as he hastened to open it. "Stay a moment."

Emma waited, wondering if she was about to be sent back to Washington post haste. The Colonel's face lit with pleasure as he scanned the page. He glanced up at her, grinning.

"Ask Reid to step in here, will you?"

She found the adjutant at his desk in a nearby tent. He smiled as she came in.

"Thompson! Welcome back."

"Thank you. Colonel Poe wants you."

"I am his, then. One moment."

He blotted the page he'd been writing, covered it with a ledger, then rose and returned to Colonel Poe's tent with Emma. The Colonel was pacing thoughtfully, but stopped and looked up as they entered.

"It's come," he said. "Call the brigade staff in here, if you would, Thompson. Reid, you know what to do."

Reid grinned, glanced sidelong at Emma, and left. Emma hastened to do the colonel's bidding, wondering what was afoot.

When she had gathered all the brigade staff who could be found, they more than filled the back half of the large wall tent that served as Poe's office. His aide-de-camp opened the canvas that divided the front reception area from the office, and still the staff was crammed in shoulder to shoulder. Emma took up a place near the door to await events.

Colonel Poe stood talking to the brigade quartermaster, but glanced up as Reid came in carrying a large basket. He was followed by an orderly burdened with a crate that clanked of glass. Both were set on the colonel's desk, and Reid proceeded to open the crate, which contained a dozen bottles of champagne.

The orderly took wine glasses out of the basket and arrayed them on the desk, and Reid stood ready to open the first bottle. Colonel Poe stepped forward, a document in hand. Emma recognized it as the letter she had carried.

"Gentlemen, I have just received notice from Washington. President Lincoln has nominated me Brigadier General."

A burst of exclamation followed, punctuated by the popping of a cork, which thumped against the canvas roof. Colonel Poe—General Poe, now—shook hands with all his staff, and the champagne flowed free. Emma took a glass, but spent more time watching all the others than drinking. Everyone was discussing the promotion in tones of excitement and anticipation. General Poe would accomplish great things, his staff all told one another.

By the time the impromptu celebration began to break up, dark had fallen and Emma's stomach was growling for supper. She set her half-finished glass of champagne on the desk alongside the crate of now-empty bottles, and finally had opportunity to congratulate the new general.

"Thank you, Thompson," Poe said, beaming as he shook her hand. "You may expect more good news in the near future."

"Good news is always welcome," Emma replied, wondering if the Colonel had picked up Reid's habit of cryptic utterances. "I am sure we can only benefit by your advancement."

"Some more than others," Reid said, coming up to join them. He winked at Emma and received a slap on the back from General Poe.

"Join me for dinner," Poe said. "We have much to discuss. You, too, Thompson," he added, nodding to Emma.

"Oh—thank you, sir, but I have the mail—"

"The mail, ah yes. It can wait an hour. I want to talk to

you."

Mystified, Emma accompanied Poe and Reid to dinner along with a half-dozen officers of the brigade. The meal was quite good, prepared by Poe's favorite cook who had been with him ever since Williamsburg, and was accompanied by yet more champagne.

Being the only private at the table, Emma felt somewhat cowed and took little part in the conversation, most of which revolved around the brigade's readiness for the battle that would take place if ever Burnside's pontoon bridges were built. Various officers who were not present were discussed, their merits compared, their likely performance in battle judged. Emma felt as if she did not belong in such a meeting, and waited for the meal to end so that she could escape.

"Now, then, Thompson," the General said, turning toward her as the dessert was being served. "I need a new postmaster for the brigade, and I think you are suited to the position. What say you?"

Caught off guard, Emma dropped her fork with a clatter. "P-postmaster?"

"Yes. And mail carrier, you would have that to do as well. Do you think you can handle all the brigade's mail?"

Poe looked at her with one eyebrow slightly raised. Emma swallowed and straightened her shoulders.

"Certainly, sir."

"Excellent. Reid will write up the order."

Emma glanced across the table at Reid, who smiled with conspiratorial warmth. "Congratulations," he said softly.

Near Falmouth, Virginia, 1862

Emma felt her cheeks grow warm, and busied herself with cutting the piece of pie set before her into ever-smaller bits. Already the general had moved on to some other topic. A lively discussion was taking place, but Emma never heard a word of it.

Postmaster and mail carrier for the entire brigade! It was quite a jump in responsibility. She knew she could handle the work, but was still a bit breathless at the sudden change.

When the dessert was cleared and brandy and cigars came out, Emma excused herself on the grounds of the Second's mail, still waiting for delivery. General Poe waved her off with a friendly smile, and Lieutenant Reid accompanied her outside, pausing beneath the awning over the tent's entrance. Rain pattered on the canvas, and a chill breeze made Emma pull her greatcoat closer around herself.

"Congratulations again, Frank."

"Thank you. I hardly know what to think!"

"Oh, you've earned it, be sure. The colonel—the general, I mean—likes to have efficient men around him." Reid smiled lazily, and added, "You'll have to reside at headquarters, you know."

"Oh—I hadn't realized."

"You may share my tent, if you like. I have plenty of room."

Emma stared at Reid, surprised and discomfited by the invitation. She would have to live someplace, and she knew no one else at headquarters any better than him. Fear tightened her shoulders, but she did not know how to refuse —could not form a plausible reason to refuse—and a part of her was actually glad of the prospect.

"Thank you, that is very kind of you."

"Not at all." Reid's smile flashed. "I enjoy your company. Bring your traps up tomorrow. General Poe will expect you to assume your new post at once, though I must warn you, the order may take a few days. We are rather swamped at present."

Emma bade him goodnight, musing as she rode back to the Second's camp. She could scarcely believe the change in her fortunes, even now.

In the drizzling rain she delivered the mail to men who scurried out of their warm tents as she arrived, stood shivering as she called their names, and scurried back again just as quick, letters or packages tucked beneath their coats. She smiled at them fondly as she handed out these treasures, thinking of this as a leave-taking, though she would still be delivering mail to the Second. She would still see these men, but she would no longer be living among them.

When her satchels were empty she saw to her horse's needs, then returned to F Company's street and her own tent. Halsted was there, sitting by the stove and reading a newspaper by the light of a candle.

"Evening, Frank," he said. "Welcome home."

"Thank you. Where are Robert and Sam?"

"Picket duty."

Emma sat on her bed and gazed around the tent. She should pack up her traps, she supposed, not that it would take long. She could make everything she owned ready for travel in five minutes.

She pulled off her boots, sighing at the ache in her left leg. Stretching it out before her, she drew up the other and rested her chin on her knee, watching Halsted. After a few minutes he folded the paper and looked up at her.

"How was Washington?"

"Buzzing with anticipation."

"Hm. They're in for a disappointment. Lee's got the jump on us. He has guns all over the heights, did you see?"

"Yes."

"No point in even building the pontoons now."

Emma made no comment. From what she had heard at headquarters, Burnside's plans were moving forward, regardless of Lee's guns.

"I've received a promotion."

Halsted raised his head, looking surprised. "Corporal?"

"No, no—but, postmaster. For the brigade."

"Whew! The whole brigade? We'll never see you!"

Emma smiled. "I'm afraid you are right. I have to move up to headquarters."

Halsted gazed at her for a long moment, his brow creased with concern. "Will you be all right?"

"Yes. Thank you—I shall never forget the help you gave me when I needed it most."

"Well...well. Good luck to you, then. We'll miss you."

"And I you. But you will see me. I'll still deliver the mail."

Halsted shook his head, chuckling. "The precious mail."

Emma smiled, then crawled beneath her blankets, letting the exhaustion of a long and surprising day carry her to sleep. The last thought in her mind was of letters, stacks of letters like mountains, all sliding into each other.

In the morning she packed up her kit and brought Ben down to camp. She was strapping her bedroll to his saddle when Bostwick and Houlton arrived, bleary-eyed, from picket duty.

"What's this?" said Bostwick. "Are we marching?"

Halsted came out of the tent. "No, Frank's leaving us. He's going to live with the shoulder straps up at headquarters."

Laughing, Emma explained her promotion. Her tentmates expressed dismay, congratulated her, and abused her as a traitor almost in the same breath. She shook hands with all of them and promised to remember them.

"God bless you all," she told them, feeling a sudden threat of tears.

"You take care of yourself, Frank," said Houlton. "We'll miss you."

"Here—wait a moment." She tugged at the strap on a saddlebag and dug inside for the small leather box of watches. She opened it and held it out. "Pick one, each of you."

"Frank, no," said Bostwick.

"Yes, yes! I doubt I'll have time to be selling them anyway. Please take one."

They each chose a watch, and amid thanks and well-wishes she mounted and left them, feeling she was leaving a part of her life behind. She rode through the Second's camp—her camp no longer—and up the long hill to brigade headquarters. On the way she passed Chaplain Brown and paused to greet him.

"Hello, Frank! We have not seen you at a meeting in some while."

"Yes, I'm sorry. I have been sent to Washington so often—"

"Is that where you are going now?" He glanced toward her traps strapped to her saddle.

"No, I'm moving to headquarters. General Poe has made me postmaster for the brigade."

The chaplain's brows rose. "Has he indeed? Well, congratulations. I hope you will not forget your friends when you are dwelling among the exalted."

Emma laughed. "No. I'll come to a meeting soon, I promise."

When she reached headquarters she found that Reid was away. She went to his tent, from which he was also absent. Emma had visited him here a number of times, but now that she was to live here she saw it with new eyes. She stood in the doorway, afraid to set her belongings inside.

It was an officer's tent, much larger than those given the enlisted men, furnished with a small camp table and two folding chairs in addition to the stove. Reid's cot looked hastily made. A large chest stood at its foot, with a spare blanket draped over it. Clothing hung from a row of pegs suspended from the ridge pole, and a pair of shelves made from boards and bricks stood along one wall, filled with mess kit, several glasses, a half-dozen bottles of wine, one of brandy, and an assortment of knick-knacks.

Reid had more space than Emma and her three tentmates had shared, yet she hesitated to claim any of it. She could not shake the feeling that she was an intruder. At last she piled her belongings in a heap in the front corner of the tent and left to report to headquarters.

General Poe could not see her at once, she was informed by his aide-de-camp, Lieutenant Keller. She sat kicking her heels for a time in the outer office, finally succumbing enough to boredom to ask Keller if she could help him with any of his work. He seemed to resent the offer.

She was on the point of giving up and going to see if more mail for the Second had arrived. At least she might keep herself occupied with that, but as she stood up General Poe summoned her into his office.

"Good morning, Thompson. All settled in are you? Good.

Go on up to division headquarters, ask the quartermaster there if our new flagstaffs have arrived, and see what newspapers you can find—the steamer captains often have the latest issues—then fetch down the mail. You'll deliver our headquarters mail first, of course, then you can deliver to the regiments. Oh, and take this with you."

He handed Emma a pouch fat with messages. She nodded, swallowing. In less than a minute he had assigned her more work than she usually did in a week.

"Will there be anything else, sir?"

Poe raised a brow at her and smiled. "No, that will do. Be sure to take a pack mule along—you cannot bring all the mail on your horse. You will find a string of animals picketed by the creek, tell Dodd I sent you to choose one. And step in here when you get back."

"Yes, sir."

Emma hastened away to retrieve Ben and claim a mule. Division headquarters was in Falmouth town, and as she rode along its streets she could see the Confederate pickets in Fredericksburg across the river, close enough to throw stones in some places. Cannon frowned over the town from the heights beyond. Emma found herself in agreement with Halsted; it was not even worth attempting to assail such a fortified stronghold.

She completed the errands Poe had given her and returned with her pack mule burdened with mail—four large sacks, which she spent the better part of the day sorting, resulting in a large sack for each regiment and another nearly as large for brigade headquarters. Having nowhere else to sort, she made use of the table in Lieutenant Reid's tent to organize the mail, then hastened to General Poe's office with a satchel full of the headquarters mail over her shoulder.

"He can't see you, he's with the chief of ordnance," said Keller. "Is that the mail?"

"Yes."

"I'll take ours."

Emma handed him the stack addressed to "Headquarters, First Brigade, First Division," but kept back the correspondence addressed to Poe. The ADC glanced at the letters and held out his hand.

"I'll take the general's mail as well."

"He asked me to see him when I returned."

"Very well, but you'll have to wait. Might as well make your deliveries meanwhile."

Emma saw the sense in this. With a glance toward Poe's inner sanctum, she left, conveniently forgetting to hand over the general's letters.

She set out to make the rounds of all the offices at headquarters, and made a number of new acquaintances along the way. By the end of an hour she had learned a great deal about the organization and staff of the brigade, and returned to Poe's office weary from walking.

"He's with the adjutant," said Keller when Emma came in.

She was about to sit down and stretch out her leg when Reid poked his head around the doorway. "That you, Thompson? I thought so. Come on in."

General Poe glanced up from his desk, a stack of reports in one hand. "Ah, good. Did you find yesterday's papers?"

"And one from this morning, sir. There was a packet just come in." Emma took three newspapers from her satchel, along with the general's mail. "These are your letters, sir. Should I leave them with your aide if you are busy?"

"Anything that isn't marked 'Urgent.' Those and any mail from division headquarters or Washington you must put straight into my hands."

"Yes, sir."

"What about the flagstaffs?"

"Not yet arrived, sir."

"Hmph."

She waited while he sorted through the letters, handing several of them to Reid. The adjutant grinned at Emma.

"Not yet drowning?"

Emma smiled. "Not quite. I have left rather a large heap of mail in your tent, though."

Reid burst out laughing. "Why, thank you!"

"You have your own office for that," Poe said, glancing up with a frown. "Didn't Keller tell you?"

"No, sir, but then I didn't ask."

Poe shook his head, grumbling. "Get him to show you the postmaster's tent. It's over by the quartermaster depot."

"I'll show him," Reid offered, standing up. "I need to have a word with the quartermaster anyway."

"And send Keller in here on your way," said Poe, frowning at a letter he had opened.

Thus dismissed, they left at once, Reid tucking the letters the general had given him into his pocket. He glanced sidelong at Emma as they left the tent and strode across the camp toward the depot.

"Keller was friends with the last postmaster," Reid said. "Don't let him give you trouble."

"Oh. Thank you, I won't."

"There's a certain amount of maneuvering that occurs at headquarters."

Emma chuckled. "I don't think there is an organization anywhere that is free of maneuvering."

"No? But you will find more of it the closer to Washington you get, and that includes the army."

"I beg to dispute. I am informed on certain authority that quite the most desperate political machinations in the world take place within the Ladies' Christian Circle of Flint, Michigan."

Reid laughed. "And who is your informant?"

"Miss Daphne Little, who is a member in good standing."

"Dear me, a young lady correspondent? Frank, you dog! You've never mentioned her."

Emma looked at him with an innocent expression she knew would be disbelieved. "We are merely friends."

Reid laughed again, louder. "Now I know why you enjoy the mail service. You must comb each batch of letters for one in Miss Little's hand!"

Emma laughed, and protested. They were both still laughing when they reached the depot.

"Here, this is your office."

Reid pointed out a small wall tent alongside the larger tents of the depot. Emma looked inside and exclaimed at the several full mail sacks lying on a long table inside.

"That'll be the outgoing mail from the regiments," Reid said. "All you have to do is forward it along, usually. Looks like it's been a day or two."

More work. Emma drew a breath and managed to smile. "Well, thank you. I had better get started."

By evening she had taken care of the outgoing mail and delivered the mail for three of the regiments, leaving the Second's for last. She had spent as much time in the saddle as on foot, and was sore in a variety of ways from riding, walking, and lifting heavy sacks. And still the Second's mail remained to be sorted and delivered—she was their only mail carrier.

She sighed as she looked at the bulging sack. After supper, she decided. She was quite hungry, and suddenly realized she had no idea where she was to mess. She went back to Reid's tent to fetch her mess kit, and encountered him coming out.

"There you are! We wondered if you had fallen into a ditch."

"Not yet, thanks be given. Can you tell me where I am to mess?"

"Headquarters mess, dear boy. Come along."

"Isn't it officers, though?"

"Mostly. Best be sure your buttons are polished." Reid grinned. "No, it's everyone, except on very formal occasions, when you lowly fellows will get your dinner in the kitchen."

He led her to a large tent filled with tables and benches, quite the nicest such accommodation she had seen. There were certain advantages, it seemed, to serving at headquarters. Her meal included applesauce and baked squash as well as meat and soft bread. Afterward, Reid led her off to his tent.

"I'll be working late tonight at the general's office," he said, "so we'd best get you settled in now."

Reid commenced discussing, largely with himself, where to put Frank's bed. He decided on moving the shelves, though Emma protested the necessity. In the end Reid prevailed and the two of them shifted the shelves and all their contents to the front of the tent, after which there was room for Emma's bedroll along the side. She laid out her bed and placed her few belongings beside it, still not quite believing this was her new home.

"Thank you," she said. "This is very good of you, sharing your tent. Are you sure I shouldn't sleep in the postmaster's tent?"

"There'd be no room for you, most nights. I'd sooner share

with you than some other. I've been lucky to be alone for this long." Reid retrieved his overcoat from one of the pegs. "And now I must leave you, my lad. I'll be back later to join you in a nightcap. Oh, no—you don't. Well, you can watch me have one. God knows I'll need it tonight!"

He was gone on the words, leaving Emma to admire the luxury of her new accommodations. She checked that the fire in the stove was banked, brought in an armload of wood, then made her way back to her office to tackle her regiment's mail.

For the second night running she delivered it in the dark. Her spirits were lifted by seeing her comrades, however, including her tentmates, who all came out to greet her. She returned to headquarters weary but content.

Reid was not in his tent. Emma built up the fire and took off her boots. Her left foot was throbbing. She rubbed it a little, then made up her bed and climbed into it. Strange to sleep in a bed in camp, even if it was only a cot.

She woke to the scrape of a boot on the ground, and started up, not remembering at first where she was. The shadow moving in the tent was Reid's, she knew from the way his hair fell forward over his brow.

"Only me, lad. Sorry to wake you."

Emma relaxed. "S'all right."

She watched through drowsy eyelids as he poured brandy into a glass, drank half of it in one breath, then sat with the glass dangling from his fingers, leaning forward wearily. In the dim tent he seemed dejected, no hint of his customary cheer.

"Hard day?" Emma ventured.

Reid gave a low huff of laughter. "Not so hard as yours, I imagine. No, but there's some news, and it isn't good."

He drank another swallow of brandy. Emma could smell it, even across the tent.

"All the materials for those cursed pontoons have arrived at last," he said. "The engineers are ready to begin construction."

Emma stiffened, remembering the dozens of cannon in plain view on the heights across the river. "They won't, will they?"

He raised his glass and tipped it back to drain it, then ran his free hand through his hair, pushing it back from his brow. Emma heard him sigh as he reached for the bottle.

"I don't know, Frank. No one knows what Burnside'll do."

She kept silent, knowing they were both thinking the same thing: McClellan would not have gotten them into such a fix.

Fredericksburg, Virginia, 1862

A week later, General Poe was summoned, along with all the other general officers in the Army of the Potomac, to Lacy House in Falmouth for a meeting with General Burnside. In his absence, headquarters was unnaturally quiet. Emma could feel the tension in the air as she made her rounds with the headquarters mail. There was no laughter. No one spoke of what might be going on in that meeting.

Emma retired to her office, alone with her mountains of letters and packages. Sorting them was a soothing task, though it left her mind too free to think of what might be coming. In the middle of December, when by rights the army should be ensconced in winter quarters, it looked very much as if they were about to be ordered to advance.

She carried the mail to the regimental camps, where the mood was not so gloomy. They did not know, yet, and Emma said nothing to her friends. If the news was bad, they would hear it soon enough.

She sent off the outgoing mail, then returned to head-quarters to learn if there was any news. A glance at ADC Keller's face told her that General Poe had not returned. It was evening by now, and she went to the too-silent mess tent, where she sat with Reid over a desultory meal for which neither of them was hungry.

"Better eat it," Reid said with a crooked smile. "Might be crackers tomorrow."

Emma stirred her stew. "It cannot be going well, can it? If it's taking this long?"

"My guess is, they're trying to talk him out of it."

In this bleak mood they spent the evening together, retiring to Reid's office after supper, where Emma watched him file paperwork. She had yawned twice, and was considering giving up and going to bed, when General Poe walked in.

"Good," he said, looking at Jamie. "Come with me. You, too, Thompson."

Emma jumped up from her chair and followed them to the general's office, where Poe waved her and Reid to the chairs before his desk. His ADC hovered in the doorway.

"Yes, come in, Keller," Poe said. "I have one or two things for you to do."

The general sat down, looking infinitely weary, and gazed at the neat stacks of paper on his desk, seeming lost in reverie. Emma and Reid exchanged a glance.

"Sir?" Reid said.

The general looked up at him and sighed. "Burnside wants to advance. There's been a great deal of argument, and there will be more tomorrow, I suspect, but so far he will not budge."

Emma felt a tightening of dread within her chest. She thought of the guns on the ridge and closed her eyes.

"It will not be tonight, at least," Poe said. "We have that much. I'll have some errands for you, James. And I must write some letters this evening. Thompson, will you see that they go out at once?"

Emma nodded, then listened as Poe recited a succinct list of tasks for Reid, all directed toward preparing the brigade for battle. All the while he was writing, making notes and lists. Occasionally he would pause to dictate a message or an order to Keller, who had brought in his writing board and sat frowning in concentration, pen scratching away at a furious pace.

Feeling slightly helpless, Emma wondered if she was caught inside a dream. Wished it, more like, and knew it was all too real.

Reid stood up and went out to carry out Poe's orders. He paused in the doorway and Emma glanced up, meeting his gaze. Something was in it that she could not quite read—regret, perhaps. A corner of his mouth quirked in a half-smile, then he was gone.

Eventually Poe sent Keller off as well, and commenced writing his letters while Emma waited. When he finally handed them to her, she saw the names she had expected: his wife, Nellie; friends in Washington; friends at home in Michigan. The letters that might be the last. They went out before every battle, from every private and every general and everyone in between who could set pen to paper. Her outgoing mailbag would be heavy tomorrow.

There had been no announcement, and Poe had enjoined them to silence, but the soldiers always knew of such things. She wondered if the word was spreading even now.

"Thank you, Thompson," Poe said wearily. "You'll take them to the depot at once?"

"Yes, sir."

"I have half a mind to send you to Washington."

"I had rather be with you, sir."

Poe looked at her and smiled. "You're a good man, Thompson. A bonnie, brave lad, as Jamie would say. Off with you, now, and get some rest."

She left, pausing to look into Reid's office before heading for the depot. He was there, making lists of his own, frowning as he wrote by candlelight.

"I'm taking mail to the depot. Would you like to send a note to your wife?"

Reid looked up in surprise, then his mouth twisted in a wry smile. "I suppose I should. Can you wait a minute?"

"Of course."

She watched him scrawl a hasty message. He handed it to her, then rubbed his hand over his face.

"God knows where we will be this time tomorrow," he muttered.

"In God's keeping," Emma replied, to which he gave her a quizzical look.

The one thing she and Reid had not yet discussed at length was religion, she realized as she saddled her sleepy horse. She thought about this while she rode, wondering if Reid was devout. If there was ever a time for prayer, it was now.

She felt a pang of guilt for her recent lack of devotion. Since coming to headquarters it seemed she simply didn't have the time. Her Bible lay untouched beneath her bed; she had not yet managed to attend a prayer meeting. She missed it now, and thought fleetingly of paying a late visit to Chaplain Brown.

In the end she decided to wait. Perhaps tomorrow the generals would prevail upon Burnside to change his plans. She would certainly pray, tonight, but she didn't wish to trouble the chaplain. She wished Jerome were here, for he would have talked with her.

She decided to write to him. A last letter, perhaps, she thought with a wistful smile. There was no one to whom she felt closer.

When she reached the tent Reid was there, pacing restlessly back and forth. He scarcely glanced up in response to her greeting. Emma left him alone, took out paper and pen, and sat at the table to compose a note to Jerome.

"Writing to your lady friend?" Reid said, a sharp edge to his voice as he paused, standing over her.

Emma dipped her pen. "To my friend at Camp Parole."

"Jerome."

"Yes."

Reid commenced pacing again. Emma did not think he was drunk; his eyes seemed sharp and not at all glassy. Not knowing how to ease his agitation, she ignored him. Perhaps he was thinking of home. Perhaps he had his own regrets.

She wrote Jerome a long, candid letter. She had not even told him of her promotion, she realized, nor of General Poe's advancement. She knew Jerome was also fond of their commander, so she described Poe's celebration. The scene had a certain poignancy now in her memory—Poe was probably the newest general going into this battle, and it would be a shame if his first battle at that rank was also his last—but she kept such reflections to herself.

Reid stopped pacing all at once and sat on his bed, dropping his head into his hands. "It's no use."

Emma glanced up, wondering if he wanted an answer. She had finished addressing her letter to Jerome, and was considering writing a brief note to Miss Daphne, but she put the pen down.

Reid ran his hands through his hair, then looked up at Emma and laughed softly.

"What?" Emma said.

He shook his head. "Nothing."

Emma watched him reach for the brandy bottle on his shelf. He looked at it, turning it round in his hands, then set it down again, to Emma's relief. Almost immediately he stood up and reached for his greatcoat.

"I'm going out for a walk. Don't wait up."

Emma watched him shrug into the coat, concerned by the

trouble in his face. She wanted to ask him to pray with her, but doubted that he would, in this mood. Instead she rose and saw him to the door.

"Are you all right?"

He looked at her, a smile twisting his mouth. "I will be. You needn't worry, Frank. But thank you."

He caught her hand and squeezed it, the heat of his flesh surprising her as it had before. He let go at once, and slipped out into the darkness, leaving Emma to wonder alone.

Next morning Reid gave no sign of his previous agitation. He and Emma both rose before dawn and set about the day's business. General Poe returned to Lacy House and headquarters returned to silent waiting, though the faces of the staff were now more grim than anxious.

Emma went about her duties, forwarding three large sacks of mail. When the day's end came, General Poe returned, his face grave.

He said nothing, but went about issuing orders as he had done the previous night. Emma again waited for letters to carry. This time they were all to division headquarters.

She rode into Falmouth, and if she had not already suspected the truth, she had no doubt whatever now. Lacy House was ablaze with light, and a long line of wagons waited on the road outside Falmouth, filled with equipment and silent men.

She delivered her messages and returned to brigade headquarters, where General Poe dismissed her for the night. Reid had disappeared somewhere; he was neither in his office nor their tent. She took out her Bible, added wood to the fire and left the stove's door open, settling down to read by its flickering light.

Reid came in not long afterward, gave her a nod in greeting, and proceeded to climb into his bed. After a while Emma began to feel drowsy, and closed her book, setting it back beside her bed. She put another piece of wood in the stove, then shut the door, casting the tent into darkness.

"Did you write to your family?" Reid asked after a moment.

"I have none," Emma said. Truth, for all she knew.

"My parents are in Scotland."

She had no response to this, and lay thinking instead of her own parents. She wasted no sentiment on her father, but her mother she truly missed. And her sisters, and poor Thomas. She hoped they were well. She wondered if they thought her dead.

Startled awake, Emma sat up. The sun had not risen, nor had Reid. Some distant sound had waked her. She got quietly out of bed, put on her boots and coat, and left the tent.

A heavy fog lay on the ground. She stood listening for a moment, hearing indistinct noises in the distance along with the sounds of the camp stirring.

A smell of baked bread wafted from the kitchens. Emma followed it, got herself a cup of coffee and a handful of bread still hot from the oven, and went to General Poe's office. Keller was there, busy at his desk, his face set in a grim expression. The general was also present, slowly pacing in his office. Emma suspected he had not slept.

Hoofbeats approached. A courier came into the tent and handed a message to Keller. He glanced at it and at once took it into Poe's office.

The message was a summons; the brigade was to be roused and assembled, ready for battle. Emma's first errand of the day was to carry the order to the headquarters of each regiment. By the time she had returned, brigade headquarters was bustling.

The brigade moved forward into Falmouth along with the rest of the division, and fell into line before the river. Sounds of splashing water and clanking machinery issued from in front of them; the pontoon bridges were being built. Sitting her horse with the brigade staff, ready to ride courier if called upon, Emma could have no doubt that the Rebels across the river heard as well.

As dawn approached the fog began to break up. Emma glimpsed one of the bridges, half-built, then someone's gasp drew her notice to the far shore, where ranks of Rebels stood waiting. The fleeting fog concealed them again. Emma's neck prickled.

They won't make it, she realized. *There is no way the bridges can be finished before dawn.*

The next gap in the fog confirmed her fears. The Rebels opened fire on the engineers working to assemble the pontoons. She saw a man fall from the bridge into the river; another stepped forward to take his place.

From then on the musketry was more or less continuous. As the sun rose the fog faded completely, exposing the engineers working on the bridges to a murderous fire. Federal cannon opened on the sharpshooters in reply, raising a deafening roar, but the sharpshooters merely hid among the houses and continued to pick off the engineers.

At last some of the Seventh Michigan were sent across the river in boats to chase the Rebels from the town, leaving the engineers to finish their work unmolested. Within an hour the bridges were done and the army began to file across them into Fredericksburg.

By evening the town had been ravaged. As she carried a message for General Poe, Emma passed burning houses, set alight by the shelling. The smell of destruction filled her nostrils and roused a deep instinct to flee. Looking up to the Rebels entrenched on the heights above the town, she feared there would be a bitter price to pay.

Poe's brigade was assigned to the command of General Franklin and the task of guarding the lowest pontoon bridge. Returning to Poe's position, Emma found him frowning so grimly that she was moved to offer a word of comfort. "Never fear, sir. Your men will stand with you."

He glanced at her and gave a cough of laughter. "Those who are well enough to stand. Keller's come down sick. I've just sent him to the rear. Ghastly timing."

Or convenient, Emma thought, then banished the uncharitable suspicion. "May I have the honor of serving in his place, General?"

"That's good of you, Thompson. I wouldn't ask it."

"I am asking it. Please, sir. I would be honored to be at your side tomorrow."

Poe gazed at her, apparently touched. "Very well, then. You shall be my acting aide-de-camp, and God help us both."

"He will, sir," Emma said, smiling.

"You'll need a sash to wear."

"I'll find one."

She did manage to find one, asking around at division headquarters the next morning, and as she tied it around her waist she knew a fleeting wish that Damon and Captain Morse could see her. At least she would look smart today, whatever else happened.

From their position near the bridge, she could see the heights above town. Cannon fire and musketry were a constant roar, but as yet no troops ventured into the open field between the town and the fortified heights.

Emma was in the saddle constantly, carrying messages and orders back and forth between General Poe and headquarters. She closed her thoughts to the bullets that whined around her as she rode, placing her trust in God. If she had work yet to do on this earth, she would be spared to do it.

Troops began to advance on the heights, and as quickly began to fall. By noon the attack was unleashed in full force. Regiment after regiment marched across the open field, only to be slain by the murderous gunfire or the sharpshooters lying behind a stone wall at the top of the hill. Dead and wounded began to pile up on the field. Emma gritted her teeth and kept riding, thankful that her own regiment was safe for the time being at least.

Charge after charge was made on the heights, none of them coming close to the stone wall. By mid-afternoon thousands had fallen, and still the order was to charge, and charge again.

Passing by a brigade that awaited their turn to advance, Emma saw an officer shoot himself in the side, then protest it was an accident as he was carried to the rear. She felt a moment's regret that the wound was not fatal. Never before had she seen a man shoot himself in order to save the Rebels the satisfaction of doing so.

She returned to General Poe, who stood grim-faced near the bridge, watching the slaughter on the heights above. With him were some officers of the 2nd and the 20th Michigan. A sober-faced major with apple cheeks watched Emma's approach and asked her if their turn had come.

"I fear so, sir. General Sumner's division has spent itself."

There were no more brigades to be sent up that terrible

hill. She had seen the pitiful remnants of the division trying to organize.

"But we have received no orders, Major Cutcheon," added General Poe with a sidelong glance at her.

Emma bowed her head, acknowledging this mild reproof, and went away to give her horse some water. She had only spoken the truth, but she understood the general's desire to assuage the fears of his officers.

No order for advance came from General Franklin's headquarters. Poe's brigade remained in place by the bridge, guarding the means of retreat. Wounded straggled across the bridge, though in smaller numbers than at the other bridges.

In the evening, Emma accompanied Poe to General Franklin's headquarters, a rough ride over three miles of ditches, ravines, and hills. The night was bitter cold, and the moans of the wounded haunted them from the heights.

Passing a graveyard, Emma heard the voices of men raised in prayer, fortifying themselves against whatever fate would greet them come daylight. Her heart was heavy with sorrow. So many had died in the futile attempt to storm the heights. Would it be the same again tomorrow?

Dawn brought no renewal of attack, however. Instead a truce was negotiated to allow the removal of the wounded from the field. Many were beyond help—frozen during the night, and propped up to shelter the living. When she was not busy carrying messages, Emma helped move the wounded to Lacy House, which had become a hospital. Surgeons worked feverishly in every room of the elegant mansion. The generals had gathered with Burnside once more at another house, arguing what to do next.

Evening came, and with it the order to retreat quietly under cover of night. Emma nearly wept with relief, and also with sorrow for all that had been lost. She stayed in the saddle, sitting at attention beside a silent, grim-faced Poe as the Union troops filed back across the bridges, abandoning Fredericksburg.

When all had crossed, Poe's brigade followed and went back to their camps, dejected. The enormity of the defeat weighed in the silence broken only by shuffling feet and muffled hoofbeats. The night was cold again, with cruel stars glittering above.

Poe went to his office and commenced writing. Emma carried a last message to headquarters, riding back to Falmouth on the mud-torn road, then the general dismissed her for the night. She tended her weary horse and retired to Reid's tent.

Reid was there, sitting at the table with his head on his arms, the empty brandy bottle before him. Emma took off her greatcoat and hung it up. It was cold in the tent, so she opened the stove and lit a fire, staring at the new flames taking hold.

She heard Reid sit up, and glanced at him. Their gazes met and held. The look on Reid's face was awful, a look of utmost disillusionment and despair. It pierced her heart, and brought all her own feelings to the fore. She felt a tear slide down her cheek.

Brushing it away, she put more wood in the stove. Reid stood up and came around the table to squat beside her. The yellow flames lit his face and glinted on his pale hair as he held out his hands toward the heat. Long-fingered, elegant hands. Emma stared at them, glad they were intact, not torn by shot or broken or severed by the surgeon's knife.

"I thought I had seen the worst at Antietam," he said, his voice hoarse.

Emma's throat tightened. It was true; this had been the worst she had seen of the war. She thought of the thousands lying slain on the field, and shivered.

Reid put a hand on her shoulder. She started to pull away, but he drew her closer instead, holding her against his chest with his arms wrapped tight around her. Off balance, she collapsed against him, then gave into the need for comfort, feeling the tears pour down her face as she returned the embrace.

Reid gave a small, gasping sob, his hold tightening even more. Emma felt his cheek against hers, rough with stubble where hers was smooth. He smelled of sweat and mud and, faintly, of horse.

He drew back his head and gazed at her, frowning in distress. Emma tried to gulp back her tears. She sniffled, unsuccessful, and Reid raised a hand to wipe her cheek. Then, frowning even more intently, he kissed her.

Emma gasped in surprise, then had no time for more as Reid kissed her again fiercely. He knew; he must know—she was lost, but it seemed not to matter. Only his lips on hers mattered, only the fire that bloomed inside her, despair seeking release in passion.

He pulled at his own clothing, then at hers. Scrambling out of their coats on the dirt floor of the tent, they clutched at each other, kissing again and again, pausing only to deal with a button or suspender strap.

Uttering a curse of frustration, he rolled away from her and pulled off his boots, then his trousers. Emma removed hers as well, shivering with excitement more than cold as she sat in her long underwear and shirtsleeves. She knew she should not do this, but she was beyond caring, and she doubted now that he could be stopped even if she tried.

And she didn't want to try. She wanted his fire, his passion. He reached for her and she came willingly.

His hand fumbled between her thighs, sparking fear and anticipation in her. He gave a grunt of surprise and looked up at her, blue eyes staring wide. He reached a hand up inside her shirt and found her breast.

"Christ!" he whispered, his face astonished.

"I-I thought you knew," Emma said.

He shook his head, then frowning more fiercely than before, bent to kiss her again.

Emma's head reeled. She could scarce form a thought as he pulled off her clothing and dipped his head to kiss her breasts, one and then the other.

If he had not known—then he had wanted—Frank, he had wanted Frank!

His hands roamed her body, rough against her skin. His kisses were rough also, but not cruel. She returned them eagerly, shivering as he moved closer and she felt him press between her thighs.

She yielded to him, not sure what to do but willing to follow his lead. He leaned harder against her, shifting back and forth, and she felt a small, sharp pain as her flesh gave way.

He raised his head and stared at her. "Sweet Jesus!"

Emma gazed back at him, the planes of his cheek and jaw sharp in the firelight, then his face contorted and he slammed himself into her again and again. Emma closed her eyes, half-enduring, half-enjoying his savage lust.

It was over quickly, and he collapsed, gasping, his weight heavy upon her. Emma lay still, feeling trapped, yet also floating in a strange euphoria. Her body was uncomfortable in a number of ways, but they were all small and unimportant.

It was Jamie who was important now. Her lover.

He raised himself on one arm, taking some of his weight off her, to her relief. With soft eyes he gazed at her as he ran his fingers into her hair. He bent to kiss her, this time with extreme gentleness.

"You fooled us all," he whispered, smiling.

Emma smiled back, then closed her eyes. Her world had changed. She would leave it to the morning to sort out how.

When she woke, she was in her own bed, with the first faint light of dawn glowing blue against the tent's walls. Confusion was swiftly followed by memories that made her gasp in astonishment at herself. She felt flame rise to her cheeks.

Turning her head, she saw that Jamie lay in his cot, asleep. He must have put her to bed before seeking his own rest. A soft snore spoke of his contentment.

She had sinned, and now she understood sin's attraction. Lofty words and thoughts were easy until the body's imperative asserted itself. Physical needs could only be denied for so long; it appeared that this was such a need, for she felt its stirrings again as she gazed at Jamie's face.

She closed her eyes, too weary to embark upon a philosophical argument with herself. Unaccustomed aches reminded her of her sin, and warned of a new danger to be guarded against: pregnancy.

The thought made her angry; not with Jamie, but with herself, for taking the risk. She had sworn that she would never be the drudge her mother had been, never subject herself to a husband's authority.

Well, Jamie was a husband, but he was not *her* husband. She would not allow him to dominate her.

And Jamie's Mary must never know. She would not wound that lady if she could avoid it.

If she became pregnant, she would deal with it somehow. There were means; during her time in the hospital she had more than once received visits from women requesting certain herbs. She hoped it would not come to that, for it was a terrible choice to make.

Jamie stirred. She turned on her side, the better to watch him.

In sleep his face was peaceful, sweet as a child's. A shock of sandy hair had fallen across his eyes, and she wanted to reach out and smooth it back.

She felt a warmth for him stir in her heart. He was wild, impulsive, and (she suspected) not very devout, yet she was fond of him. She was one of the few who had seen his gentler side: the Jamie who doubted, who knew fear.

How would they go forward now? Impossible to continue exactly as they had been.

A clatter out in the camp startled her, making her glance toward the door. Voices were raised briefly in dispute, then subsided. The kitchen crew, she thought. At work preparing their breakfast.

Looking at Jamie, she saw that the noise had waked him. He smiled back at her, then stretched luxuriously. His blanket slipped down, revealing his bare chest. Emma felt a glimmer of heat in her gut.

"Well, my dear," he said in a voice she could just hear, "do you care to tell me your name?"

A tingle of fear went through her. Only Jerome knew her name. But Jerome was far away, and Jamie was waiting.

"Emma," she whispered.

He smiled. "And what led you to enlist?"

"I wanted to serve my country."

"Your adopted country."

"Yes."

He propped his head on his elbow, lazy, almond-like eyes watching her. "It must have been difficult to arrange."

She swallowed. "Not as difficult as you might think."

"Oh?"

"I will tell you, some time, but now I have a question for you."

He gave a nod, inviting her to continue.

"Last night..."

He waited, his gaze unblinking, a hint of a smile on his lips. Emma swallowed.

"I am wondering about your interest in a young private."

"Ah." His eyes narrowed. "Yes, I knew you must wonder about that. You need only think a little and you will find the answer."

He sat up and reached for his shirt. Emma watched him pull it on, watched him hunt down his trousers in the heap of clothing on the floor.

"These are yours," he said, tossing her trousers to her.

"Jamie—"

"Still thinking?"

"Jamie, you are married. Why...?"

"Thousands of men, far from home and family. Men with desires that do not diminish. I personally prefer not to seek solace among the camp followers."

"Oh, no! They are ridden with disease!"

"Yes. But a fair young private..."

Emma's cheeks burned afresh. She caught up her undershirt and put it on, then reached down to pull her long underwear from the pile.

Jamie, a sodomite? Was that a greater sin than the one they had committed together?

Fidelity mattered little to him, it seemed. But then, it mattered little to a great many men. How many others would seek the alternative he spoke of?

Her mind was reeling.

"It's more common than you think," he said, sliding his suspenders onto his shoulders.

He was assuming the guise of Lieutenant Reid. How on earth was she supposed to behave toward him?

Jamie stood and came to her, picking her shirt off the floor and inspecting it with a frown. "Have you a clean one? I fear this is rather spoiled, and one of the buttons is loose."

Emma took the shirt and held it to her chest. Confusion, doubt, and dread conspired to render her speechless. She felt very small.

Her blanket shifted as he sat beside her. She stared at the stove, unwilling to meet his gaze.

"I should not need to tell you," he said softly, his warm breath brushing her ear, "that I much prefer an Emma to a Frank."

She swallowed.

"And you need not fear that I will betray you. I had far rather keep you to myself."

She looked at him, then. He smiled, then took her breath away with a sudden kiss. His arm slid behind her, supporting and embracing her. He smiled again as he released her, then rose and reached for his boots.

"We'd best get a move on. Don't want to be late for breakfast."

Emma was accustomed to living a double life, but this new one was the strangest yet. Inside the tent she shared with Jamie was a haven of warmth and silent tenderness. Outside, the cold stabbed at her and the bitter losses of the army's defeat returned to weigh on her heart, reflected in the sad faces at every hand.

Lieutenant Reid was carelessly friendly to her in public, though now and then a glance spoke more than others knew.

She had no doubt of his affection for herself, for he showed no hesitation. Jamie was a generous lover; in their tent he taught her new sensations every night, and roused feelings in her she had never imagined.

There were worries. At first she feared he would betray her somehow, either deliberately or accidentally, but as the days passed she grew more confident.

That she must share him, she accepted as fact and privately regretted on many levels. She wished no harm to the faceless Mary back in New York. She felt badly about wronging her, but she was certain that if she had not become Jamie's lover, someone else would have.

Jamie never spoke of his wife, and Emma thought it was not her place to raise the subject. She occasionally encountered a letter addressed to him from New York, in a feminine hand. She always left them on his bed, as she did the rest of his mail.

She struggled daily with her conscience. She knew what she was doing was wrong, but she also knew a greater happiness than she had ever felt before. It was a quandary she could not resolve.

She had another, more pragmatic worry. The possibility of pregnancy. Earlier in the year a corporal in a regiment stationed not far from the Second had fallen ill while on picket duty, the illness proving to be labor of childbirth. That woman had been treated kindly by her comrades in arms, and sent home to her parents with her new baby. Emma had no home to go to.

Riding, she had heard, was dangerous for a woman who might be in a delicate condition. She rode every day in the course of her duties, and made sure to ride very hard indeed.

As a last resort, she could go to the hospital and find among the supplies there what would end an unwanted pregnancy. Only this knowledge kept her from fretting herself into a frenzy.

The army remained in camp on the Rappahannock, licking its wounds as the winter's cold deepened. Emma dealt with mail and ran errands for General Poe, and spent a good deal of her spare time in the hospitals.

Gradually the anguish of Fredericksburg receded to a dull sorrow, though the Northern press was full of wailing and woe. General Burnside was cursed by his men, yet Washington sent no new commander to replace him.

A few days after the battle Emma came into Poe's office with the general's mail. Keller was still sick abed, and she now shared his duties with a clerk, Sergeant Covington, who glanced up as she came in.

"Someone was looking for you earlier," Covington said.

Emma handed him a stack of letters. "Who?"

"A private. Didn't give his name. Said he knew you from the Second Michigan."

"I know dozens of privates in the Second. What did he look like?"

Covington shrugged, uninterested. Emma gave up the lost cause and went into the general's office.

An hour later she rode down to the Second's camp with their mail. She no longer distributed it herself, but gave each company's mail to their commander, as she did with the other regiments of the brigade. She had just dismounted before Captain May's tent and was digging I Company's mail out of her satchel when she heard a familiar voice.

"Frank!"

Turning, she gasped in astonishment. "Jerome!"

Jerome smiled broadly and held out his hand. Emma put hers into it. He shook hands warmly, clapping her on the back.

"You've been exchanged at last!" she said, marveling at how well he looked.

He nodded. "All of us who were captured at the hospital. I thought of writing, then decided I would reach you faster than any letter."

Emma laughed. "Yes, I sent one to you at Camp Parole. It is probably trying to find you."

"Well, I shall look forward to receiving it eventually."

"Don't, it's quite gloomy. I wrote it the night before Fredericksburg."

Jerome's face became serious. "We heard about the battle when we reached Aquia. I was worried for you."

Touched, Emma smiled. "Well, I'm fine as you can see. Oh, Jerome, it is so good to have you back!"

Captain May had come out of his tent, and Emma hastened to hand him the mail for his company. He glanced at Jerome, then began looking through the mail.

Reminded of her duty, Emma caught Jerome's arm. "I must finish my rounds. Will you walk with me?"

"Of course. I hear you've moved up in the world."

Emma laughed as she started up the street with him, leading her horse by the reins. "Yes. Oh, it must have been you who asked for me at headquarters earlier."

"Yes, I've been looking for you since yesterday."

"Well, I am in the saddle a great deal."

"How is your leg?"

Emma glanced at him, wondering if she had been limping. She scarcely noticed her injury any more, except when the cold made it ache, or when she was very tired.

"Much better, thank you."

"I am glad. I have prayed for you often."

Emma felt her cheeks grow warm. "And I for you, Jerome."

Not often enough, lately. Since Fredericksburg, she had not shown her face at a prayer meeting. She felt the prick of conscience more sharply than ever.

227

Jerome walked with her through the rest of the Second's camp, then up to Burnside's headquarters to collect the next shipment of mail. They chatted and debated as if they had never been separated, or indeed, never at odds, and Emma felt a quiet joy in the return of her dear friend.

They came back to brigade headquarters and Emma proudly showed Jerome her office, which he duly admired. He offered to help her sort the mail.

"Ah—I know what you want," she said, grinning. "You want to look for a sample of Miss Corey's handwriting!"

Jerome stiffened. "No, indeed. I only wished to be of help."

Emma felt badly for teasing him, though she had only meant it in fun. Recalling her former bitterness over Miss Corey, she realized that now she felt none of it. She wished him joy of her—and sincerely wished that Miss Corey might return his regard, since that would please him.

She emptied the mail onto her table and began to sort it, keeping her eyes on the letters. "Did she not write to you at Camp Parole?"

"A few times."

He said no more and she did not press him. Instead she talked of the army's disgust with their commander, and asked if he had heard any news in Aquia.

"Nothing concrete. I think Lincoln doesn't know who to give the command to next."

"He won't give it to McClellan."

"I fear not."

"My fear is that he will find someone even worse than Burnside."

"God forbid."

They finished sorting the mail and packed it away ready for delivery in the morning. Emma looked at her watch and realized they had missed the dinner mess.

"Eight o'clock! You must be starving! Why did you not say something?"

Jerome smiled. "Is it that late? I hadn't noticed."

"Come on, we can scrounge a bite to eat from the kitchen. I know the cooks."

"Frank always knows the cooks!"

Emma grinned. "Well, I bring them little things from town when I'm sent with dispatches. You'd be surprised what a cook will do for a couple of lemons! Come along!"

She led him from her office toward the brigade's mess tent, pulling her overcoat tight against the cold. Jerome's greatcoat looked new; he must have been issued a new kit upon his return.

The frozen mud crunched beneath their feet as they hurried toward the lighted mess tent. Emma pulled aside the door flap and nearly collided with Jamie, who was coming out.

"Oh!" she said, falling back.

"Well, come in, don't stand in the cold!" Jamie said, grabbing hold of the flap. "I've been looking for you."

Suddenly nervous, Emma stepped inside and gestured for Jerome to join her. Jamie looked at him, then turned an inquiring gaze to Emma, his brows drawing together in a frown.

Emma cleared her throat. "This is my friend, Jerome Robbins. He has just lately arrived from Camp Parole. Jerome, this is Lieutenant James Reid."

Jamie's gaze shifted to Jerome and narrowed. With trepidation Emma sensed his gathering anger, then he suddenly clicked into cool formality and extended a hand to Jerome.

"How do you do? I've heard a great deal about you."

"Have you?" Jerome glanced uncertainly at Emma, then shook hands. "How do you do?"

Jamie gave him a perfunctory smile, dropped his hand, and turned to Emma. "The general wants you," he said, eyelids drooping lazily.

"Oh. Right away?"

"I imagine so."

Jamie's tone was sardonic, which Emma knew implied a dangerous mood. She turned to Jerome.

"I'm sorry—"

"Not at all," Jerome said hastily, taking a step backward toward the door. "I'm glad we had as much time together as we did. I will see you tomorrow."

"Yes." She smiled. "Good night, Jerome. Be careful walking back."

He nodded and waved farewell, then disappeared into the darkness. She took a step after him. Behind her, Jamie let the canvas fall, shutting away the warmth of the mess tent.

"How long has he been here?"

She looked back at Jamie, silhouetted against the lighted canvas. "Since yesterday, but I only met him late this afternoon."

"What a joyful reunion that must have been."

"Yes it was," Emma said, biting back her annoyance at his tone. "He is a dear friend."

She stared at the darkness that was Jamie, unable to make out his face. After a moment he brushed past her.

"Best get to Poe's office. He's waiting."

With that he was gone, striding into the night. Emma pressed her lips together and hastened to do his bidding.

General Poe wished her to carry a message to division headquarters. By the time she returned, her stomach was growling with hunger, but the mess tent was dark. She looked after her horse and headed for her tent, thinking she would make do with some apples she had in her haversack.

Jamie was there, sitting before the open stove with a bottle in one hand and a glass in the other. Whiskey, it smelled like. Emma wrinkled her nose, then quietly took off her greatcoat.

"So, the prodigal returns," Jamie said, lifting his glass without looking at her.

Emma sat on her bed and began to unlace her boots. "Do you mean me, or Jerome?"

"Both." He laughed, rather nastily, emptied the glass and refilled it.

Emma quietly took off her boots, then reached for her haversack. She got out an apple and bit into it.

"Hungry, are we?"

She could hear the anger in his voice, behind the laziness. She swallowed, apple skin catching in her throat.

"I missed supper."

"Yes, you did."

"We were talking. Jerome helped me with the mail."

"Very helpful indeed, your Jerome."

"Jamie—"

He turned his head, spitting the words. "What else did he help you with?"

"Nothing. He's a friend."

"Oh, aye, that I know! You canna stop talking about him!"

His eyes flashed, and Emma glanced fearfully toward the neighboring tents, mere layers of canvas away. He understood, for he put down his bottle and glass and stood up, seizing her by the shoulders and hauling her to her feet.

"I was tired of him before ever I met him," Jamie hissed in her ear.

"Please—"

"Was he your lover? Is he?"

"No! You know he isn't!" she whispered angrily.

He stared at her, scowling, breathing whiskey fumes into her face. Emma realized she was trembling, which made her even more furious than Jamie's behavior. At last he eased his grip on her shoulders.

"He knows, though."

Emma swallowed. "Yes."

He turned from her, knocking over his glass with a foot, spilling whiskey on the floor. He snatched up the glass and bottle, and for a moment Emma feared he would hurl them into the stove, but instead he set them on the shelf.

His hand was shaking, Emma saw. Rage, or fear, she wondered? Perhaps both.

"Jamie—"

"How does he know?"

His back was to her. She saw the tension in his shoulders, and longed to rub it away.

"I told him."

A pause. "Why?"

Emma closed her eyes. "For a very foolish reason."

She heard Jamie turn, and opened her eyes. He was staring at her, mutely demanding explanation. She went over to his chest and sat on it. After a moment he sank down beside her.

"I was jealous of a young lady he was writing to," she said quietly.

Jamie let out a crack of hard laughter. "You thought to supplant her in his affections."

"I suppose so. I said it was foolish. I never had any chance of that."

He seemed mollified. Emma sensed the anger drain from him, though he still frowned as he gazed at her. She knew this frown; it was need, not wrath. She touched his hand, and just that quick he caught her to him, kissing her all over her face.

"I'll not share you with him," he said roughly.

Emma put her hands against his chest and gently pushed away until she could look up at him. "I must see him, though."

He scowled. It was jealousy; she ought to be flattered.

"Jerome does not know about us," she added, "and I don't mean to tell him, but he will think it strange if I refuse to spend time with him. May I not see my friend?"

Jamie stared at her, his brows still knit. "If you swear that's all it is."

"I swear it, Jamie," she whispered as his arms closed

around her. "I swear."

She did see Jerome, at least once every day, for he was always in camp when she came with the Second's mail, and he always accompanied her in making her rounds. He seemed rather intimidated by Jamie and was astonished to learn he was her tentmate, but she coaxed him to visit her at home one evening when she knew Jamie would be there.

Initial stiffness between them gave way as conversation revealed their mutual interests, particularly in Washington's policies and the future leadership of the Army of the Potomac. By the end of the evening she had the satisfaction of knowing that each of them had risen in the other's esteem.

On Christmas Eve, Jamie wanted to host a celebration in their quarters. He invited a select group of his friends, some from the headquarters staff, several others officers in the 79th New York. Out of courtesy he insisted that Emma invite Jerome, but she was not surprised when the invitation was declined.

"Chaplain Brown is holding a midnight prayer service," Jerome said quietly. "I thought you might like to attend with me."

Emma hitched her near-empty mail satchel up on her shoulder as they walked to K Company's street. "I would like to, but I doubt I can get away. I ought to stay and play host."

"To a party of officers?" Jerome gazed at her in his uncompromising way. "They are not your friends, Frank."

She shrugged. "Some of them are. Anyway, I should be there."

"Well. In case I don't see you, have a Merry Christmas."

He held out his hand, and Emma clasped it warmly. "Merry Christmas, Jerome."

She watched him walk away, back to his own camp. A drizzle of rain began, and Emma hastened to make her last delivery and hurry back to headquarters. She went to the kitchens, where preparations for the morrow's Christmas dinner were already underway.

"Bennett," she called to a cook, staying in the doorway to keep out of the way.

Bennett, a stout fellow whose face was perpetually flushed, hastened over to her, dusting flour from his hands. "Hallo, Frank."

"Is my pudding ready?"

"Steaming on the stove, next to the coffee. You can take it whenever you like."

"I'll take it now, if you don't mind."

"Don't you want to keep it hot?"

"Yes—may I not take the pot?"

Bennett frowned and glanced sidelong at his fellow cooks. None seemed interested in their conversation.

"All right, if you bring it back before morning. We'll need every spoon for tomorrow."

"Thank you! I'll bring it back promptly, I promise!"

Bennett fetched her the pot, and Emma used the sleeves of her greatcoat to keep it from burning her hands as she carefully carried it to her tent. She deposited the pot atop the stove, which was just large enough to support it.

"What's that?" Jamie asked.

"The surprise I promised you. Christmas pudding."

She lifted the lid and looked in. A bundle of cloth swathed the pudding tin, which rested atop an empty tin can in a pool of hot water. The aroma of savory spices rose up with the steam, overlaying the sharp evergreen scent of the boughs with which Jamie had decorated the tent. Emma smiled. At least it smelled like Christmas.

Jamie peered into the pot over her shoulder. "Ha! You must have bribed the cooks a pretty penny."

She closed the lid. "I made a good negotiation. You're welcome."

"Thank you, Frank."

He caught her by the elbows and pulled her toward him, grinning, but with guests soon to arrive they dared not indulge in such play. Emma gently pulled away and took off her greatcoat, while Jamie returned to straightening the wine glasses arrayed on the table, borrowed and scrounged for the occasion.

Beside them stood a dozen bottles of wine and champagne, a basket of fresh bread, a plate of sliced sausages and a round of cheese. The repast had cost Jamie a week's pay.

Before long the guests started arriving. Emma welcomed

the headquarters folk, and watched Jamie joyfully greet his friends of the 79th, who arrived all together carrying more bottles and singing a ribald song.

Emma was slightly acquainted with them from having delivered their mail, but the names went by too swiftly for her to retain them all, and there were too many "Mc"s to keep straight. They all spoke with a Scottish burr far more pronounced than Jamie's. She guessed that it was a point of pride among the Highlanders.

Emma watched them make themselves at home on her bed and in the chairs she had gathered for the occasion. She sat on an upended cracker box in one corner and tried to have a conversation with two of the headquarters fellows, but as the wine and whiskey began to flow the noise in the tent made it almost impossible to hear one's own voice, let alone another's.

Her instinct among such company was to stand back and observe. She fended off frequent offers of drink, and watched Jamie, glad that he was happy. He traded outrageous stories with his friends, and occasionally they broke into song, more and more often as the evening wore on.

When the cheese and the sausages had been eaten, Emma judged it time to serve the pudding. She had listened to Bennett's instructions for unmolding it, and decided to take less care than that, since she made it a point never to demonstrate competence in cooking matters. Consequently, the pudding emerged somewhat lopsided and broken, but no one complained. One of the Scots broke into a song about Christmas pudding, and was joined by the others, who quickly fell to making up verses of their own, each a tribute to some officer of the brigade.

Emma collected the pan with its lid and the pudding tin, and quietly slipped out to carry them back to the kitchens. She did not see Bennett, though a couple of bakers were busy at long, flour-covered tables. She left the pan on another table and went back outside.

The night was clear and cold, the sky bristling with stars. Emma thought of that Christmas star that was a sign from heaven, and smiled. Disinclined to return to the tent, and quite certain she would not be missed, she turned her steps instead to the camp of the Second Michigan.

Chaplain Brown's tent was as crowded as Emma and Jamie's own, though far more quiet. Jerome saw Emma step in and smiled, offering with a gesture to make room for her on the chest on which he sat.

The chaplain smiled, too, though he did not pause in his reading. Emma sat down and breathed a small sigh of relief, finding this company far more congenial than that in her tent.

Inevitably, as she listened and prayed, she thought of her sins and regretted them. She was deceiving herself, living with Jamie. There could be no hope for a union between them. They were too different, he with his decadent pleasures and she with her hope of devotion.

She was weak, to remain with him. Weak and a sinner, yielding to temptations of the flesh. She should leave, but to leave would take greater courage than she could muster.

Jamie was powerful—he could ruin her. He need not even denounce her to do it; a word or two to General Poe and a few others, a mere hint of her implied incompetence or dishonesty, and he could completely destroy her position.

Perhaps it would not be so bad, to return to being a private soldier. Even as the thought occurred, she knew she would hate it. The freedom of being postmaster gave her many advantages, not the least of which was the avoidance of living in close quarters with men who might discover her.

Halsted and the others would welcome her back, of course, and she knew she would be safe with them. The thought gave her no comfort, though.

Perhaps the deception she practiced was an even greater sin than her affair with Jamie. The deception, after all, had led to the rest. Yet she had entered into it with pure intentions, had enlisted with pure intentions. Where had she gone astray?

The meeting ended with singing. Emma joined in softly; her singing voice did not bear scrutiny, but she wanted to participate in the hymn. Feeling somewhat less burdened by guilt, she resolved to try, at least, to find a resolution to her situation.

The hymn ended, the meeting broke up. Emma waited her turn to shake hands with the chaplain.

"Thank you for coming, Frank. It's good to see you here."

"Thank you, sir. I have missed these meetings. I will come again soon."

She left with Jerome, talking in soft voices as they walked slowly through the streets of camp to his tent. Jerome's mood was pensive, and she had her own problems to ponder, problems that she could not share with him.

She still loved Jerome with all her heart, but she saw him a little differently now. There were moments when she could imagine seducing him, but these were only idle thoughts. She would not add that to her catalogue of sins.

"I am glad you came to the meeting," he said, stopping outside of his tent. "How did you get away?"

"Oh, I wasn't missed. It was quite a noisy affair. Is, I should say—I am sure it is still going on."

Jerome glanced at his tent as if wishing he could invite her in. He had tentmates, though, and the hour was late. Emma smiled and offered her hand.

"Well, good night, then. Merry Christmas."

"Merry Christmas, Frank."

He shook her hand and held onto it, gazing at her with what she thought was earnest concern. Emma felt a small flutter in her heart. She knew it was folly, but she could not help her feelings.

"I hope we can talk again soon," Jerome said.

Emma nodded. "Yes, I would like that. Perhaps you can come with me on my rounds."

"But I already do that!"

Emma grinned. "I mean all of my rounds. You'll need a horse."

She bade him farewell and walked back up to head-quarters. It was deepest night, now—late enough that there was no singing or revelry, early enough that only the bakers were awake. The camp was quiet, even her own tent as she approached it issued no sounds except snoring.

She went in quietly and discovered the source of the snoring—a large Highlander, stretched out on her bed. Another was asleep in a chair with his head on the table amid a clutter of bottles and glasses. Jamie lay face down on his cot with one arm draping down to the floor. His head was turned sideways and his face, in the quiet of sleep, looked like a young boy's.

Emma opened the stove, stirred the embers into life, and added wood. She sat for a while, thinking over the evening, then said a silent prayer, curled up in her greatcoat before the fire, and went to sleep.

Jamie was slow to rise the next morning. Emma brought him coffee, which he sipped sitting up in bed, bleary-eyed. The Highlander was still snoring on her bed. She left Jamie to recuperate at his own pace from an evening which he assured her was most enjoyable, and rode up to army headquarters to see if there was mail.

She was not obligated to work on Christmas, but she knew that a letter or a package from loved ones would be especially welcome today, and it gave her pleasure to be the source of such cheer. The day was brisk and with little traffic to hinder her, she retrieved the mail, sorted it, and had all delivered before the headquarters mess was summoned to Christmas dinner.

Returning to their tent, she found Jamie putting the wine glasses into the basket that had held the bread. The Highlander was gone, and though the tent was rather a shambles, at least it was their own again.

"You have a letter," Emma said, holding it out to him.

It was a New York, feminine hand letter. Jamie took it, glanced at it, and set it on the shelf, then pulled Emma into his arms.

"You left last night," he said, kissing her ear. "Where did you go?"

"To a prayer meeting."

"Be serious."

"I am serious. You can ask Chaplain Brown of the Second if you do not believe me."

He leaned back and gazed at her, frowning slightly. "Of course I believe you."

"I am a Christian," she said.

"We're all Christians."

He kissed her, lighting desire within her, and also trouble in her heart. She tried to pull away.

"Jamie—"

He pulled her back sharply, kissing her face, her throat. "You go to a prayer meeting and now you don't want me, is that it?" he whispered hoarsely.

She closed her eyes, dizzy with wanting him. "Jamie, please. They'll be calling us to dinner."

He let her go abruptly and turned away, returning to the wine glasses. Bereft, Emma stood watching him for a moment, then bent to pick up a glass that was on the floor by the stove. Jamie took it from her with a smile that was brief, but lifted her heart. He cared for her; he was not angry. It was enough.

Soon the summons to dinner was heard, and they walked to the headquarters mess together. The mess tent was bedecked with evergreens, and the labors of the cooks were duly appreciated by all. Turkey and chicken, both rare treats for the army, were served in abundance, along with potatoes, carrots, and applesauce. General Poe had provided wine for the celebration, and many a toast was drunk.

It was well into evening by the time Emma and Jamie returned to their tent. Jamie's spirits were cheerful, to her relief.

"The officers of the 79th are hosting a party this evening," he told her. "Shall we go?"

Emma hesitated. "You go, Jamie."

"Won't you come with me?"

"Will it be like last night?" She gestured to the mess still remaining in the tent.

He grinned. "Probably."

"Then I'd rather not. I'm sorry, Jamie. It isn't fun for me."

"Why? You have a wonderful sense of fun!" He caught her by the waist, spun them both around, and kissed her.

"It's just—a little too wild for me, is all."

"You'd rather stay home and pray?"

"Jamie—"

"I'm sorry. All right, you needn't go."

He pulled her close, holding her tenderly, kissing her with slow softness, rousing her feelings as he knew so well how to do. Emma closed her eyes, giving in. She would always give in to him, she knew.

"Are you planning to see Jerome instead?" he breathed into her ear.

"I might. Does that bother you?"

"In a word, yes."

His grip tightened, his kisses deepened. He caught her up and carried her to his cot, pushing aside the tangled blankets. He claimed her there, playing her desires as a master musician played his tune, making her forget everything but his touch.

Some time later, Jamie got up and pulled on his clothes. Emma lay watching him move about the tent in near-darkness. He had a silent grace that she always admired.

He was preparing to leave, she realized. Going to his party with the 79th. She felt sad, as if some failing of her own had caused this, though she knew that was untrue.

Jamie came to the bed and sat beside her. "I have something for you."

He folded her hands around a small, heavy package wrapped in paper and string. Emma sat up, untying the string while Jamie kissed her shoulders and got in her way. Laughing, she pulled away the paper from a book. She could not see it well, but she knew by touch that it was a book of quality, the binding of leather with raised gilt lettering, the pages cut square and gilt-edged.

"It's beautiful."

Jamie chuckled. "You can't even see it."

"It's still beautiful. What is it?"

"Robert Burns. I know you enjoy poetry."

"I do indeed. Thank you!"

He kissed her. "Merry Christmas."

She threw her arms around him and returned the kiss, then scrambled up. "I have a gift for you, too."

She knelt beside her bed, moved aside an empty bottle, and pulled out her old cracker-box desk, which now served as her storage chest. Beneath her writing paper and a stack of magazines was a small jar wrapped in cloth. She brought it out and gave it to Jamie.

"I won't try to guess," he said, sliding an arm around her waist. "What is it?"

"Brandied cherries."

"Mmm." He kissed her. "Will you share them with me?"

She laughed softly. "I might have one."

"I'll make you want more."

He pulled her close and kissed her thoroughly, then let go and stood up. He put the jar on the shelf.

"We'll save them for later."

Emma watched him put on his greatcoat and pick up a bottle of wine. He must have obtained it during the day, for last night every bottle in the tent had been consumed. Her spirits sank a little.

"Sure you don't want to come along?" Jamie asked.

"I'm sure. Enjoy yourself."

"Thank you, I will."

He went out, leaving her alone in the cold and dark. Shivering, she got into her clothes and hastened to build up the fire. She lit candles as well, excusing the extravagance because it was Christmas.

With the tent warm and lit, she felt better. She did not wish to go out, though. Instead she tidied as much of the mess as she could, then sat down to enjoy her new book.

Jamie wouldn't get up at all the next morning. She knew he had come in very late, for his shuffling step had awakened her, but they hadn't spoken. She breakfasted alone in the mess tent and brought him back a cup of coffee, but he only groaned and turned his head away.

"I'm sick."

Emma felt his brow. It was a little warm, but she suspected the cause was not illness, exactly.

"Stay and get well, then. May I borrow your horse?"

"Hnh?"

"Jerome has offered to ride with me on my rounds."

"Unh."

Taking this for assent, she left him to enjoy the fruits of his excesses, and led his horse down to the Second's camp. Jerome greeted her with pleasure and accepted her invitation to ride to army headquarters. He stood back before mounting, admiring the bay.

"That is a splendid animal!"

"It's Lieutenant Reid's."

"Won't he want it today?"

Emma shook her head. "He's ill."

"I am sorry for him. Are you sure you would rather not take care of him?"

"I would, but the mail must be delivered," she said. "I'm not a nurse, now. He'll be all right."

They rode up to headquarters, chatting companionably. She was always comfortable with Jerome, she reflected, a thing she could not say about Jamie. Jerome confided that he was thinking more seriously of studying medicine, which she approved. His friend Dr. Clelland had offered to help him, and Dr. Bonine, now the brigade surgeon, had also given his support.

Returning to Emma's office, they sat across from one another at her work table and set themselves to sorting a mail that was rather heavy with belated Christmas greetings. She found such a letter addressed to herself, in Miss Daphne's hand, and tucked it into her pocket. A short time later she encountered another familiar hand.

"Jerome."

He glanced up from the stack he was sorting. "Yes?"

Emma smiled as she handed him the letter. His face lit as he recognized Miss Corey's writing. His hand moved to open it, then hesitated.

Emma stood up. "It's chilly. Why don't I go fetch us some coffee?"

His cheeks colored slightly as he smiled. "Thank you. That would be excellent."

She smiled back, and left him to enjoy his letter in private. On her way to the mess tent she stopped to look in on Jamie. He was still in bed, and she slipped away without disturbing him.

She idled in the mess tent, chatting with Bennett until she deemed she'd given Jerome had enough time to read his letter twice through. Returning with two steaming cups of coffee, she found him standing outside the office.

"Getting a breath of air?"

He nodded. "Admiring the sky."

Emma glanced at the gray overcast. Only a man in love could find anything to admire in it, she decided. She handed him a cup of coffee and went inside, and he followed.

"I trust Miss Corey is well?" she said, smiling as they sat down at the table.

"Yes, quite well."

"I am glad for you."

He glanced at her, looking doubtful. Emma laid her hand over his.

"I mean that most sincerely," she said.

Jerome looked at her hand. She withdrew it, wrapping it around her tin cup instead.

"If I had met you some years ago I might have been much happier now," she said, and a little thrill of fear went through her. She had not been so open with him on this subject in many months—since their disagreement in fact.

"But Providence has ordered it otherwise," she added, seeing the trouble in his face. "Jerome, I would not change now if I could. I do not love you less because you love another, but rather more, for your nobleness of character, displayed in your love for her. May God make her worthy of so good a husband."

Jerome glanced up sharply. "I have not asked her to be my wife."

Emma sipped her coffee. "Well, why don't you?"

His eyes lit with exultation. "Do you think I should?"

"Oh, Jerome!" She laughed, set down her cup, and reached for a stack of mail. "If you do not, the angels will weep in heaven."

He was silent for a few minutes. Emma sorted mail, pleased that she had at last been able to tell him, without awkwardness, that she approved of his courtship. She sensed his gaze on her and looked up.

"You have changed," he said, a thoughtful expression on his face.

"For the better, I hope."

Jerome only smiled—a bemused smile, one that sent a small chill across her shoulders—and picked up a handful of mail.

Lebanon, Kentucky, 1863

The New Year brought changes at last. Burnside, after one disastrous wallow in the mud, was at last removed and command of the army given to Joseph Hooker. Poe's brigade returned to the Peninsula, then was abruptly transferred to the Army of the Cumberland and sent to Kentucky. General Grant had his eye on Vicksburg, and the President had given his support to the cause.

Emma's life continued much as it had been, though a persistent cough troubled her. The climate was sultry, and the taste of metal on her tongue informed her that malaria hovered, seeking weakness in her by which it might strike again. She asked her friends on the hospital staff for some quinine, and took care to get plenty of rest.

She walked a strange path, trying to balance between her faith and her actions. She and Jamie had their differences, more often than not over Jerome despite her protests that their friendship was innocent. The differences were always made up, though, and she could not tear herself away from Jamie.

He received more and more letters in his wife's spidery hand. He read them and put them away, never commenting. He answered at least some of them, Emma knew, though he never gave his outgoing mail into her hands. She glimpsed his letters occasionally as she picked up the headquarters mail bag.

One afternoon late in March, not long after the brigade's arrival in Kentucky, she came into their tent after making their rounds, and found Jamie sitting on his cot with a letter dangling from his hands. It was from his wife; she had left it on his bed before delivering the rest of the mail. His frown told her it could not be good news.

She swallowed as she took off her greatcoat, fearing the import of Jamie's silence. He had not moved. She sat down on her own bed and waited.

At last he rubbed a hand over his face. "My father-in-law has died."

Remembering the elegant gentleman at Willard's, Emma

knew a pang of sadness. "I am sorry."

"I think I shall have to go to New York."

Shock kept her silent. Apparently she had deceived herself, despite knowing better, into believing that their idyll might last forever.

He set the letter aside and put his head in his hands. Emma didn't know whether she should try to comfort him.

"I'll ask for a furlough," he said.

"The General isn't granting furloughs, I thought."

"Only in extreme cases of need, and this is one. My wife is ill."

She knew this; Mary had been ill forever it seemed. Feeling an uncharitable anger toward her, Emma stood up and went to the stove. She could not raise a spark from the ashes it held, so she busied herself kindling a new fire, coughing a little as she inhaled the disturbed ash. Jamie watched her in silence.

She wanted to ask when he meant to go, when he would be back, but she was afraid. She was also angry, an unjustifiable anger, a hard knot in her chest. She knew she could not safely discuss his intentions, so she kept silent.

Jamie said nothing more on the subject. That night, he held her tightly, touched her passionately, kissed every inch of her, all in silence. Emma returned his kisses, choking back tears.

The next day another letter came from New York. Emma wanted to throw it in the fire, but instead she brought it back to the tent, and since Jamie was there she handed it to him. Unable to bear what it might contain, she left, riding her rounds with a heavy heart. She went to the general's office on her return, to see if he had any errands for her.

"Yes, I do, Thompson," he said, glancing up from his desk. "Sit down a minute."

She sat, waiting for him to finish a letter. A dispatch pouch sat waiting on the corner of his desk. The general finished writing and sealed his letter, sliding it into the pouch before tying it shut and handing it to Emma.

"Sad news about Jamie," he said. "He had a brilliant career ahead of him."

Emma stared at him, frowning. "What do you mean?"

"Didn't he tell you? He's resigned his commission. His

letter's in there, with the others. Has to take his wife back to Scotland. She's ill, you know."

Emma felt as if the world had tilted beneath her.

"Yes, I know," she said faintly.

She managed to get out of the office without disgracing herself, though General Poe looked at her a little oddly. She rode hard for headquarters, only slowing for the sake of the horse. The pouch she carried burned in her heart, and she had wild thoughts of throwing it into the river, then jumping in after it.

She was too much a creature of duty, however. She delivered the dispatches and returned to camp at a more modest pace, too numb to be angry. After tending her horse she went to her tent. Jamie was there, pacing. He turned as she came in.

"Thompson. I—I must tell you—"

"General Poe told me."

"Oh."

They stood staring at each other. Emma felt the tears she had held back all day rising. She couldn't fight them any more.

"Why?" she said. "Why resign? You spoke of taking a furlough—"

"General Poe refused. You were right."

"But when you explained—"

"He is not in a position to grant them, he told me. I had no choice—I have to go."

She stood staring, tears running down her face. Jamie came toward her, drew her to him.

"Emma, I'm sorry," he whispered.

"No!"

She pulled away, gasping, and ran from the tent, wiping at her face as she fled. Wishing to avoid others, she went into the woods and walked there until she was calmer. She remembered being lost in the Chickahominy swamp, and laughed bitterly at herself, the laughter turning to a fit of coughing. She was just as lost now as she had been then, not in flesh, but in her soul.

She came out of the woods, finding herself near the Second's camp. She thought of seeking Jerome, then the chaplain, but decided neither could help her. In the end, she returned to her tent. Jamie was not there, nor did he return that evening. She lay alone, fevered and unable to sleep, and by morning she felt truly ill.

She saw little of Jamie for the next few days. He spent his nights elsewhere—in the 79th's camp, she learned from a comment she heard there while delivering mail—though his things remained in their tent.

She went about her duties in a haze of numbness, and lay at night tossing in her bed, unable to rest. Jerome noticed her heavy-eyed appearance and commented upon it. She told him she thought she was suffering a relapse of malaria, and spent her spare hours in her tent.

One day a shell burst in camp just outside her tent, killing and wounding several soldiers nearby, and sending fragments of shell and a cloud of smoke into the tent. A freakish accident, and it broke Emma's spirit. She wept inconsolably, for hours at a time. For two days she was unable to deliver the mail.

On the third day she dragged herself up and went to headquarters, returning with her mule heavily laden. She sorted all the mail and took the headquarters mail to deliver, placing several letters in the General's hands.

"Thank you, Thompson."

He seemed preoccupied, and Emma, feeling unusually sensitive, dared to speak. "Is something troubling you, sir?"

He glanced at her, blinking. "Yes. I am leaving."

"Leaving?"

"I'll be announcing it tomorrow. The Senate has declined to approve my promotion to Brigadier. As I resigned my Colonelcy to accept it, I now have no position in the volunteer army. I'm going back to the Engineers."

"Oh, sir!"

"No one is more sorry than I." Poe smiled sadly and offered his hand. "Good luck to you, Thompson."

Emma shook it, numb with despair. Her comfortable world was crumbling around her. The next general—the next colonel of the Second, for that matter—might not be so generous a friend.

She walked slowly back to her tent, trying to imagine a life without Poe, without Jamie. She saw only blackness before her.

Jamie was there, sitting at the table, writing. He put down his pen when Emma came in.

"General Poe is leaving," she said.

"I heard."

She sat on her bed, gazing around the tent that had been her home for six months. Some other home, next. Such changes had never bothered her before, but now she felt unwilling to let go.

Jamie rose and quietly came to join her. He sat beside her and took her hand. She wanted to pull it away—her anger rose to choke her—but she sat still.

"Can we not part friends?" he asked softly.

"You are the one who is leaving."

"I have no choice. You know that."

"There is always a ch—"

A fit of coughing seized her. Jerome waited in silence, his hand clasping hers tightly. He knew that he could do nothing for her.

Nothing. Nothing was left.

She regained control of her voice. "There is always a choice. It isn't that you can't choose. It's that you won't."

She stood up, pulling her hand away. Anger flashed in his eyes, but she no longer feared his anger. She was too full of grief to feel anything else.

She left the tent and stumbled away, dizziness assailing her. She walked on, not daring to admit how truly unwell she felt.

As she drifted toward the Second's camp, she felt her carefully constructed world coming apart. Her friends and supporters, leaving. Her health abandoning her. She coughed again, and pictured herself lying feverish in her tent, no one there to guard her. If she were to become delirious, and be carried to the hospital, it would mean an ignominious end to her career.

She paid a visit to Chaplain Brown before seeking out Jerome. She said nothing of import to either of them, only that she had been unwell, and was sorry to grieve them with her absence. Chaplain Brown accepted her words at face value, but Jerome was more alert.

"Is there anything I can do?" he asked.

She shook her head, smiling. "No, but thank you, Jerome.

I'll always remember your kindness."

He gave an exasperated laugh. "Well, you're not dying, anyway!"

"Not quite."

She left him, and went back to brigade headquarters, to the hospital there. She sought out the Chief Surgeon, whom she found in his office.

"Dr. Bonine."

"Thompson! Come in, dear boy. Sit down. How are you faring?"

"Not very well, sir. I think it's the malaria again."

"Let me give you some quinine."

"I had rather you gave me a furlough."

Dr. Bonine looked at her, raising an eyebrow. "Are you that ill?"

Emma blinked back sudden tears. "Indeed, I am quite ill. I need time to recover. Please, sir, will you help me?"

"I would, with all the will in the world, but there are no furloughs being issued just now."

Emma closed her eyes, unsurprised. She'd had to try, though.

"You do look pale. Let me have a look at you."

Emma stood up hastily. "Thank you, sir, but there's no need. I know what is the matter."

Dr. Bonine frowned up at her in concern. "You never would let anyone help you, for all the help you gave others."

"I'm best on my own, sir."

"I heard you had injured your leg."

"It's better now. Thank you, sir," she said, and left.

Jamie was not in the tent when she returned to it. She was glad; nothing more could be gained by talking with him. She pulled out her cracker box, took her remaining watches, her Bible, and her letters, few as they were. A handful from Miss Daphne, the rest from Jerome. She tucked them into her pocket, and picked up the volume of Burns that Jamie had given her.

It was a handsome book, indeed. Red leather binding with gilt letters. She had spent hours enjoying its contents, all the more because it was a gift.

She pushed the cracker box away, stood up, and walked over to Jamie's cot. Laying the book in the precise center of it, she stood over it for a moment, then turned and walked out of the tent.

She didn't stop walking until she reached Cairo.

Washington, D.C., 1883

"You shouldn't have left the book."

Emma looked up at Jamie, roused from her musings. He had been silent a long time, and she knew he was thinking back also. She gazed at him, marking the changes in him, the lines on his face and the silver in his hair. For all that, he was the same.

"Why not?" she said. "It is customary to return gifts when one ends a connection."

"But it angered me. If you hadn't left it I wouldn't have gone to Robbins."

Emma felt heat rising into her cheeks. "And told him everything about us."

"I'm not proud of it."

She sighed. "Well, it doesn't matter now."

"Did he ever forgive you?"

"No."

She stood, walking slowly a few paces to stretch out her aching leg and foot. Jamie stood up as well and she paused. He stepped toward her.

"Let me take you to dinner, for old times' sake." A corner of his mouth curved upwards. "I'll take you to Willard's."

Emma sighed. "I am married, Jamie. And so are you."

His smiled faded. "My wife died in Scotland."

"Oh." She could not bring herself to say she was sorry. "You never remarried?"

He shook his head, and the glint in his eye was one she remembered. She repressed a shiver, not entirely of fear.

The door into the congressman's office opened, and a stream of visitors and secretaries, including Mr. Glass, emerged. Emma watched the majority of them leave, then stepped up to the desk. Mr. Glass glowered at her and pointedly took out his watch.

"It is seven-thirty, ma'am. The congressman is seeing no one else today."

Jamie came up as well, walking around the desk. "I've remembered something I wished to say to him. It will just take a moment."

He smiled—his most engaging smile—and slipped past the secretary, who allowed it. Emma clenched her teeth in frustration.

"May I make an appointment for tomorrow, then?" she asked. "I can come as early as you like, and will take only a few minutes of the congressman's time."

Mr. Glass frowned, and reluctantly turned a page in the appointment book that lay open on his desk. He was still peering at it when footsteps sounded, coming from the office.

Emma looked up to see Jamie returning, his arm through that of an older man. Congressman Cutcheon was tall, with white hair and whiskers and apple-rounded cheeks. She saw in him the shadow of a younger man, a major in the army.

"Here she is," Jamie said, gesturing to Emma.

She looked at him, wondering what he'd done now. Did his thirst for vengeance live on, even after twenty years?

The congressman stepped up to Emma, peering at her face. She returned his gaze, unsure whether it would be wise to smile.

"By Jove! So it is! Frank Thompson!"

Emma swallowed. "Yes, sir."

"I remember how you rode through a hail of bullets all day at Fredericksburg! You know, we wondered what became of you in Lebanon. Not like Thompson to desert, we all said!"

"No...well. I had my reasons."

"You should listen to them," Jamie said. "It's a fascinating story."

"Well, and so I shall!" Cutcheon took her hand, patting it. "Come and dine with me, Mrs.—Seelye, was it? And tell me all about it!"

Emma felt hope rising in her. She glanced at Jamie. "Thank you, sir."

"You come, too, Reid," said Cutcheon. "We'll have a good talk about old times!"

Jamie met Emma's gaze and held it a moment, then his eyelids drooped lazily. "Thank you, sir, but I'm otherwise engaged this evening. I feel certain that Mr. Seelye would like to join you."

The congressman stepped aside to speak to his secretary. Jamie retrieved his hat from the chair where he'd left it. Emma took a step toward him.

"Thank you, Jamie."

He smiled, the crooked smile. The heartbroken smile. Emma watched him turn and walk out of the room.

He was like her. He never looked back.

Author's Note

Anyone who undertakes to write about Emma Edmonds, whether in fiction or non-fiction, must inevitably speculate. For some aspects of her life there are no records; others are documented, but sometimes only in hints, and her own memoir is an inextricable blend of fact and fiction.

What is certain is that she enlisted in the 2nd Michigan Volunteers as Private Franklin Thompson in May of 1861, and served until deserting in April of 1863. She married Linus Seelye on April 27, 1867, and bore him two sons, both of whom died on the days of their birth. The Seelyes then had a daughter and adopted two orphaned boys.

Emma Seelye began pursuing her claim to a pension in 1882. Her campaign consisted mainly of writing to her former colleagues and soliciting their support in the form of letters. She did not visit Congressman Cutcheon in Washington; that is a dramatic device of my own. He did, however, remember Frank Thompson and introduce a bill to strike the charge of desertion from Thompson's record. In 1884, Emma received her pension: $12 a month.

Of her relationship with James Reid very little is certain, but Jerome Robbins's journal confirms that she shared his tent at General Poe's headquarters, and refers to her as Reid's "pet." Her desertion gave rise to speculation about her connection with Reid, and the fact that she left just a few days after Reid tendered his resignation begs the question of whether it was truly illness (as Emma claimed) or despondency over his imminent departure, along with that of General Poe, that drove her to abandon her army career. With her friends and supporters leaving, her position at headquarters became much more dangerous.

James Reid appears to have vanished from the pages of history after leaving the army. While Emma did not, as far as we know, encounter him again, she did see many of her old army friends, including Captain William Morse and her former bunkmate Damon Stewart. She was mustered into the

Grand Army of the Republic in 1898, the only woman to receive that honor, and died later that year at the age of fifty-six.

Like her fictional counterpart and inspiration, Fanny the Pirate Captain, Emma Edmonds is a larger-than-life example of a woman who, through the exercise of courage, initiative, and talent, could transcend the social barriers of the nineteenth century to achieve as much as any man.

Suggested Reading

Edmonds, S. Emma E., *Nurse and Spy in the Union Army*, W. S. Williams & Co., Hartford, 1865.

Gansler, Laura Leedy, *The Double Life of Sarah Emma Edmonds, Civil War Soldier*, Free Press, New York, 2005.

Burgess, Lauren Cook, *An Uncommon Soldier: The Civil War Letters of Sarah Rosetta Wakeman,* The Minerva Center, Pasadena, 1994.

About the Author

P. G. Nagle is the author of seventeen novels and two collections of short fiction, and co-editor of two anthologies. A native and lifelong resident of New Mexico, she has a special love of the outdoors, particularly New Mexico's wilds, where many of her stories are born.

Her shorter work has appeared in national magazines and anthologies. She is a founding member of Book View Café Publishing Cooperative.

Nagle lives in the mountains in New Mexico, surrounded by coyotes, birds, and starry skies, with her husband and two furry muses.

Made in the USA
Lexington, KY
07 November 2015